HOLY MURDER

POLYGAMY'S BLOOD

Bethy –Chriey

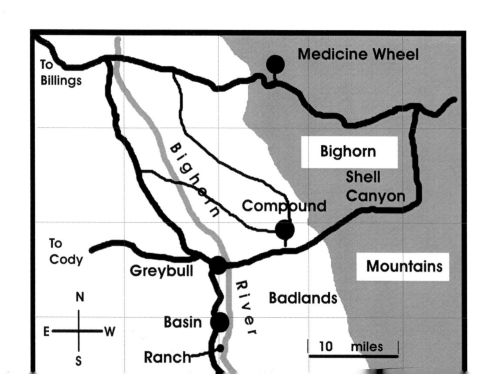

HOLY MURDER
POLYGAMY'S BLOOD

by
James R. Spencer

Other books by James R. Spencer

- *Beyond Mormonism: An Elder's Story*
- *Have You Witnessed to a Mormon Lately?*
- *Hard Case Witnessing: Winning "Impossibles" For Christ*
- *Heresy Hunters: Character Assassination in the Church*
- *Bleeding Hearts and Propaganda: The Fall of Reason in the Church*
- *Mormonism's Temple of Doom**
- *Whited Sepulchers: The Hidden Language of the Temple**

The Mormon Dilemma (video)**

* with William Schnoebelen
**with Ed Decker

To the young women
of Mormonism
who are forced
to marry old men

Acknowledgements

First and foremost, there are some I want to thank, who—for one reason or another—cannot be named here. Some of those choices were theirs, some were mine. Know that your secrets are safe with me.

Dick and Cici Landis read this initially and made important contributions, as did my daughter, Erin Morgan. Paul Andrews helped me envision some key characters and dialogue. My proofreaders, Cynthia Schnereger. Russ Bales, Cherie LaPorte, and Sandy Barrow saved many a disastrous error. I'm sure there are more errors that I have not yet corrected. (Please email any you see so I can correct future editions)

Flora Jessop shaped this manuscript simply through my contact with her and her passion for the Child Brides. You will recognize Ed Decker in the story; his insight continues to inspire me.

Members of the Through the Maze Newsletter family have followed the development of this project and have contributed to its completion. My family and friends have put up with the laborious creation of this book, in some cases stretching their patience—thanks for hanging in there!

PROLOGUE

*P*rophet Ronald Hansen III closed the door to his bedchamber and stepped out onto the wooden walkway. Katherine, one of his wives, was still asleep. The sun was just rising over Wyoming's Bighorn Mountains. From his viewpoint on the second floor of his personal residence, the Lion House, he watched a golden eagle working the currents wafting up the red sandstone hills across Shell Creek to the north. The eagles made a nice living off the ground squirrels, prairie dogs, rock chucks, and rabbits. Hansen loved to watch them working, admiring the economy of their movements changing direction and altitude effortlessly. This male was small, the larger females reached wingspans of seven feet. "May account for their monogamy," he had once joked to the Elders.

Hansen shook his head. With such order and beauty in the world, how could it have reached its current state of pollution? Outside the boundaries of the Prophet's compound the world continued in its sinking spiral—downward into a cesspool of sin. How many men in the world are true to the wives of their youth? How many? Almost none! *Gentiles pointed accusing fingers at the compound and spoke of "moral issues." But Hansen had married, loved, and protected all his wives, while men in the outside world divorced and had sexual relationships with many women, leaving in their wake bastards, disease, and brokenness. They polluted their bodies with excessive amounts of alcohol, tobacco, and drugs; they polluted their minds with pornographic filth; they polluted their race by marrying dark-skinned and cursed peoples.* So who has the moral problems?

Hansen descended the stairs and walked across the compound as it began to come to life, a small city stirring in the dawn. The sister-wives who prepared this week's meals scurried around, the smell of frying bacon filling the outdoor dining area.

Hansen loved eating outside in the summer because it allowed the entire family to break bread together at one time. In the winter months the meals were staggered because no more than 25 could be seated at the two long tables in the inside dining room.

Now, on the outside dining patio, a plain woman in an ankle-length dress placed clean, white china plates on one of the half dozen oak tables that were bolted to the concrete pad. Overhead a latticework shaded the patio.

"Good morning, Sarah," the Prophet said, as he attempted to pass by her.

"Ronald. Good morning to you, dear! What a beautiful morning."

Sarah set the stack of plates down and positioned herself in Hansen's pathway. Hansen could not walk past her without being obviously insulting, so he stopped and waited for Sarah to get to the point she always got to. She would have to get there in her own way.

"So have you been on your morning walk, Ronald?"

"Not yet, Sarah."

"You are looking very handsome this morning, Ronald."

"Thank you, Sarah."

Silence.

"You are looking very pretty yourself, Sarah." He immediately regretted the politeness.

"Am I really?" Sarah asked, drawing close to him.

Although he tried to avoid it, he could not force himself to ignore her heavy movements, her obvious adoration, her fawning manner; behavior that once endeared her to him, now repulsed him.

"Ronald, you haven't visited me in some time." She pursed her lips in a mock pout. Hansen felt his stomach tighten.

"Oh, it hasn't been that long, Sarah."

"Six months."

"No! Really?"

"Six months and three days," she said and smiled.

He was trapped.

"Well, I have been busy." Then hurriedly, *"But not that busy. You will see me soon, rest assured."*

"For sure?"

"Sarah," a trace of irritation now, *"what did I say?"*

She stepped back, her eyes involuntarily widening.

"Oh, of course I believe you. I didn't mean to question..."

Hansen lifted his hand in a dismissive motion.

"Sarah, I don't want to be rude, but I really have to be somewhere." He glanced at his watch.

Sarah's face reddened. She looked at the stack of dishes.

"Yes, Ronald. Of course. You run along. I have my work to do."

He hesitated.

"And...and you do such a fine job, Sarah. I appreciate all you do. We all do."

Now she waved her hand.

Hansen, his face coloring, strode away.

These were the encounters he hated most. And the ones he least understood. It seemed as if they happened more and more these days. He smiled to himself. Most men would be elated to have more than a dozen women anxious for sexual favors. Well, not all of them were anxious. Melissa was not anxious. Which further confused him. Melissa, the one he really wanted, didn't want him anymore. He dropped that thought immediately.

Of 65 children born to his wives over a period of 31 years, 30 were still home. The others were married and living outside the compound. Two sons and their families lived within the compound itself; another six children and their families lived nearby. Some of the kids, in spite of Hansen's best efforts, had thrown the traces and left the faith. All of them were still on friendly terms except three children born to Alma, his first wife, who had left him in the fifth year of their marriage. She and her children had left the faith—eventually becoming "born again" Christians—and viewing Hansen as a cultist. None of the eight grandchildren born to Alma's children had ever been permitted to see their grandfather.

Across the common area Hoyt Akers was waving at Hansen. Akers was Hansen's helicopter pilot and a faithful member of the Church. He walked toward the Prophet and nodded politely.

"Mornin President."

"Good morning, Hoyt, how you doing?"

"It is well with me, President." He then smiled and added, "It is well with my whole house!"

"That's good, brother Hoyt, that's really good." Hansen said.

"President, I got something I want to bring up in the

council meeting this morning."

"Of course, brother. What is it?"

"Well, I think the Lord is giving me another mate."

"Really? Who is it?"

"Maggie Balsom."

The Prophet stared at Akers. Akers dropped his eyes to the ground. "At least that's what I think the Lord is saying to me."

The Prophet smiled and let his arm fall around Akers. "Well, brother Hoyt, you bring that up in the meeting and we'll hear from God on it."

"Yes, sir." Akers said.

"Don't look so glum, brother. God will have His way. Do you believe that?

"Yes, sir. I do, sir."

"Things will work out fine, brother. Whether or not God has Maggie for you I cannot say, but life goes on no matter what. Isn't that true?"

"Yes, sir."

"We'll see you in the meeting. Now excuse me, I have business to attend to."

As Akers drifted off, Hansen walked quickly back to Lion House. On the ground floor porch he passed 10 doors on the west side of the building, turned right, passed three more bedroom doors, then stopped and knocked lightly. He waited five seconds, as was his custom, and turned the doorknob. The doors to the bedrooms of his wives were never locked.

No one within the compound except the Prophet ever so much as approached this part of the Lion House, which was nestled within its own brick walls—actually a compound within the compound. The Prophet entered.

"Melissa?"

The woman standing across the room was tall and slender. She had dark eyes and long midnight-black hair and looked, to Hansen, a decade younger than her 35 years. Her silk nightgown hung gracefully over her hips. The gown was split up the side to the waist revealing a long, slender leg. She looked at the Prophet with a directness that few women— and no men—affected in his presence.

Inclining her head she said, "Ronald."

"Can we talk, Melissa?"

"Certainly." *She moved over to a chair, sat down, crossed one leg over the other, and pulled her gown over the exposed leg. She resolutely placed her hands on the arms of the chair.*

"You look peaceful, Melissa."

"I am at perfect peace, Ronald."

"Is that so?"

"Yes, it is."

"Well, I find that a little strange…"

She did not answer.

"I find that strange because we have not been together to honor the marriage bed for six months."

"Has it been that long?"

Hansen laughed softly and shook his head. "Melissa," he said. "You just get better and better."

She said nothing.

"Melissa, I want you to come back into full favor in the family."

"At what price?"

"The same price we all pay."

She shook her head slowly. "I told you I can't do that, Ronald. I am your wife. At least I have been..."

"You are my wife!"

"All right. All right, I am your wife, but..."

"Melissa, I don't want to hear your objections again."

"Well, then what do you want?"

The Prophet stared at her and worked his jaw muscles. "I've already told you what I want."

"Then," Melissa said, "I think we have nothing to talk about."

"Melissa! Melissa!" His eyes flared in anger. He took a breath and waited a moment. "Melissa," he said in a softer voice, "don't make me go down this road."

Melissa sighed. "I don't have a choice."

"Nonsense. Of course you do. You simply need to return to the Principle..."

"Ronald, I can't do that. I think you know that. You should know it. You should know me..."

"I think I do know you," the Prophet said.

"Perhaps you do. If you do, then you know I cannot

return to the Principle." She gathered the gown together at her throat.

The Prophet was silent for a full 30 seconds. Then he said quietly, "Melissa, do you know me?"

She said nothing.

"Do you know me?" he repeated.

She sighed. "Yes, Ronald. Yes, I think I do."

The Prophet looked down at the floor. He stared at the dark Berber, following the patterns with his eyes. A tear rolled down his cheek and dropped onto the carpet. He looked up at her. He stood and continued to stare at her for a few seconds, tears rolling freely down his face. He shook his head, turned, and walked quickly out of the room.

CHAPTER ONE

Apale and nearly full moon hung in the western sky, casting ghostly sagebrush and cottonwood shadows on the alkali patch where a man crouched against a concrete cistern. The moon, when it had risen out of the badland bluffs across the river six hours earlier, had been an orange beauty; now it looked like a bleached skull. The man waited in the chill morning air, cradling a twelve-gauge shotgun that had belonged to his father. The man felt his 58 years as he turned his ear toward the lane leading to his driveway.

Four feet from the man a jackrabbit, frozen in the moon-light, stared at him. Across the river sandstone bluffs rose like parapets. Jan Kucera wished he would quit thinking in funerary terms. Even more he wished Monster were with him.

Crouching in the dark, Jan took deep breaths of pungent, sage-scented night air. Breathing deeply made him lightheaded, but helped calm him. He laid the old Winchester atop the cistern his father had poured from concrete he had mixed in a wheelbar-row. The cistern had held the family's drinking water.

Jan heard the distinctive clicking of a diesel engine and watched a shadowy black pickup truck creep down his driveway, lights out, its tires crunching the pea-gravel. The pickup stopped. Two dark figures slid out and made their way to Jan's bedroom window. Standing tiptoe, they sprayed the darkened room with automatic weapons. Then they went to the front door, where the shorter of the two blasted the doorknob until his gun emptied. The other would-be assassin kicked the door open and went in. Thirty seconds later he came out and scanned the yard for Jan's pickup.

"Somebody warned him," he said. "Get the cans."

They lifted two five-gallon gasoline cans from the camper shell of their truck. Leaving their weapons on the tailgate, they carried the gas cans to the porch. Jan stood up and pumped a shell into the shotgun chamber. With his right hand he punched the radio control switch in his jacket pocket, activating 6,000 watts of halogen light, transforming the yard into near daylight. The gunmen froze like the jackrabbit.

Jan interrupted the stillness of the night, "Set the cans on the deck and keep your hands where I can see them." The short, stocky gunman glanced toward the truck. Jan triggered the shotgun and blew the gas can out of his hands. The man went down screaming as Jan jacked another round into the shotgun.

*   *   *

John Broadbeck, at his desk in the Big Horn County Sheriff's Office in Basin, wiped gun oil off a Ruger Super Redhawk with a nine-inch stainless steel barrel. The huge 44 magnum looked delicate in his meaty hands. Sheriff Broadbeck had locked the two young shooters from Jan's place in a holding cell and was waiting for the county ambulance to transport the injured one (whose hand Jan had wrapped in a tea towel and then wrapped again with duct tape) to the hospital for treatment

A pungent odor drifted on the air in the sheriff's office from the 100-year-old basement walls of Big Horn County Courthouse. In the daytime, light poured into the office through large windows, but at night the place was borderline dungeon. The room was decorated in Louis L'Amour basic, right down to the longhorn steer horns on the wall above the desk. A gun rack along the back wall housed a dozen rifles and pistols, all locked in place by a steel rod running through the trigger guards.

"Jan," Sheriff Broadbeck said, "these two are about as likely to give up Prophet Hansen as Bill Clinton is to keep his pants on. They know the Constitution better than Sandra Day O'Connor— not to mention they have better ankles."

Raising his voice so the young men could hear, the sheriff said, "But they're two sweeties, all right. Think Hansen is tiring of his 13 wives and turning to soft young men?"

"What about it, boys?" John Broadbeck yelled over his shoulder without turning his head, "The Prophet added you two sissies to his harem?"

Broadbeck's voice, Jan thought, rolled out of his massive chest like music from the subwoofers the teenagers cranked up full volume in their cars while romancing their dates on the dark lanes around his ranch. The edge of Sheriff Broadbeck's mouth twitched slightly. Jan assumed harassing the two shooters amused the sheriff.

Jan had known John Broadbeck since they were kids. "Monster John," as he was known during high school. Broadbeck stood six-four, and had been a 240 pound vision as a linebacker, strong and quick. Even now, wearing a slab of fat like a Kevlar vest, he could pick up two men, one in each hand, and throw them into his cruiser—something he occasionally did. He had once arrested Jan's older brother, Buzz, on a bad check charge in the Stockman's Bar.

The sheriff had walked in smiling and waving a warrant. Buzz later told Jan he had been so drunk and so terrified by the leering figure stalking him across the barroom floor that he ran outside, jumped into his car, and slammed the door. The problem was, he wasn't all the way in the car and slammed his head in the door. The sheriff said it was the easiest arrest he had ever made—"The perpetrator knocked *himself* out!" All that before Buzz drank himself into the grave, another victim of the brutal lifestyle of the Wyoming oil patch.

The assorted drifters, unemployed roughnecks, and drunks throughout Big Horn County feared Monster; most everyone else respected him. At the Stockman's Bar, Dooley piled sandbags at one end of the barroom and took $100 bets that Monster could plug a silver dollar clean through at 25 feet—one shot off a quick-draw. If he missed or broke the rim of the coin, Dooley paid the bet. Dooley split the winnings with Monster and the bettor got to keep the dollar—and Monster's good will. A silver dollar with a hole through it often deflected a speeding ticket in Big Horn County.

"What about you?" Monster John was saying to Jan. "You ain't goin back out to the homestead tonight with Hansen's Avenging Angels looking for you like you're Salman Rushdie?"

"Well, I don't think they will do anything else for a day or so," Jan said.

Monster snorted.

"Well, *hombre,* flaunting your invulnerability before Prophet Ronald Hansen III is about as smart as dating O. J. Simpson's girlfriend. I wouldn't be in a hurry to challenge Hansen to finish the job he began tonight."

"That he began two years ago," Jan corrected.

"OK, two years ago."

"With Emma's murder," Jan said, his voice rising.

"I know, I know partner…We'll bring the Prophet down, Jan."

"Will we?"

Monster was silent, then he said, "If we don't, I guess you'll be a dead man."

"Yeah," Jan said, "I will if we don't stop him."

"I'm as frustrated as you are, boy. But it ain't over 'til it's over."

Jan knew Monster was smarting over his failure to make a case against Hansen for Emma's murder. Nobody, before this time, had been able to stand up to Monster Broadbeck in Big Horn County. Normally, Monster would have—by whatever means—enforced his own "natural justice." But Hansen had erected a wall of defense that even Sheriff John Broadbeck had been unable to breach. "Redoubtable," was how the sheriff had once referred to Hansen in Jan's presence, Monster staring out the window of his office chewing on an unlit Pall Mall.

"Look, John," Jan said, "I really don't know where we go from here. I know you're my only real ally. The Feds have demonstrated that they are powerless to move against Hansen. I thought maybe I could get past all this…" His voice trailed off.

Monster was silent for awhile. He continued to play with the Ruger, snapping the cylinder open, examining the load, popping the cylinder shut.

"Anyway," Jan continued, "tonight has taught me one thing for sure—this certainly isn't over. It will never be over until I—or we—end it."

Monster slipped the Ruger back into its holster. "We'll end it all right."

"Let's talk about it in a day or so," Jan said. "Right now, if you think you're safe with these two hitmen, I think I'll slip over to the café for a short stack and coffee."

"Ginny workin this morning?"

Jan ignored the question and said. "By the way, John, I don't think there's any point in sweating these guys."

"Yeah, yeah. I know, *amigo,* I'm not going to waste county water by rinsing their hair in the toilet. As I said, they won't give up the Prophet."

Jan headed out, Monster throwing him a set of keys to an extra county vehicle to drive home, saying he would have a deputy pick it up later. Monster would hold the gunmen until federal agents made the four-hour drive from Casper to pick them up for arraignment on automatic weapons charges.

*   *   *

Basin City was beginning to glow in the early dawn as Jan walked from the sheriff's office toward the Basin Café. The buildings of the block-long main street had survived from Jan's youth. A few modern facades covered the brick and sandstone structures, but new construction was financially out of the question—the town was dying. Business went to Worland, or Billings or Casper. Gone were the shops of the 1950s. Back then Basin supported two drug stores, three saloons, a pool hall, a bakery, two grocery stores, a couple of clothing stores and hardware stores, and two cafés. You could spend all Saturday afternoon at the Wigwam Theater watching two movies, three cartoons, a serial, and a newsreel. Back then Ethel's Variety Store had merchandise stacked to the ceiling, everything from thread to greeting cards, candy to shoe polish. Ethel could find anything you needed—if you had enough time for her to dig through all the stuff.

When Jan was a teenager, he would hang out with Ginny Hollingsworth at Larry Lowrey's Drug Store listening to the jukebox and drinking graveyard Cokes. A couple of years later he would hang out at the pool hall smoking Camels and playing pea-pool for dimes. Eventually he hung out at the city reservoir drinking Coors.

Since Emma had died he hung out at the ranch, drinking way too much whiskey.

*   *   *

At the Basin Café Virginia Hollingsworth was looking almost as good as she had in high school, remarkably trim for her 55 years. She still had the graceful moves that had fascinated him—and all the other boys at Basin High School—back then. In the two years since Emma's death, Virginia had watched Jan through soft eyes.

Jan took a stool at the counter, one of those his father had used 50 years earlier when he had pancakes and bacon before beginning his workday. Ginny moved toward him.

"Coffee, Jan?"

"Yeah, coffee, Ginny."

"What brings you to town so early?"

"I had a load of trash to drop off."

Ginny glanced up quizzically. The landfill wouldn't open until 9:00 a.m. and it was not yet 6:00 a.m.

She slid a cup of coffee in front of him and leaned against the back counter, then folded her arms across her chest and squinted her eyes like someone facing into bright sunlight. She did that, Jan remembered, years ago, when she was a self-conscious teenage beauty. Her auburn hair today was shoulder length and naturally curly, lying in soft springy layers around her face. High cheekbones and faint red eyebrows framed dark chestnut-brown eyes. And she still had freckles.

"Anything else?" Ginny asked.

"Not right now."

"Are you doing OK, Jan? You look…well, weary."

"I've had a bad night."

She was silent. After a moment, she squinted her eyes again, smiled sweetly, and flowed off toward the kitchen. Jan inhaled the warm steam off the cup, rolled it around and watched the reflection of the lights dance on the surface of the coffee. Ginny—the one woman as kind-hearted as Emma had been.

* * *

After breakfast, as Jan drove the six miles home he reflected that his mother had always referred to the family homestead as *the ranch,* even though they had never run cattle there. They had grown some alfalfa, a little grain, and melons. Still, it was always *the ranch.*

Approaching his lane he deactivated the security system: interruptible laser security detectors set at waist level at random intervals along the half-mile lane that was the only vehicular approach to his place. The security system's signal had alerted him to the pre-dawn visitors and saved his life. Other mantraps guarded the trail from the river to the house. Monster Broadbeck had conceived, ordered, and installed the system.

Jan sat in the county vehicle in his driveway. He leaned against the door and scanned the acreage before him. Some 115 years earlier, Jan's great-grandfather homesteaded this brush patch along the muddy Bighorn River in North Central Wyoming. Jan's great-grandfather, his young wife, and their five-year-old daughter—who was to be Jan's grandmother— wintered the first year in a hole dug out of the bank of the river. Jan imagined his great-grandfather gathering scrub brush for a fire and pondering why he had left Maryland to come to a place like this—a place then where only trappers, Indians, and bushwhackers moved among the cottonwoods. Jan wondered if his great-grandfather realized he was building a frontier community that would one day become a civilized outpost in the Wyoming scrub. He doubted his great-grandfather ever imagined that 100 years later the city fathers would name a quiet, tree-lined street after him in Basin City six miles downstream from the homestead. Basin, after a fight with the tiny community of Otto, won the County Seat of Big Horn County, insuring the leg of the CB&Q railroad would run two blocks east of Basin's main street. Jan's great-grandfather built a house halfway between Main and the rail bed. He established the first store in the new community, and the first bank—then died young on his kitchen table, attended by a physician trying desperately to force a breathing tube into his infected throat, which was closing in a pre-antibiotic world.

As a boy, when Jan had lived on the ranch in the basement house, he had investigated the charred hole where the dugout's old chimney had come through the top of the bank. Eventually the dugout had eroded away, given up with 50 feet of riverbank to the incessant flooding of the Bighorn. After World War II the federal government constructed the Boysen Reservoir 80 miles upstream. Before that Jan's dad had fought the floods every year, sandbagging the house and wading waist deep into the barnyard to rescue chickens and pigs.

The old basement house wasn't much of an improvement over the dugout—nothing more than a large cement cellar with a flat roof. Yet, Jan had been at peace there with his parents, his older brother, and two older sisters. Fifty plus years later when Jan repurchased the place he constructed the new log structure over the old cement walls of the original basement. But the peace he had hoped to replicate on the ranch had morphed into a nightmare.

Stepping out of the county vehicle onto the driveway, he smelled the river and the odor of the horses in the corral. The sun was now warming the June morning. Across the river he saw an eagle perched on a dirt pinnacle, twisting its head as it surveyed its domain. A casual observer would never spot him blending into the sandstone, but Jan knew the dark silhouette.

He walked over to the corral and threw some hay to Brutus,

the big gelding paint, and Trudy, the small bay mare. The ponies watched him with huge black eyes while they ground pungent stalks of hay with their big molars. Jan stroked their powerful necks and drank in their smell. They stepped gingerly back and forth as they watched him and chewed.

"Not today, kids," he said. "Your old man is too tired. We had a big night, remember? Hope you weren't as scared as I was by the fireworks."

He walked up the wooden steps to the house. The screen was hanging by one hinge. The hardwood door was ruined. Inside he inspected the bedroom trashed from the gunfire. Window glass littered the entire room and the bed looked like someone had run a Rototiller over its surface. Jan decided it was time to order the pillow-top king-sized bed he had seen in Billings. He would need a new bureau, and from the looks of the closet doors, a new wardrobe.

The far wall, constructed not out of logs but drywall, was destroyed. Bullets had ripped the plasterboard from the two-by-fours and the entire wall would need to be replaced. Surprisingly, only one computer monitor on the other side of the wall was shattered, at least three slugs had imploded the CRT and passed through the monitor case before lodging in the exterior log wall. The copier was missing a corner but it made a perfect test copy when he tried it. The Internet connection was operable. Not bad.

Then Jan saw the picture frame on the floor. He froze. Slowly he reached down and picked it up. Turning it over, he saw that the glass was shattered and a bullet had pierced the picture exactly between Emma's eyes. Jan shook the remaining glass onto the floor and pulled the picture out of the frame. With a pair of scissors he carefully cut a rectangle out of the center. Holding the 2-by-3-inch segment by one corner, he looked at Emma. Then he pulled out his wallet and placed the picture in the plastic pocket over his driver's license. From now on, when he opened his wallet for any reason, he would see Emma with the bullet hole in her face. He thought it might help motivate him.

Back out on the porch a warm morning breeze had come up. Jan gazed at the concrete pad where the two-car garage had stood until Emma died there two years earlier. A few burned timbers from the building were stacked to one side of the pad, reminders of the explosion that had been intended for him. A wave of fresh grief washed over him, a sensation he experienced with increasing—instead of *decreasing*—frequency. The shrink in Billings said that was a bad sign. But Jan could not let go of the memories, as if doing so would somehow take Emma even further from him.

He stood frozen in place as the movie played in his mind—the front door slowly floating toward him into the kitchen, hinges flying in slow motion. A coffee cup lazily floating upward, turning over, pouring its contents out, and drifting slowly down to shatter on the floor. He could hear the explosion coming from the garage and could see, through the front door, timbers from the garage sailing in an arc as though lofted by an unseen hand. Two vehicles were on fire, his Jeep Cherokee was missing its roof and, of course, Emma was dead. Her Nissan Sentra was blown 10 feet outside what had been the wall of the garage.

A crazy cosmic flip-flop killed her instead of Jan. The bomb was meant for *him*. It was in *his* Jeep. Their routine never varied: she left for her real estate office in her car while he cleaned up the breakfast dishes and got to his current writing project. His Cherokee sat alone in the garage until he needed to run to town for office supplies, or to a spot on the ranch for some chore or other. But that morning Emma was to take his rig to work so he could take her car in for an oil change. When she keyed the ignition to his Cherokee, she died.

He had known, the moment he ran through the doorway toward the flaming garage, that she was dead.

CHAPTER TWO

Tuesday, the morning after the two religious fanatics attempted to kill Jan, Monster assigned a deputy to watch Jan's property. Toward evening Monster's chief deputy, Harold Eisenstadt, wheeled into the driveway at the ranch. Jan saw him park the patrol car under the large tree in the front yard. Harold tended Jan's horses and checked the security system when Jan was out of town. Jan thought his kindness was out of respect for Emma and for Jan because he was Monster's friend. Loyalty was Harold's middle name.

The deputy uncurled himself from the vehicle and walked to where Jan was sitting on the porch drinking a glass of Seagram's VO and ice. Jan drained the glass then set it under his chair.

Jan never got over how skinny Harold was, but he never forgot that Monster said he was probably the toughest lawman in the state. Harold was wearing an exact replica of Monster's Ruger on his hip. Everyone in the county knew that Harold idolized the sheriff and modeled himself, as much as possible, after his boss. "Not a shame to imitate the best," he told people who asked.

Jan thought back to the night he and Monster were having a steak at the Crossroads when Harold came in to report an incident that had occurred in Shell, the tiny village at the foot of the Big-horns. He had been in a beef with a couple of Mexican illegals outside the Shell Saloon.

"They had Orville Bishop's prize bull, Damnation, in the back of a beat-up cattle truck," Harold had told the sheriff. "When I approached them they menaced me with a couple of rusty revolvers. They were drunker than Icy Shultz on payday."

"That drunk?" Monster asked.

Harold smiled. "Well maybe not *that* drunk. Anyway, I looked straight into the eyes of Louie Ortiz. Got him lookin close at me, almost nose to nose. His partner, a little guy they call 'Gringo'…you remember him…"

"Little guy we found under Marjorie Leonard's bedroom window last fall…"

"That's the guy. Anyway, Gringo is watching me watching Ortiz. Little smirk on Gringo's face. I just keep looking at Ortiz, but I quick punch Gringo in the nose. Then Ortiz looks at Gringo and I knee *him* in the groin. He goes down screaming."

But now Harold approached the porch, tipped his hat to Jan and placed an ostrich-leather boot on the first step. Harold's skinny leg looked to Jan like it belonged on a giant grasshopper, not a man.

"Hey, Jan, good to see you. Musta been quite a scare last night."

"Yeah, it was. But I wasn't as scared as the two Hansen thugs were when they saw the sheriff."

Harold guffawed.

"Harold, you look like you're set to spend the night. You don't have to do that."

"Monster's orders, Jan."

"Yeah, but…" Jan let his voice trail off. Harold smiled quietly at him. No way he was leaving the ranch before dawn.

Jan sighed.

*   *   *

Wednesday morning Jan awoke with a headache. He looked at the VO bottle by his bed and mentally recounted the drinks he had consumed the night before. It was a morning ritual. After the double-shot Harold had caught him with in the early evening, he had drunk no more until bedtime. He allowed himself three double-shots before bed. Any more than that he considered failure; any less than that and he was certain to be awake most of the night. His shrink said, "I don't care what sedative you choose. All medication has risks. It's up to you." So Jan settled on three double-shots. But sometimes it became four or five. He always regretted that. Especially during his morning workout.

After he showered, he had breakfast on the coffee table in the greatroom. Emma had loved the house. It was a kit constructed from Northern White Cedar from the Boyne Valley in Michigan. Emma and Jan had spent five months overseeing the construction crews. A 25-by-30-foot greatroom with a panoramic view of the river opened into the kitchen area. The master bedroom and office were also on the first floor. Above were two guestrooms, a landing overlooking the greatroom, and a door to an outside balcony overlooking the river.

Jan rinsed his plate in the kitchen sink and put it in the dishwasher. He stepped outside onto the porch—actually, Emma said it was a veranda because it ran the length of the south side of the house—and was pleased to see that Harold's cruiser was gone. He checked the security control panel and confirmed what he instinctively knew he would find—Harold had armed the perimeter security when he left at dawn.

Looking south from the porch, he spotted the two horses in the tall sagebrush. Trudy was scratching her back against a cottonwood. Brutus was pawing at the earth, maybe looking for a wild onion. The horses had the run of the 500 acres. It was all barbwire fenced, with the house, yard and outbuildings separated from the pastureland by a pine rail fence. Along the river, willows formed their own barrier, but not enough to stop cows from the Mink place from coming in and competing for what little grass was available for the horses. Jan had recently heard about a man from Manderson who was restoring his pastureland through a natural grazing program. He made a mental note to call the guy.

A symphony of fragrances swirled from the acreage: buffalo berry, wild rose, and squaw bush; cottonwood, ash, and salt cedar; wild licorice and asparagus. The morning sun had risen above the badlands, Jan could see golden ripples on the muddy river and knew if he were to walk along the river, enormous carp would churn up, frightened into activity. Across the river and beyond the 100-foot bluffs lay hundreds of thousands of acres of badlands as barren as anything the West had to offer, stretching to the foothills of the Bighorns.

Jan went back inside and snapped the rubber band off a large chart that lay rolled up on the oak dining table. The schematic of the Hansen compound lay before him. It was a 36-inch by 48-inch blueline drawing that had been pieced together by the Bureau of Alcohol, Tobacco, and Firearms in Washington and had come to Jan through Monster Broadbeck. He also had four satellite photographs of the compound and surrounding area. Hansen was known to stockpile heavy weapons at the compound, but his extreme care in acquiring the weapons had precluded warrants so far. Hansen did everything with military precision. Monster said the ATF brass believed the compound was a powder keg.

Despair engulfed Jan as he looked at the satellite photographs. Getting to Hansen seemed impossible. And he wasn't sure what he would do if he did get to him, but Jan would never be safe in Wyoming as long as Hansen remained in power.

Jan traced his finger over U.S. Highway 14 on the map. The compound was nestled three miles north of the highway, five miles downstream on Shell Creek after the stream emerged from Shell Canyon, a prehistoric crack in the Bighorn Mountains. Shell Creek ran west from the mouth of the canyon twenty miles until it emptied into the Bighorn River just north of the town of Greybull. Greybull was eight miles north of Basin, 14 miles north of Jan's ranch.

Months earlier Jan had driven up to the entrance of the compound, 10 miles east of Greybull toward the majestic Bighorns. Five miles before entering Shell Canyon he had turned left onto a dirt road and traveled two miles north. Fronting the compound were a thousand acres of hay fields—also Hansen's property. A hurricane fence topped with razor wire flanked the last half-mile approach to the only entrance into the compound. A gate and armed security guards closed each end of the corridor. Two razor wire fences separated a 100-foot no-man's-land that was patrolled day and night surrounded the perimeter of the compound.

Jan had learned that Hansen seldom left the compound or his 13 wives, and when he did he was usually in a convoy of at least three vehicles with several armed bodyguards. Sometimes he flew out of the compound aboard a six-passenger Sikorsky S-76 helicopter. Hansen reportedly had fitted a 50-caliber Heckler & Koch machine gun under its nose cowl. At 175 miles an hour, Hansen could be in Billings—80 miles north—in 30 minutes. He kept the church's Gulfstream V jet at the Billings airport. The jet could accommodate 19 passengers in a pinch and had a range of 6,500 miles. Hansen could be in Argentina in seven hours. Jan had heard rumors that Hansen had a community prepared some-where in the Argentinean interior where he would be welcome and where extradition would not be a problem.

The best estimates suggested that 200 people lived inside the compound—a handful of the highest officers in the Church, each with their several wives and children. About 700 others lived in homes and trailers within 10 miles of the compound. Some 2,000 other baptized members of the cult were scattered through-out Wyoming, Montana, Utah, and Idaho. Other polygamists in Oregon, Nevada, Arizona, and California were closely aligned with, but not official members of, the sect.

Jan picked up the phone and dialed Monster's cell phone.

"Yo!"

"John, you busy? I'm thinking of coming in for lunch."

"Meet me at the Crossroads. How about 1:30?"

"I'll be there."

*   *   *

Jan knew Monster liked to have a big lunch after the crowd cleared at the Crossroads, the only eatery in Basin other than the Basin Café. The Crossroads was the only place in town with what passed for a formal dining room, which in this part of Wyoming meant tablecloths. A bar took up the front of the building. The sheriff was waiting at a table in the rear of the dining room. From his vantage point, Monster could see the wide entryway to the bar and the side-street entry to the dining room itself. His back was to the wall.

"Get any rest yet, *muchacho?*"

"Enough. I'm good to go. I just need to think through a few things."

"Well, you're better at thinkin than I am."

Monster was leaning back in his chair, his Stetson on the

chair to his left. Jan sat across from him, now wondering if Monster meant anything deeper by the remark. Sometimes Jan felt as though Monster viewed him as too intellectual for his own good. Jan knew he did tend to analyze things too much. Emma had said it was his Piscean nature—two fish swimming in opposite directions. He could see both sides of every issue, which made him a good reporter, but not a good decider. But now he decided Monster meant no slight by his comment.

The waitress took their order, automatically bringing coffee for Jan. She was wearing a button on her apron that said "Beware, Attack Waitress!" The lunch special was sauerkraut balls. Monster jumped on that.

"John," Jan said, "I just want to review the situation at the Hansen compound. Actually I want to think out loud about this whole…well…situation."

The sheriff nodded but said nothing.

"I can't escape the conclusion that I—*we*—are going to have to bring Hansen to justice with no help from *anybody* else. The ATF—the Feds—they aren't going to do anything."

"Matter of fact, my boy, I am meeting with George Olson later today. But you're right, the *federales* are so busy watching the border for ragheads they have precious little interest in patriotic religious whackos. Especially after the lessons they learned from their over-exuberance at Ruby Ridge and Waco."

Jan nodded. Things had changed big time after 9-11. During the 1980s, ATF agents were spread throughout the Rocky Mountains, focused on hotspots like Ruby Ridge in Northern Idaho where Randy Weaver and federal agents turned a standoff into a bloodbath after Weaver refused to surrender to a federal arms warrant. Weaver's wife was killed in the battle, as was a federal agent. Weaver was acquitted under the spectacular defense machinations of Gerry Spence, the buckskin-clad attorney from Jackson, Wyoming.

The ATF, of course, had also botched the arrest of David Koresh—the Wacko from Waco—and his followers, the Branch Davidians. And the Oklahoma City bombing flowed, according to some estimates, out of the Branch Davidian fiasco. After the Twin Towers disaster, non-Islamic religious zealots were pretty much overlooked. Hansen's group, although watched by the Feds and considered dangerous, was not considered a real threat to anyone but themselves. Oh, Hansen was capable of ultra-right-wing machismo and saber-rattling, but the federal government actually looked at him as a *resource* in many ways—an armed, patriotic militia. Hansen, until recently, had hobnobbed with Wyoming governors and congressmen. Only in recent years, as his actions grew more erratic, had state powerbrokers begun to shy away from him.

Jan saw that the relative isolation of the West allowed radical religious groups to flourish; groups like the Church Universal and Triumphant near Bozeman, Montana. That church, known as CUT, had migrated to Montana under the frenetic leadership of Elizabeth Claire Prophet. There she ordered her followers to build underground bomb shelters and stockpile automatic weapons. White Supremacists had saturated Northern Idaho. Mark Fuhrman, the alleged racist LA cop, moved to Northern Idaho after the O. J. Simpson trial. Bo Gritz, the ultra-conservative one-time presidential candidate, also had a compound there. Beyond that, scores of *posse comitatus,* Book of Revelation survivalists, and other anti-government extremists roamed throughout the West.

After Muslim terrorists destroyed the World Trade Center, things began to change in the skinhead movement. The extremists softened their criticism of the federal government and took lower profile positions. Some of them actually became very friendly with certain government agencies. Some of them were US operatives in pre-war Iraq.

Mormonism's Fundamentalists, however, were slow to warm to the Feds. Possibly because a new taste for prosecuting bigamy was arising in the West. Tom Green had been convicted and sent to prison for keeping five wives in the Utah desert. Mormonism's polygamy deeply rooted itself in the West. It had originally found safe harbor the Salt Lake Valley in the 1850's. The church grew, isolated as it was from mainstream America, until dozens of Mormon splinter groups existed in polygamist enclaves—as many as 50,000 in the western United States. Many of the little groups were radical, socially isolated, and—in Jan's mind—dangerous. Hansen's group, The Church of the One Mighty and Strong, was one of the larger factions.

"What's the meeting with Olson about?"

"Not sure, *amigo,* but I know it relates to Hansen. You know Olson wants him bad."

"Well, I think the ATF is tired of squandering resources here. Two years and no arrest on the horizon." Jan chewed his lower lip, a nervous gesture he had developed in childhood.

"That frustrates George as much as anyone," Monster said. "Since 9-11 resources are spread thin."

"I suppose so. But you'd think with—what—three agents full-time here…"

"Five, counting the two running the Ops Center on C1MS in Casper."

"C1MS?"

Monster laughed. "Yeah, you know to the Feds, everything has to be an acrostic. It's how they refer to Hansen's group. C1MS stands for The Church of the One Mighty and Strong. Anyway, the ATF doesn't maintain a regional office in Wyoming, the nearest is Denver. So, they set up a temporary Ops office in Casper where two agents work the peripherals of the case. They fly all over the

West interviewing disaffected members of C1MS, conducting phone interviews, updating the database—stuff like that. The Casper office is linked to Denver and Washington, D.C. headquarters with secure phone lines and encrypted satellite data links."

"Well, how long do you think they will continue to waste resources on a non-Islamic quasi-terrorist?" Jan asked.

Lunch arrived. Monster turned his attention to the waitress.

"Dating any biker hunks these days, Debbie?"

"Not since the last time I went out with you, Sheriff."

Monster hooted. He poured an enormous glob of catsup over his sauerkraut balls. Jan winced.

"Anyway, *compadre,* as you know, Olson has two other agents undercover in Big Horn County. Darrel Southwick, poses as a fertilizer salesman. He calls on farmers throughout the county, but mainly the hay producers near the C1MS compound. The locals are always anxious to gossip about the fun and games at the compound."

Jan knew the other undercover agent, a 50-year-old named Franklin James, who posed as an insurance executive retired to a life of nature photography. James was free to hang out in the cafés and bars, and to drift throughout the county with fishing gear and cameras. Since the C1MS compound was less than five miles from the mouth of Shell Canyon—one of the most scenic areas in the West—James spent much of his time in the area climbing the red sandstone hills with camera and telephoto lens.

George Olson himself was known openly as a federal agent, but not an ATF agent. He had an office in the courthouse basement with the words "IRS Special Agent" painted on the door, a purposeful misdirection. Olson spent most of his time in the office communicating with his two undercover agents over scrambled voice links and communicating as well with Casper, Denver, and Washington, D.C. As a purported IRS agent, none of the locals pressed to get to know him. At the rear of his small office, a door opened into a cavernous storeroom that the ATF had taken over. No one but the sheriff, the county commissioners, and the district judge knew the real reason a federal officer was stationed in Basin, or that the storeroom housed sophisticated electronic communications gear and an arsenal that could equip 30 imported agents in the event a raid ever *was* ordered on the compound. Jan fully expected the operation to end soon.

"Well," Jan said, "You go ahead and meet with Olson. But in the meantime, we need to start working on our own plans."

"I'm ready to rock 'n' roll!"

Jan chewed his lip. "Thing is, I just can't get my mind around Hansen…"

"You don't need to get your mind around him, you just need to get your hands around his neck."

Jan smiled. "I've been studying the history of Mormon polygamy…"

Monster interrupted. "You need to go to Seattle and talk to Deck Edwards."

"Yeah, I suppose I should. Haven't seen him for a while so it would be a chance to pick his brain and enjoy his company. You're right. I really do need to talk to him again. I'll make a trip right away."

"Good idea."

"Anyway," Jan continued, "Deck once told me that there is something very interesting in the name of the Hansen cult—The Church of the One Mighty and Strong. Deck says the concept of "The One Mighty and Strong" runs throughout all the Mormon splinter groups, particularly the polygamous groups. The phrase itself comes from the Mormon book of scripture called *The Doctrine and Covenants*—a compilation of purported prophecies primarily from the founder of Mormonism, Joseph Smith."

"Old Joe Smith…"

"Anyway, there is a supposed prophecy in the book that cryptically mentions 'The One Mighty and Strong,' who would supposedly rise up among the Mormon population one day to set the Mormon Church straight after it had fallen into error. The error was that the Church gave up polygamy."

"Giving polygamy up? That's the *error?* And our Prophet Ronnie Hansen is this mighty strong guy?" Monster shook his head incredulously.

"Yeah, I guess so. And it seems wherever you turn in Mormonism you run into polygamy."

"Yeah, I know, I thought about going into it myself, but with my marital record I figured it would just turn into multiple *divorce!*"

Jan, ignoring the digression said, "Of course, the Mormon Church, almost from its inception, practiced polygamy. Officially, Utah Mormonism denies that. The official Church position is that polygamy was never really practiced before Brigham Young led the Church from Illinois to the Salt Lake Valley in 1847. Of course history disputes that. Nevertheless, Mormons openly engaged in polygamy for more than 40 years in Utah. Polygamy was the major story in the West during that time. It caused a huge stink throughout the country. It was condemned in the halls of Congress; Mormon leaders were vilified as lecherous despoilers of virgins. The United States nearly went to war with the Utah Territory over the practice."

Jan paused, pursing his lips, "What I haven't been able to figure out is why and how polygamy has persisted up to the present time. But I think it has something to do with The One Mighty and Strong. The best I can tell is that there was some sort of secret commission or something set up to keep polygamy alive but underground. The Mormon Church sent Hansen's granddad up here. Maybe he continued polygamy up here as a secret mission—a commission of the Church."

Monster speared a kraut ball and shook his head. "And Ronnie Hansen is part of that? Ronnie, Ronnie, Ronnie," he said.

Monster was silent for a while.

"You know, bro, I agree with you. I think you need to see Deck Edwards *now*."

"I'll make a reservation out of Billings tomorrow."

"I'll drive you up," Monster said.

"That isn't necessary."

The sheriff stopped chewing and stared dead-eyed at Jan, the jocular mask falling away and the predatory lawman surfacing. Jan knew Monster would stare at him until he reversed his position. Jan had seen the unaided stare bring startling confessions from Monster's interrogees.

Jan sighed. "OK," he said, "I'll call you tonight and tell you when to pick me up."

Monster smiled. "You're buyin lunch, right?"

"Absolutely."

*   *   *

Back at the ranch, something deep within him drew him down the gently sloping path that led to the river and the boathouse. He had told Emma that calling the shed a boathouse was an exaggeration, but she always used that word. In reality, the shed only had room for the 16-foot aluminum boat Jan used to navigate to the glory hole upstream from the dock. The glory hole produced the Wyoming State record sauger, along with record ling and catfish. Mostly, though, the river gave up only whitefish and carp. The streams of the Bighorn Mountains produced beautiful pink-fleshed brook trout and that's where Jan really liked to fish. Still, he enjoyed taking the boat upstream to the confluence of the Bighorn and the Nowood

Rivers, just off the point of land marking the southern and western edge of his property. There he would tie up and fish, and watch the sun go down.

Emma had liked to sit on the rough-beamed deck that supported the boathouse. In the summer the shed doors were left standing open and the boat was tied at the pier. On hot afternoons, with the shed shading the sun and the river running coolly before them, she and Jan would sit there for hours. Those peaceful times haunted Jan more than any single memory of Emma.

When Emma had replaced the living room couch, she suggested that the old one should be moved to the boathouse for the summer. The boathouse stayed dry because Jan had tarpapered it on the sides and had nailed composition roofing material to the roof.

"Why do you want a couch down there?" Jan had asked.

Emma had merely smiled demurely in reply.

So it was that warm summer evenings found them snuggled together on the couch with the moon on the river and the smell of her hair in his nostrils. Mosquito netting covered the front of the boathouse, but did not obstruct the view. Across the river the badland foothills dissolved into the water. For Jan, life had never been better.

Now he sat on the dock in the gathering dusk, his feet inches above the river. He sighed, got up and took a bottle from a shelf. He twisted the cap off the fifth of whiskey and filled a shot glass. He poured the shot into the river. Then he refilled the glass and drank it. It had become a ritual. His drinking bothered him. He had never really cared much for booze. He spurned drugs not wanting to trade lucidity for numbness. But that had changed since Emma's death. Since then he could not—*could not*—expect to sleep without the medication. Damned if you do, damned if you don't. The blast that killed Emma had blown a huge hole in his guts. He knew booze could never fill the hole. But that wasn't why he drank. He drank to avoid the nightmares.

The balmy evening breeze caressed his body, warming him on the outside while the whiskey warmed him on the inside. He wondered why he still felt cold.

CHAPTER THREE

J an rose early the next morning and walked the mile and a half from his house up the lane that led over the railroad tracks and up a steep hill to the junction of County Lane 48. He walked fast and pumped three-pound hand weights shoulder high, supposedly doubling the aerobic value of the walk. He followed County Lane 48 to its junction with Orchard Bench Road, a blacktop leading to U.S. Highway 20 and into Basin. Orchard Bench Road was a farm-to-market route for the irrigation farmers on Orchard Bench—the Swancutts, the Greeleys, and the Rogers. The land produced sugar beets, beans, hay, and some grain. The road ran down the middle of the five-mile wide greenbelt of irrigated crops that lay between the Big Horn County Canal and the river. The land sloped from the canal eastward to the river. Main irrigation ditches—six feet deep and wide—carried water downhill to the farms before dividing into smaller feeder ditches that watered the crops. What little water was left rejoined the Bighorn.

Standing at the junction of County Lane 48 and Orchard Bench Road, Jan wiped the sweat from his face and surveyed the old Rogers place where he had worked summers in his youth. O. J. Rogers had bred beautiful palomino stallions. Every year during the county fair he rode a huge stud in the parade. His tack sported a robin's egg blue leather saddle with silver ornaments and a matching bridle. Rogers' high-spirited horses pranced and snorted in the parades, wild-eyed under the restraining rein of the old man.

Jan worked summers bucking hay on the Rogers place, irrigating, and feeding stock. After school in good weather he mended fences. On hot summer days he drove his stripped down 1932 Model A (purchased in 1957 for $50) to the canal to swim in the muddy water. His favorite spot was upstream from the mile-long concrete siphon snaking through Antelope Creek wash. Steel bars formed a grill over the opening to the siphon now, but not when he swam there in his youth. Had he been caught in the rushing water entering the siphon he would have drowned. Lanny Ford, three years older than Jan, threw a live dog in the canal at the mouth of the siphon and then raced his car to the other end to watch the bloody carcass come out.

At age 58 Jan was aerobically fit, although he always carried at least 20 pounds too much, sometimes more in winter. Just under six feet, his best weight was 200 pounds. He thought he carried that well. He had begun walking regularly in Los Angeles when he headed the Associated Press Bureau and after he met Emma who was a marathoner. After they moved to Wyoming, she had continued to run four mornings a week, except during the winter when she worked out two evenings a week at a gym in Worland. Jan didn't run—even for her—and he never liked working out in the gym, though he would often drive down with her and drink coffee and read. His walking program fell apart in the winter.

He turned and began the mile-and-a-half trek back to the ranch. As he turned into his driveway, Jan unbuckled the belt that positioned the speed holster holding the SIG-Sauer P232 in the middle of his back. He picked up the security keypad on the porch and rearmed the perimeter, then slumped down in the big bentwood rocker and mopped sweat off his face with a towel. It was already over 80 degrees, the precursor of a hot June day. Jan loved the hot, dry Wyoming summers. He lived for days like this. "Another summer," he remembered saying to Emma, embracing her as she left for work. "I'm the luckiest man on the planet." The last words he said to her. Almost exactly two years ago.

He had misplaced the summer of her death altogether. It went up in the smoke of the explosion, clouding his mind for months. He drifted in a sea of self-pity, alcohol, and grief until he slowly began to function. By the following summer—last summer—he was at least able to begin to work again. And when he began to work, his focus shifted.

When Jan left the AP at age 52, he and Emma had moved to Wyoming. They purchased the ranch and supported themselves through his freelancing and her real estate business. She had done well in that profession in California. Wyoming licensing was among the easiest in the nation. Her winsome personality and brains quickly carved a piece of the Northern Wyoming real estate pie, mostly ranch sales and commercial property.

Since moving back home to Wyoming, Jan had written for a variety of magazines and newspapers. He interviewed celebrities who retired to the Wyoming mountains or who had summer homes in Jackson Hole, or near Sheridan, or Cody, or Bozeman, Montana. He also did some work in Utah and Nevada. Occasionally he worked political stories in Oregon, Washington, Colorado, and at least once in New Mexico. Sometimes his old contacts drew him into a story in California. Following Emma's murder he was unable to work for a year, and when he finally did go back to work he found that polygamy and Mormon Fundamentalism dominated his writing.

At first Jan had taken on the Hansen cult as simply another intriguing story. Of course he realized that journalists sometimes touch nerves and get into trouble. He had received death threats when he investigated organized crime in Southern California. That's when he bought the SIG-Sauer. But it simply hadn't occurred to him that the stories on the Hansen cult would place him in danger in Wyoming. Certainly it had never occurred to him that he would endanger Emma.

As the fog began to clear from his mind in the months following Emma's death, he was stunned by the thought that Ronald Hansen might be behind the murder. But there was no hard evidence connecting the murder to Hansen. At first, Jan suspected the murder had its origins in an old Mafia grudge from his LA days. But as his mind began to clear and information began to filter through Monster to him, it became clear that Hansen had ordered the hit—the hit meant for Jan but killing Emma instead.

Jan had struggled to see Hansen as the murderer. He remembered Hansen from grammar school. In fact, a memory going back more than 50 years to the first grade resurrected itself. Hansen—Jan could see him in his mind's eye—dressed in farmer-style overalls, common enough then in the small rural community. Hansen had brought for show-and-tell a working model of a hay bailer. He had made it by hand, carving each wooden piece with skill far advanced for a child of six. He had a toy John Deere tractor to pull the bailer. Jan had been impressed.

It was all downhill from there for Ronnie Hansen. As the years wore on, Ronnie became less and less like his classmates. His clothes were hand sewn and from an earlier era. Hansen was quiet and, Jan remembered, had a superior air about him. He didn't participate in team sports or other extracurricular school activities in high school. He didn't date. He often spent his lunch hours reading the Book of Mormon. And, although Big Horn County hosted a large Mormon population, the Mormon students had nothing to do with him. Jan had not really understood why. Something about polygamy, he had heard. He also heard the word "apostate" applied to Hansen, but he didn't even know what the word meant.

Basin High School graduated 18 students in 1960, Hansen among them. Jan, troubled after his parents' divorce, had dropped out of school the year before and joined the Navy, finishing his high school work by correspondence and eventually getting a high school diploma signed by the Big Horn County School Board. He did that for his mother.

Jan, when he finally accepted that Hansen was behind Emma's murder, was stunned. He was amazed that, accompanying the rage he felt toward Hansen, he also felt pity for him. The picture of little Ronnie and the hay bailer in the ridiculous overalls and mop of blonde hair superimposed itself over the now tough, sophisticated Ronald Hansen, III, leader of a large, prosperous, and weird sect. The only time Jan had encountered Hansen since moving back to Wyoming was at the Big Horn County Fair. That was just a few months after Jan moved up from LA with Emma. Young bodyguards had surrounded Hansen, and he had three or four of his wives with him. Hansen looked coolly at Jan and nodded. Jan had smiled thinly and held up a finger in recognition.

The more Jan learned about Hansen and the unusual social forces at work in the West, the clearer the picture became for him. As he talked to the locals in the area about Hansen, he learned more from what they would *not* say than by what they *would* say. There was fear in the air. One man, a bearded grizzly bear disguised as a farmer, spoke quietly about his ex-wife who was now one of Hansen's wives. "Started out simply enough," the man said. "Jennifer began attending what she told me was a Bible study. One day I came home and her clothes were gone. She left me a note."

As Jan studied the polygamy phenomenon and its connection to the Survivalist/Christian Identity Movement, Jan began to get a handle on Hansen. He learned that 30,000 polygamists inhabit Utah and perhaps as many more live in the surrounding Western States. He learned of exit groups like Tapestry Against Polygamy, a group made up of former polygamous wives who had escaped the system and who now provided shelter for women trying to escape. The Utah newspapers were full of horror stories of young girls who were forced into marriages with uncles and who were sometimes beaten when they attempted to leave the system. Utah had mostly ignored polygamy until the state woke up to the fact that polygamist men had only one wife of legal record and often signed up the rest of the wives for state welfare benefits which annually drained millions of dollars from state coffers.

The most important thing Jan had learned was that Hansen viewed any attack on himself as an attack on the Kingdom of God. But Jan had not known that when he published his *New York Times* story—"Mormon Polygamous Sect Stockpiling Weapons and Hatred in Wyoming." He had no way of understanding that the story immediately targeted him for removal by Hansen. That realization came to him too late—after Emma's murder. It finally came home to him late one night as he listened to an interview with Salmon Rushdie on BBC radio. As Rushdie explained how his written words had purchased a death sentence for him from a Muslim Ayatollah, Jan realized he was under the same sort of threat. He finally came to realize that he was on an unchosen but certain collision course with Hansen.

Even though Monster Broadbeck had pulled strings and got the FBI involved, forensics could produce no evidence linking Hansen to the murder. Eventually it came down to what Jan called a certain *knowing*. Monster fully shared Jan's convictions.

As the impact of Hansen's responsibility dawned on Jan, he discovered other feelings within himself—fear, hatred, rage, and a desire for vengeance. Those feelings grew in intensity, although he tried not to nurse them. He tried to subdue them. He thought he was going crazy. Fear totally overcame him. He was afraid to walk from his house to his pickup. It was then that he invested several thousand dollars in electronic security at the ranch—security that had paid off and saved his life two nights earlier.

After Jan lived through the raw emotions, he settled into a studied determination. He realized he had been driven into a death struggle that *required* a response. He determined to rise to the challenge. Hansen had not only killed Jan's wife, but he was committed to kill Jan as well—no matter how long it took.

Jan weighed other options besides confrontation. He could run. That was a very real option for a while. He finally realized he could not exercise that option, although he wasn't sure why he couldn't. He tried to convince himself that his desire to get Hansen was rooted in some kind of moral high ground—like justice. Revenge was a worthy enough passion, but Jan considered himself neither philosophical nor religious. However, he believed revenge—if it weren't God's jurisdiction—*ought* to be. Justice wasn't enough to motivate him either, maybe for the same reasons. He admired people who understood things like revenge and justice, and who stood for those concepts—the Nazi-hunting Jews, for example, determined to bring the perpetrators of the Holocaust to justice—but those abstract concepts did not move him personally.

In the end, Jan could not form a rational backdrop for the rage he felt. This rage was different from anything he had ever known. Anger was no stranger to him, and impatience—he had often been told—was one of his primary faults. But rage was only a word until it dawned on him that Ronald Hansen had murdered his wife in cold blood. The rage he felt became palpable, like an evil twin stalking him. And he knew it would never go away.

Actually, it was worse than that. The rage might be eradicated, but at what cost? Jan believed that if he were to bring Hansen to justice the rage would subside. But the problem was, given Hansen's resources and the government's state of paralysis, the term "bring to justice," meant, in the final analysis, that Jan had to murder Hansen. At first he said he had to *kill* Hansen, but reason told him that entrapping a man in order to kill him may be justifiable in some cosmic way, but it was, nevertheless, murder. Jan wanted to be straight with himself about that.

Jan had known cops in LA who had "crossed." They crossed over and took up the methods of the criminals they pursued. They used the term "crossed." That meant they went from being the good guys, who used civil methods, to being bad guys who used evil methods. Their motives and methods became hopelessly scrambled. In the end, they "crossed."

Jan had discussed this with Monster. "Yep," Monster had said, "that's true. When you dance with the devil, *he* doesn't change, *you* change." Where, Jan had asked, was Monster in all this? Monster had smiled enigmatically.

What Jan had hoped would become the warm autumn days of a man in full maturity, had become instead a winter. Ronald Hansen had turned his life turned topsy-turvy. Would Jan cross? Would he become a murderer? If Ronald Hansen had forced that upon him, it made him hate the Prophet even more.

By the end of the first year following Emma's death Jan recognized he was on dangerous ground. He needed a reason to live; some positive reason for life beyond his desire to eliminate Hansen. He needed something to help him endure the darkness. It was then that he mentally retraced the steps that had brought him back to Wyoming. He knew the answer for him—for now—was in this *land,* this *place*—the place that had drawn him home. And now, he believed, this place would provide him with reasons to live.

So it was that finally, even as he continued to live in the

palling shadow of Hansen, he had begun to suck life out of the earth—the earth of his ranch. He drew life out of the hot Wyoming air on his face, out of the smell of the sage at night, out of the view from the crest of Mount Baldy, out of the drift in the muddy Bighorn. He was no conservationist, no New Age tree-hugger, no mystical medicine man; but somehow the permanence of the huge cottonwoods—drawing life from the river through the dust—moved him. The serene silence of Dead Horse Gulch carried him to a place in his memory nothing else could. If ever he was in love with something other than Emma, it was this place. He believed in the land as strongly as Hansen believed he was God's mouthpiece.

*   *   *

Jan showered and ate his ritual breakfast of three eggs, four strips of crisp bacon and whole-wheat toast, slathered with butter. Emma had marveled that his cholesterol was never high. "The only thing my dad left me," he had told her. "Good fat genes."

He placed his overnight bag by the door and took the metal pistol case from the closet. He unlocked it, and placed the nickel-plated SIG-Sauer with tritium night sights into it. He put two boxes of ammo—380 APC slugs, 9mm shorts—into another lockable container along with an extra clip. These two boxes could be legally checked through from Billings to Seattle.

The wedding clock on the piano was gently chiming 11:00 a.m. He had an hour. He walked to the first bedroom down the hall from the living room. Opening the closet he slid the suits and dress shirts to the center. On the back wall of the closet at the far right end of the wall was an almost invisible finger hole. Placing his finger in the hole, he slid the dark panel to reveal an opening through the back of the closet. He entered a narrow passage that housed a stairwell. Going down the stairs, he entered what had been his home more than 50 years earlier—the basement house.

The basement house had been constructed as merely four poured concrete walls that rose three feet above ground. A flat roof had covered the structure, which included a kitchen, a living room, and three bedrooms. The whole area comprised barely more than 1,000 square feet, but it had housed his mother, father, and four children. They lived there until he was six years old and then moved to town. Jan had repurchased the land from the lawyer who had bought it from his mother 35 years earlier. He had considered filling the basement house in, or building the log house somewhere else on the 500 acres, but somehow he couldn't bring himself to do that. He built the new house directly over the old one. Now the basement was a storage area filled with filing cabinets and outdated computers.

There was a hole in the wall Jan had broken out with a 16-pound sledge. It was three feet wide and led into a dirt passageway. Last summer, as Jan had begun to understand the depth of the peril he faced from Hansen, he had used his backhoe to dig a trench from the outside wall of his home toward the river—to the boathouse. The trench was six feet deep and three feet wide. He had covered it with corrugated metal sheets and pushed a foot of dirt over the top. The trench ended under the boathouse, a hinged door opening through the floor.

Jan went to an old dresser and pulled open the top drawer. He withdrew a leather shoulder holster and went back upstairs. There he put the shoulder holster in his overnight bag, then he stepped out on the porch to wait for Monster who would drive him the hundred miles to Billings. Since Emma's murder, the sheriff always insisted on accompanying Jan on any drive that took him more than twenty miles from home. He especially worried about the long stretch of Highway 310 between Greybull and Lovell. "Great place for an ambush," Monster had once said.

Jan's cell phone rang and Jan heard the sheriff's voice.

"Coming off Orchard Bench onto County 48," Sheriff Broadbeck said. "Hit the eject button or whatever you do."

CHAPTER FOUR

J an watched the champagne-colored Porsche 996 churn a dust
cloud coming down the lane. Monster pulled into the driveway grinning from the cockpit. The sheriff sprung the front boot
and Jan threw in his bag and computer. Jan climbed into the Porsche
and snapped his shoulder harness and seat belt, again wondering at
the ample interior; plenty of legroom for Monster to fit—if not
easily—at least comfortably.

"You never told me how a tinhorn sheriff drives an $80,000
toy," Jan said.

"I bought Microsoft stock in March of '86 and sold it before
the tech crash."

"Oh yeah? I heard you confiscated a panel truck loaded with
coke."

"Well, that could be true, too. But, funny thing, no one ever
pressed me on that."

"No kidding? By the way, how fast will this thing go?"

"It's spec'd at 174. I put her at 150 on the 310 north of
Greybull."

"Let's not do that today."

"Not unless Hansen's hit squad is on our tail," Monster grinned.

"You mean you'd outrun them? I thought you'd just pull over, rip the hood off their Jeep and beat them to death with it."

"See, that's the trouble with legends. What I'd really do is get a two-mile lead on them, pull over and blow their wheels off as they went by. By the way, we have plenty of time, I need to stop at the office on our way through town."

"You're the driver. I'm in good hands. And thanks for this," Jan said as he settled back into the seat for the ride through Basin and then on to Billings to catch his flight to see Deck Edwards in Seattle.

"No problem, boy. I don't want to have you on my conscience, that's all. If the Hansen disciples *are* watching you—and I think they are—I don't want you on that lonely stretch of 310 with nothing but wild mustangs between you and the bad guys."

They drove in silence until they hit Orchard Bench Road. Monster broke the ice. "How's your love life, boy?"

"John, I have no love life, I have no interest in a love life, I..."

"OK, OK, I'm out of line."

"I know you worry about me."

"Yeah, yeah."

"Thanks, but I'm *fine.*"

"Sure you are. And it's none of my business."

"You know, right now, I have bigger things to worry about."

"What's that got to do with anything? I worry all the time, but I try not to let it affect my love life."

Jan chewed his lip, then cleared his throat. "John, you ever been afraid of anything? I mean *really* afraid?"

"Sure, lots of stuff. Afraid I'll wake up some morning and

my masculine charm will have disappeared…"

"No, come on. Everybody walks in fear of you, even Hansen I suppose. But, you, what do you fear?"

"I've been scared."

"When?"

"Vietnam."

"Well, sure…"

The sheriff was quiet, then said, "Want to hear a story about Monster's fear?"

"Sure."

Monster was in a pensive mode, something Jan had never seen.

"I arrived in 'Nam in March of 1966," Monster said. "You missed all the fun."

"Yeah," Jan said, "I enlisted in the Navy in 1959. I never thought of myself as a Vietnam vet."

"No shame in that. If I'd been smarter *I* would have enlisted before I went to college, like you did. By postponing college, you wound up missing the war. The luck of the draw."

"Yeah," Jan said, "the Navy actually took me at the end of my junior year of high school. They sent me to electronics school and gave me a chance to grow up. I didn't go to college until 1969. I was a late bloomer."

Monster paused as if to consider that.

"Well, in May of '66 the largest battle of the war to that date broke out near Dong Ha. Most of the 3rd Marine Division, 5,000 men—boys I should say—headed north in five battalions. We backed up the South Vietnamese in Operation Hastings. Along with the Army and a flotilla of Navy warships shelling from off-shore—not to mention naval air power—we drove the North Viet-namese Army over the so-called DMZ in three weeks. Some Wash-ington genius called it a victory.

"At any rate, I hadn't been in 'Nam long, and I was on patrol in that stinking jungle. I took the midwatch while my platoon was hunkered down for the night. I'm green as grass and scared to death. About 2:00 a.m. it's real quiet. Hot and wet and…anyway…"

Monster was silent. Jan looked at him.

"You all right, John?"

"Anyway, like I'm saying, I been on watch for two hours. Still as a San Francisco bath house at noon. Suddenly this gook surfaces about six feet in front of me. Little kid, 16-17 years old. With a huge AK-47. I mean, it was as big as he was."

"My God!" Jan couldn't help himself.

"We both freeze. My mouth hanging open, his eyes the size of coffee cups. We stare at each other for twenty seconds, both of us afraid to move. We just stare at each other. Pretty soon he starts backing away. Keeps staring at me. Just backs out of my vision.

"Now I'm really screwed up in my head. I don't know if he is going to open up on me. I wonder should I start whanging away at him. So what do I do? Nothing. I did nothing! I sat there sweating and shaking. I shoulda woke the lieutenant. I did nothing."

"What happened?"

Monster's knuckles were white on the wheel, but his face had turned crimson. *My God, he's gonna have a heart attack.* "What happened, John?"

Sweat was rolling down Monster's cheeks. When he spoke his voice was soft, barely audible over the engine and road noise.

"About twenty minutes later we receive incoming mortar fire. The little slope went back to his platoon and spotted us for the mortars. They started pounding us. I should have known that. I *did* know that, but I couldn't think, I couldn't move."

"Well, John, who could have?"

"We lost two men from our platoon in that raid."

"John...."

Silence.

"Yeah, boy, I've been scared. Like you are now. Wasn't the worst thing I encountered, though."

Jan could see Monster wanted to talk. He wondered if he had ever told anyone this before. Monster looked over at him.

"Wanna know why I'm telling you this."

"Because you empathize with my fears?" Jan said, attempting to lighten the conversation.

Monster chuckled softly. "No, boy, because I know you can keep a confidence."

"Thanks, John."

"The one story I have never told anybody, but I think about it every day of my life—my rotten useless life."

Monster took a deep breath. "OK, so I was doing chicken coop cleanup. You know—going through a Vietcong village, checking out their pathetic little huts. 'Course all the Vietcong had tunneled halfway to hell before we hit the village. It was always that way. Except this one day."

Silence again. Jan wondered why John was saying this today, after holding it inside for more than 30 years.

"This one day I'm screaming through a village, kicking in doors, terrorizing the women and old men and kids. I go through this one door and, no kidding, here is a young kid with *another* AK-47. For a minute, I thought it was the *same* kid. Anyway, he has this piece pointed at me. He looks like he just woke up or something. Then he throws it on the floor of the hut." Monster paused.

"He throws the gun down..." Monster's teeth are clenched and he is speaking through them. He is forcing himself to continue talking. Jan starts to interrupt him, but Monster waves him off.

"He throws the gun down...and I...and I shoot him." He

sighs, "I shoot him about eight times in the chest. He's younger than I am and just as scared. Maybe he was the lucky one. Anyway, try living with *that* for 30 years, boy."

Jan was silent for a while. Then he said, "So are you doing penance now by chasing bad guys—by being in law enforcement?"

Monster knit his brows. He drew a deep breath through his nose.

"Not so much that. More like trying to balance the *world's* karma, rather than my own."

"I don't get it."

"Neither do I. I'm sure it's all jacked-up irrationality. But it goes something like this. See, I took a young innocent off the planet, so how can I allow Ronald Hansen to walk around?"

Jan whistled. "And you accuse *me* of philosophical speculation!"

Monster laughed.

"Yeah, you're right. But let me tell you something else, something for you."

"OK."

"You are determined that you want to get involved in all this, that you want to get Hansen?"

"It's about Emma…"

"I mean no disrespect, but we both know that is not true. It's about *you*. It's about your failure to protect her, your *guilt*."

"Well…"

"But let me give you a warning. If you *can*, turn back from this. Turn back now. But if you *can't*, and you do the deed with Hansen, you will have crossed the Jordan—only backwards."

Jan felt his stomach tighten. *Crossed.* He wondered where Monster came up with the biblical allusion: the Children of Israel crossing the river Jordan after forty years in the desert, crossing into the Promised Land. Monster was full of surprises.

"What to you mean *backwards*?"

Monster smiled at him.

"What you mean, I suppose, is that by killing Hansen I will be forced out of the Promised Land to wander the desert?"

"Bingo, *tomadachi*!"

"Yeah? There's only one problem with your analogy."

"OK…" Monster strung the word out.

"Yeah, John. That's because I'm not in the Promised Land right now, I'm in hell. So why should I be afraid of the desert?"

Monster shook his head and chuckled.

"Double bingo. I think you will make a *fine* killer."

Monster looked at Jan. He was laughing out loud now.

"Welcome, buddy," the sheriff said. "Welcome! You have discovered the Great Secret."

"Yeah, what's that?"

"There is no Promised Land! There's only hell!"

Monster was laughing so hard now that tears came to his eyes.

"John," Jan said, "sometimes you scare me."

CHAPTER FIVE

The Council Room was situated at the north end of the tabernacle, a building that housed a 1,000-seat auditorium where church services and semi-annual conferences were held. The council room was paneled in dark mahogany, a huge polished teak conference table sat in the exact middle of the room. A gentle, pleasant fragrance wafted from a large fresh-cut flower centerpiece on the table. Down each side of the table were plush chairs for the Apostles, six to a side. A bottle of water stood on the table before each chair. The Prophet Ronald Hansen sat at the north end of the table, flanked by his secretary and a chair for a guest, should the Prophet invite one. At the south end were three chairs. Today nine Apostles were in attendance, three were on assignment. Half a dozen invited observers and supplicants sat in chairs placed around the perimeter of the room.

"Brothers," Hansen said, "I thank all of you for being here. Let the secretary note that Elders Wainwright, Smith, and Brucellus are on assignment at the pleasure of the President."

Turning to the petitioners, he said, "Welcome to this open

meeting of the Ruling Council. As you know, we hold these particular meetings once a month and invite all members of the Church of the One Mighty and Strong who wish to attend to petition the Council. May we have the first member take a seat at the end of the table?"

A young man of about 25 arose, walked to the end of the table and sat down. He carried a file folder, which he placed carefully on the table in front of him. He wore a dark suit that fit him loosely and showed signs of wear. The collar of his white shirt was frayed and his tie was too narrow. He ran a hand through fine brown hair and licked his lips nervously. "Thank you for allowing me this opportunity," he said, looking right and left down the table. To the Prophet he said, "Thank you especially, President. It is an honor for me to be here."

The Prophet smiled and waved his hand slightly.

The young man continued. "As some of you know, I finished a mission to Arizona this spring."

One of the Apostles nodded vigorously. "And a very successful mission, if I may add that comment." He looked at the Prophet who nodded his approval.

"Anyway," the young man continued, "I really want to go to college. I don't want to get married right now. I have prepared a few pages that give my reasons, my qualifications, and my petition to the Council. I would like to leave this with you brothers to consider. I will accept your verdict no matter what it is."

"James," the Prophet said. "James, we know you well. We have watched you grow into a strong and pure young man and we have great expectations for you. Of course, we know your parents, Ralph and Donetta, and we have observed their sacrifices for the Church and their many years of service to it. We also realize that they do not have the means to send you to college, but they would spare nothing to give you every possible opportunity."

"Thank you, sir."

"Tell me, what area of study do you plan to pursue?"

"Computer science, President."

Hansen smiled. "Wonderful. And where do you expect to practice your engineering skills when you finish college?"

"Wherever the Lord directs me, sir. I will return here and seek the Council's guidance at that time."

"Where do you plan to go to school?"

"I have been accepted at UC Berkeley. But the out-of-state tuition…"

Hansen interrupted. "James, money, as you probably have guessed, is not the deciding factor in cases like this. If it is the right thing to do, the Church will provide what you need. You would, of course, be required to meet certain scholastic goals and to keep us well apprised of your activities."

"Of course."

"James, as you know, these decisions are not made lightly. The entire Council needs to seek the Lord in these matters."

"I understand that, sir."

Hansen looked up and down the table. "However," he said, "unless one of the brothers has a check in his spirit about this, I think we should just say 'Yes, and Amen' to you right now. What say you, brethren."

With one voice they said, "Yes, and Amen!"

"Wonderful," the Prophet said, "James, call at my financial secretary's office later today and tell brother Satterwhite that the Council wants to send you to Berkeley." The Prophet drummed his fingers on the table and looked at the ceiling. "And James, tell brother Satterwhite the President said to send you in good style!"

*   *   *

Three hours later, the Council meeting was dismissed. Hansen noted that Hoyt Akers, his helicopter pilot, left the meeting apparently disappointed that his petition to take Maggie Balsam to wife was temporarily set aside to give the brethren time to seek the Lord.

The Prophet asked Apostle Campbell to stay. A bowl of fruit and a pitcher of orange juice were set before the two men by a fresh-faced young girl. She poured two glasses of juice. The Prophet followed her with his eyes as she left the room.

He turned to Campbell, his most trusted Apostle. The Church knew him as Silent Bill Campbell because he didn't speak often and when he did it was always brief and to the point. Hansen called him Silent Bill for a variety of other reasons.

"Bill, I have a matter of the utmost urgency to talk to you about."

Campbell waited for the Prophet to continue.

"You know, of course," that our special mission south of Basin went wrong the other night and that our own men are in jail in Casper awaiting trial. Their bonds are set at $200,000 each."

"Yes, of course I know that."

"Well, this is not a time for recriminations. Excellent legal counselors have already visited with our soldiers there in Casper."

Campbell said nothing. He picked up his orange juice and sipped it, but continued to look frankly at the Prophet.

"What I need to know," Hansen said as he inspected a thick-skinned tangerine, "is how those two boys will fare under the thumb of the gentile storm troopers."

"I think they will crack."

Silence.

"Hmmmm, I'm *very* sorry to hear that." Hansen picked up a sharp knife and sliced the tangerine cleanly in two. He looked at Campbell.

Campbell arose, drank down the last of his orange juice,

turned, and walked out of the room.

After he was gone, Hansen shook his head. "What a smooth character you are Billy Campbell."

*   *   *

Five minutes after Campbell left the conference room, Sydney Greenleaf came in. He wore khakis and gum-soled boots. He was 35, muscular, and had a military haircut. Greenleaf crossed his hands in front of his waist, standing at parade rest.

The Prophet sat silently staring at a tangerine he rolled around on the table as though to soften it. After a moment, Greenleaf cleared his throat. The Prophet slowly brought his gaze to him.

"Oh, Sydney, forgive me. I didn't realize you had entered."

"That's perfectly all right, President."

"Kind of you Sydney. Look, yesterday you told me that Monster Broadbeck is escorting Jan Kucera to an Alaska Airlines flight in Billings."

"Yes, sir. We have a tap on his phone. He made arrangements yesterday and should be on his way right now as a matter of fact."

"Don't we have anyone inside Alaska?"

"I'll find out, sir."

"I want to know when our friend is coming home. If I am right, he will not allow Broadbeck to meet the plane. His pride will only let him go so far. So, I would like to know that."

"You want to know when he is coming back?"

The Prophet froze. He turned toward Sydney with a perplexed look on his face. "I believe that is the question I asked, was it not?" His voice was calm, but his eyes were flashing.

For an instant fear crossed Sydney's face, but just for an instant. "Yes, sir," he said flatly, "That is the question you asked."

"So will you please just get that information and get back to me."

"Absolutely, sir."

"Thank you, Sydney."

The Prophet turned back to the bowl of fruit. He neatly sliced all of the pieces in half.

CHAPTER SIX

Half the seats on the Boeing 737 to Seattle were empty on the 4:00 p.m. flight. Jan, after Monster had dropped him at the Billings airport, had boarded, settled in, and ordered a VO on the rocks. He had pulled out the slip of paper Monster had given him in the café. It said "Granny, 555-3665—maidenform."

The drive to Billings had been uneventful—no sign of Hansen's people. Jan hadn't expected any trouble when he left the ranch with Monster. He hated being chaperoned, but Monster insisted that Jan not travel Highway 310 without him. The 310 ran 25 miles north from Greybull to Lovell through an alkali desert. Only rattlesnakes, coyotes, jackrabbits, and—interestingly enough—a herd of wild horses—inhabited those dry sagebrushed hills. The horse herd had been there for a century and in the 1980's the state had erected a marker detailing the herd's history. Jan's father had walked those hills searching for dinosaur fossils, proudly displaying a fossilized dinosaur tooth for Jan. The road came within fifteen miles of the C1MS compound, and for Monster that was too close for comfort.

At lunch in Greybull, Monster had delighted the waitress—who couldn't keep her eyes off him—by ordering a 12-ounce sirloin cut in strips over a huge salad drenched with Bleu Cheese dressing, along with an order of mashed potatoes and gravy on the side. One of the customers, a man of about 50 in a snappy business suit, immediately got up and left the café when they entered. He threw a bill on the counter and glared at Monster as he left. Jan cocked his head and raised his eyebrows.

"John Duffy," Monster said. "Banker. He made the mistake of pointing his finger in my face when I brought his drunk teenage son home one night."

"And?"

"I broke his finger."

Monster took a sip from his coffee cup. "I had a talk with George Olson last night. Told him you were going to Seattle to see Deck. I pressed Olson for information on C1MS."

"He's been helpful so far."

"Yeah, he has. He wants to nail Hansen as bad as we do. But the Feds have their heads so far up their gray flannel bloomers they're paralyzed. They will never go into that compound unless they have hard evidence of violation of a federal crime."

"Such as?"

"Such as possession of prohibited firearms or other weaponry."

"How about murder?"

"There is no federal statute on murder. Conspiracy to deprive someone of their civil rights can get you life without parole on a RICO indictment, but murder has to be tried in a state court. Listen, Olson is very worried about Hansen. And he's frustrated. He feels he is not getting the kind of response from Washington that he should. He remembers the disaster at Ruby Ridge, both before and after the shootout."

"After?"

"Did you know that Lon Horiuchi, the ATF agent who accidentally killed Randy Weaver's wife during the gun battle at Ruby Ridge, spent 10 years fighting the State of Idaho to keep from being prosecuted for manslaughter? The 9th District Court ruled that Horiuchi could be prosecuted, but the Boundary County prosecutor eventually dropped the charges. Olson was galled that a great marshal nearly went to prison for simply doing his duty.

"Yes, I followed that. The 9th District is notorious for such rulings."

"Well, it just demonstrates that the bad guys still have more rights than the good guys. Anyway that—and a boatload of other stuff—means that Olson is no longer the company man he once was. As for the Hansen compound, Olson says he continues to hear rumors of a stockpile of ammonium nitrate out there. He's worried we are on the verge of an Oklahoma City, but he is convinced the Feds won't move until somebody blows the doors off the statehouse in Cheyenne or until the federal building in Billings gets a facelift. In other words, the Feds are paralyzed until there is "clear and present danger."

"To whom?"

"To anyone. If they have good intelligence that Hansen is abusing women or children—depriving them of their civil liberties—they could go in."

"Like Waco? Wouldn't that be cute?"

"Well, that's the problem, of course." Monster continued, "But if they had sufficient evidence that Hansen is conspiring to put civilians at risk they might act. But it would have to be evidence 'of the highest reliability.'"

"And how are they going to obtain such evidence?"

Monster's eyes twinkled. "Ah, my point exactly. Just what I asked Georgie boy. This is where it gets very interesting."

"Go on," Jan said rotating his index finger in a circle.

"See, they know that Hansen is a computer wonk. He considers himself very high-tech…"

"I remember he was a bright boy in high school."

"Well, get this, he has lots of computer terminals on the compound. He tracks all his financial stuff. Did you know that he owns, or controls, nearly a hundred businesses throughout the West?"

"I've heard rumors. In fact I started to look into that."

"Yeah, he's a multi-millionaire, but—get this—he stores no digital information at the compound. None!"

"How can that be?"

"He microwaves everything to computers off compound."

"Come on!"

"No kidding. His terminals operate the remote computers through the microwave links. Hey! this is the digital age, *amigo*. It's all speed of light. It makes no difference where the hardware is. And the microwave link is safer than Wyoming telephone cable. Safer, I'm told, than satellite. It can only be intercepted if you physically position an antenna somewhere along the line-of-sight transmission pathway.

"But what does all this cost him?"

"The costs are nothing for him, *nothing*. Believe me. You do not know the kind of wealth we are talking about. Remember, he is the *grandson* of the founder of the cult. Sure, his own genius has multiplied the membership 100-fold, but his dad died very wealthy, controlling dozens of businesses, from garbage collection services in cities throughout the West to mobile home manufacturing plants in Oregon and Washington."

The waitress walked up and set the plates on the table, her hip rubbing Monster's arm. He smiled at her and raised his eyebrows. She winked and wiggled off.

Monster continued, "Ronnie-The-Third has built the Church into a mega-wealthy empire. In fact, Olson says their best shot is an IRS conviction. That's part of the reason Olson chose the IRS cover. Hansen is so sure of himself he *expects* the IRS to be present in the county. "Anyway, Olson said that the microwave is a backdoor."

"What do you mean?" Jan asked.

"Well, the information that is microwaved from Hansen's compound—Olson doesn't know exactly what route it takes or where it winds up, but he's certain it passes through a relay site on Medicine Mountain."

"The Medicine Wheel?"

"Right. How's that for spooky? He apparently has a station on a piece of grandfathered private land within a mile of the Medicine Wheel itself."

"Unbelievable!"

"Well, when you think of it, it's another demonstration of our boy's genius. He's not only Jehovah's supposed spokesman, but he works powerful medicine. He has actually attracted a handful of American Indians! You ever hear about the Mormon connection to the Indians—the so-called Lamanites? He has access to the Crow Agency just over the mountain in Montana. We think another microwave transmission site may be located on the reservation. Once the signal gets to Billings, it can be transmitted over secure landlines anywhere in the world. Anyway, for our purposes, when that information is riding along the airwaves, it is accessible, it can be intercepted."

"What about decoding the encryption?"

"Jan, we are talking the *ATF* here! They can decode Allan Greenspan's bank statements."

"But Olson won't be party to some clandestine..."

"Jan, you don't know Olson like I do. All I'm willing to say at this point is that he served with Bill Degan at Ruby Ridge".

"Oh wow!" Jan said. "Marshal Degan was killed at Ruby Ridge!"

"Yep. Olson has a well of bitterness inside that cool G-Man demeanor. He told me that if we could find some way to provide him with a microwave feed, he'd find some way to turn it into usable information."

Jan whistled low and shook his head in amazement.

"Anyway," Monster continued, "as the signal leaves the compound, it must travel west before it is bounced back to the Medicine Wheel, and from there…who knows, it might wind up in some Ayatollah's bedroom. The point is that Hansen apparently can't imagine the U.S. government would build a radio tower and intercept his data. So, here's the deal, Olson guesses there is enough information within the data to do real harm to Hansen. Olson should probably get out of all this before he mucks up his retirement, but he promised me that if we can provide him with the raw data, he will make sure we get the meat of the translations. And *we*—that is you and me, *kimo sabe*—have none of the Fed's inhibitions when it comes to Ronnie's civil rights."

Jan could feel the excitement rising inside him, but he controlled it. So far what he was hearing made some sense, but left too much unanswered. It also begged a tremendous number of questions. He'd think about it.

Monster spoke. *"Amigo,* you're as quiet as a gay hairdresser in a recruiting station. You're asking yourself why the Feds don't intercept the information themselves?"

"Among other things."

"Olson says in order to do so, they would have to either finance an interception station to snake the material out of the air, or physically compromise one of Hansen's relay stations. Getting an electronic tap order is one thing. They could do that if it were a simple wiretap. But the Feds are very circumspect about physical incursion. Olson says there is no way anybody in Washington will order a crew to penetrate a private relay station in a situation like this. We are not talking international terrorism here."

"So we're out of luck."

Monster paused. "I wouldn't say that." He slid the piece of paper across the table. The paper with a Seattle phone number, a name, and the code "maidenform."

*   *   *

Jan cleared Sea-Tac, picked up his rental, a Buick Century. The girl at the Avis Wizard counter handed him the keys and said, "It's the Bordeaux Red Pearl in space 36."

"Bordeaux Red Pearl?"

She smiled, "Yep. Hope you have a date."

He smiled back and walked to the car, scanning the parking lot, his bag in his left hand and the keys in his right. Immediately after grabbing his luggage from the carousel he had gone into the nearest restroom, transferred the SIG-Sauer to the pocket of his leather jacket, and put the ammo gun cases in his bag.

He opened the trunk and deposited his bag, then took the jacket off, folded it, laid the gun on the seat and placed the jacket over it.

He caught I-5 at 188th and headed north to downtown Seattle. The drive was familiar. He arrived in the Pacific Time Zone at the same clock time he left Mountain Time Zone—4:00 p.m. He settled into the bumper-to-bumper traffic, taking nearly an hour to make the 15 miles to the Hilton. By the time he hung his shirts in the closet, it was pushing 6:00 p.m. Perfect. He picked up the phone and dialed Suntorys. A familiar voice came on the line.

"Jack, Jan Kucera."

"Jan! How ya doin, baby? We gotcha covered. $10-20, probably have ten players by 8 o'clock."

"Including me?"

"What you mean, 'including me?' Gimme a break here, Jan."

Jan laughed. "Plug a seat, I'll be there."

"You got it kid."

The best part of coming to Seattle was Texas Holdem at Suntorys on Aurora in North Seattle. Jan looked at his watch. Time for dinner if he hurried. He strapped on his shoulder holster, slipped in the SIG-Sauer and put on his worsted gray blazer. It was somewhat out of date—he had purchased it more than 30 years earlier in Hong Kong—but he told himself that in the current atmosphere of sartorial liberty, he was OK. And he was proud it still fit—at least in the summer. With his Wranglers, boots, and black T-shirt, he would be comfortable in the Seattle night. He didn't like playing cards in a jacket, let alone while wearing a shoulder holster. And, he was not licensed for a concealed-carry in Washington state, but Monster had counseled him, "Being illegal is better than being dead." Monster assured him that if he were busted in Seattle the Big Horn County Sheriff could get him released with a phone call.

Whenever he was in Seattle, Jan tried to make time for an evening or two at Suntorys. Jack Vecchio and he had been shipmates on the USS *Preble* during Jan's WestPac Cruise of 1960. They had spent hundreds of hours in an 04 deck radar room playing five-card-stud and California draw. Back then, Jan was actually a better player than Jack, but that had changed over the years. Now Jack was the professional and Jan tried to stay up to speed.

Until Emma's death he had tried to drive to Billings once a week to play Texas Holdem across the street from the Northern Hotel where, as an eleven-year-old a boy, he had stayed the night before catching the Northern Pacific to Minneapolis to visit his married sister. Now he played cards only occasionally.

As he dressed, he reflected on those childhood visits to Billings, a shopping hub not only for South Central Montana, but for Northern Wyoming as well. He remembered how, the first time he had stayed at the Northern Hotel with his mother, he had arisen early and left her sleeping in the room while he took the elevator to the roof of the hotel and helped the maintenance man raise the American flag. His mother was ashen-faced when he finally showed back up at the room. He had never previously been out of the state of Wyoming. That would have been 1953, Jan recalled.

Funny how his mind drifted to childhood scenes so much these days. His mother had taken him to a burger shop on Montana Avenue in Billings where they bought tiny little hamburgers— 12 for a dollar. And they had fried chicken in a restaurant across the street from a department store named "Fuchs." He remembered putting Worcestershire sauce on his fried chicken, developing a lifelong quirk. "Where in the world did you learn to do *that?*" Emma had asked him.

*　　*　　*

At Suntorys in North Seattle, Jack welcomed him to the club with a shot of VO. He reached across the bar and punched Jan on the arm. He insisted on a moment of conversation, even though Jan continued to glance at the game.

"That'll wait, Ace. Bring me up to speed." Jack exhaled a plume of smoke from his unfiltered Camel, picked up a shot glass, and sipped gingerly. Jack had always looked like an old man, even when Jan knew him when they were youngsters in the Navy. He had a face too small for his head and ears too big for his face. He had been bald before age 30. But behind the funny face was a mind that tracked everything at the speed of light. He had a heart as big as Wyoming in a body the size of Rhode Island, but in a fight—and Jan had been in several with him—he was merciless. "Can I help it? I'm a Sicilian," Jack would say, "I was taught how to punish people." Of course, he was not a Sicilian, but Jan had seen him take on a man twice his weight in an alley in San Francisco, Jack getting the poor guy in a headlock and running backward until the guy's head popped into a brick wall. Jack ran his card room with grace but expected—and received—instant obedience from the patrons in case of a dispute.

"How you holdin up, Jan?" asked the Sicilian.

"One day at a time, Jack. One day at a time."

"Yeah, ain't it. I worry about you kid. You getting out any?`"

"You and Monster! What's with this inordinate interest in my love life?"

Jack threw his head back and roared, "Yeah! Good ol Monster. Stick with us buddy-boy, we'll have you straightened out yet…" He laughed again, then looked down at the bar. It got quiet. "Man, when I think…"

"I try not to think any more than I have to, Jack."

"I know, boy, I know. Listen, I never told you this, but…Emma was the best."

Jan looked at Jack's striped suspenders holding up slacks that were at least an inch too big around his skinny waist. *Was Jack losing more weight?* Jan chewed on his lip and looked at the gleaming bar top. Finally, he looked up at Jack's face and nodded.

"Listen, get to your game, kiddo," Jack said. "But when you're done have a word or two with me before you go."

"You know I will."

Ten players in a Holdem game, $10-20—a perfect game, in Jan's opinion. The green felt, the heavy metal-centered plastic chips, the whir of the shuffle, the snick of the deal, the peek at the hole, the flop, the turn, the river—all these movements and sounds and tactile sensations got Jan's blood up. It wasn't so much the risk of the wager, or even the satisfaction of a hand well played. That was wonderful, but the *game itself* was the thing. Mostly he liked the men and women who played the game. He liked the conversations, the movements, the emotions, the mutual respect, and the humor that inevitably were part of a good game. The diverse personalities converging on a felt battleground with explicit rules of engagement and the chance of gain or loss—these factors combined to move his soul. For Jan, poker was every bit as much an artistic pursuit as music or painting.

His Dad, Frank Kucera, had played cards every night of Jan's childhood at the Pastime Pool Hall in Basin. Jan would slip in and lean on the rail made of gas pipe that separated the card table from the rest of the pool hall. He would stand there quietly watching his father play pan or pinochle. They used real coins not chips—dimes and quarters and occasionally a silver dollar or two would wind up in the pot. Gambling was not technically legal, but the night marshal was in the game most evenings.

After Jan had stood quietly for a while his dad would pretend to suddenly notice he was there. "Want a pop, Jan?" And Jan would take the dime over to the Pepsi machine and get an icy bottle with the most beautiful red and blue and white and black design on it. Somehow, those exquisite colors mixed with the caramel color of the soda through the glass and with the green felt, and the red and black suited cards with the red or blue diamond-patterned backs. The smoke curling from his dad's cigarette and the laughter of the man in the khaki pants and shirt and the sound of the cue ball zipping and clicking and the dull thud of the captured ball into the leather pocket and the sound of the plastic peas in the leather bottle shaken together and doled out to the players in the pea-pool game, quarters lining the pool tables—these sounds and sights and smells were layered into Jan's psyche.

Every evening after work, his dad would come home for

supper, then go to the pool hall and come home late. He left early in the morning. He would go to the same café in which Ginny now served other khaki-dressed men. And he would have a stack of hotcakes with patties of butter and syrup and a side of sausage. His dad was respected and beloved in the town. Tall, handsome, black hair slicked back, intelligent and funny. He was not formally educated, once asking Jan if *minus* meant add or subtract. He was gifted with a mason trowel. He poured a pink-colored sidewalk in the old house on main street before they moved into the new house right before the divorce. The Basin City of his childhood was pastoral and dusty, predictable and quiet. Basin and Mom and Dad...and a peace that Jan longed to recapture but knew he couldn't.

No, he couldn't recapture that. But he could catch a nut flush and check it to a possible straight and bring down the straight and a couple of two-paired hind-titters. And that was *almost* as good as the memories of the peaceful little river town of 50 years ago.

CHAPTER SEVEN

Friday morning a slate sky drizzled Seattle and obscured the Olympic Mountains. Even though Jan was a child of the desert, he enjoyed the Seattle rain. From the hotel window he watched the traffic in the streets below where amost all the cars were burning headlights.

He turned Monster's slip of paper over in his fingers, feeling vaguely stupid preparing to speak the word "maidenform." He practiced it a couple of times. "Oh, *brother*," he said and dialed.

"Yeah?" A Marlboro voice.

Jan hesitated and said the code word.

"Go downstairs and call me from one of the pay phones near the men's room."

"You know where I'm calling from…"

But the phone was dead. Jan frowned at it. What kind of melodramatic nonsense was this? But Monster doubtless knew what he was doing.

In the lobby he redialed.

"Listen closely," the raspy voice said. "At exactly 10:00 a.m.

tomorrow I'll call you on this phone and tell you where to meet me."

"Yes, but…"

Again the line was dead.

"Brother!"

*   *   *

Deck Edwards walked out his front door grinning. Jan's mood immediately lifted. The twenty-mile trip west on I-90 to Issaquah had been a wet drive—Jan decided he was no longer comfortable in big city traffic. Deck Edwards lived about five miles south of town in a rambling two-story home set on five acres. As Deck approached the car he stopped to tussle the head of Bandit, his one-eyed sheep dog. Bandit was so old, blind, and miserable that Deck had once tried to put him out of his misery by giving him 20 sleeping pills—"I'm against euthanasia in *humans,*" he had said. But when he had come home from the office that day, Bandit met him in the driveway looking healthy. Three years later Bandit continued to thrive.

As Deck opened the car door it was apparent he was in his normal state—somewhere between exuberance and bliss. His favorite saying was "I'm too blessed to be stressed." He was a habitual bundle of nervous energy. "Baby steps, Deck! Baby steps!" his wife would remind him as he brisked his way through airline terminals. He'd had a couple of heart attacks and a stroke. He was short, balding, paunchy, and talked nonstop. His conversation was always interesting, challenging, and laced with humor. He also was the world's leading authority on Mormonism. Deck's name came up early in Jan's investigation of Mormonism. Eventually he had attended a conference in Billings where Deck had been a featured speaker. They had dinner and became quick friends.

Monster met Deck when he came to Basin to testify in a trial that required an outside expert on Mormonism.

"Hey, buddy!" Deck said opening the passenger door. "Can we stop by the post office and get my mail on the way?"

"No, but we can get it on the way back. I don't want you reading mail while I'm trying to pick your brain."

"That'll work. How you doing, Jan?"

"I'm OK."

"Well, I worry about you."

"Join the club."

Deck laughed.

"Martha's for lattes and potato pancakes?"

"Martha's is perfect," Deck said. "What, No bacon?"

"Of course, bacon. I won't tell Sally. Your secrets are safe with me."

"Well, that's about as mysterious as I get, so you won't have to worry about betraying me to the enemy."

"You mean if Ronnie-The-Third hangs me by my toes I can give you up?"

"Anything I know about Ronnie I have already published."

"That's too bad, I was hoping to get something good from you."

"I don't know what you're after, Jan, but I'll help you any way I can."

They pulled into Martha's and entered to the smell of hotcakes, bacon, and Seattle's too-strong coffee. Jan wondered why coffee in the Northwest United States was so much stronger than anywhere else west of the Mississippi. He had first noticed the phenomenon on an AP assignment in Portland years earlier. It had taken him a long time to get used to the bitter brew, and he still didn't really like it. For whatever reason, however, Seattle was King Coffee, exporting fancy coffee drinks to the rest of the nation. Jan thought he drank way to many of them, but he couldn't help himself. He once contemplated writing an article about the tide of lattes spreading from Seattle south and east. He planned to track the number of latte shops opening in major metropolitan areas. He guessed he would see a pattern radiating from Seattle until it faded nearly to nothing in the Southeast. He came up with the idea while he was in Savannah where he had searched for two hours before he found anyone who could build him a drink.

After breakfast while the second lattes were being served Deck asked, "OK, friend, how can I help you?"

"First, tell me what you know—specifically—about me, and Ronnie, and Monster."

Deck's eyes sparkled at the mention of Monster. "How is Monster, anyway?"

"You know Monster. If nothing else he's consistent."

"I do, indeed. You know he once rescued me when I did a seminar on Mormonism in Lovell?"

"No, I didn't."

Deck wrapped his hands around the latte mug. "Well, it was during the 'Doc' trial. An Evangelical Christian medical doctor was convicted of abusing a dozen Mormon women during pelvic examinations over a 10-year period."

"I'm familiar with that, in fact, I have known Judge Hartman, who tried the case, since we were boys."

"I didn't know that!"

"Yeah," Jan said, "he and I were acolytes in the Episcopal Church together as kids. During the trial Hartman carried a 38 under his robes. Security was heavy."

"Jan, you surprise me, I didn't know you had a Christian upbringing."

"Not much of one. And it is well in my past…as you know."

"I'm not going to try to evangelize you, Jan."

"I appreciate that, especially knowing your religious zeal."

"I take exception to the word 'religious,' but I know what you are saying. I suppose I do come on kind of strong sometimes."

"You don't offend me, Deck. I appreciate—even *envy*—your faith. I have read your books. I know how important your—I think you call it *relationship*—with God is."

"Yeah, Jan, that's the term I use. And, of course, I use it specifically when I talk about Mormonism."

"Why is that?"

"I won't bore you with that right now, but I may return to it if it will help with your current problems. I need to know what you are really after."

"I want to get Hansen."

Deck stared out the window for several moments. The sparkle left his eyes. Then he looked hard at Jan.

"Your wife was murdered. I realize that. But are you *sure* it was Hansen?"

"If not before, I am now." He told him about Monday night's attack.

"Jan, you know, I'm a lot more concerned for your safety than I am in bringing Hansen to justice."

"If you're concerned about my safety you will help me get Hansen."

"Jan," Deck said softly, "you are not the arbiter of justice. If you are, if you take it upon yourself to exercise vengeance—to decide upon matters of life and death—how are you different from Hansen?"

"That's easy. I'm defending myself."

"Yes, of course you are. If Hansen or his people assault you, you have every right to defend yourself. But confronting him in order to murder him is not self-defense."

Jan sighed. Deck, as usual, was thinking things through and

doing it thoroughly.

"So, Deck, you're telling me that I should sit around in the dark, armed, and wait for a truckload of Hansen's disciples to come for me. Or maybe, if I'm lucky, they'll take me out on the post office steps. And, by the way, if Hansen treats my life as nothing, isn't there a good possibility that others are in danger as well?"

"The question is, Jan, who makes the decision about who lives and dies? You? Come on, you're a child of the system. You covered organized crime. Every offender in the system has some reason why it's legitimate for him to take the law into his own hands."

"Hansen is different."

"Aren't they all? Aren't all these kinds of circumstances 'special?'"

Jan looked out the window. Of course Deck was right. What gave him, or Monster, or George Olson the right to circumvent the legal system? Finally he spoke.

"How many lives did Hitler take?"

"Oh, Jan, for God's sake..."

"I know, I know. But think about it. Think about Jim Jones, think about Koresh and Applewhite. The Hansen compound is a ticking bomb and the government is not going to take action."

"Do you have any reason to believe there is eminent danger to anyone?"

"You mean besides me?"

Deck was silent.

Jan said, "You know what ammonium nitrate is of course."

Deck remained silent and grim.

"With or without your help," Jan said.

Deck sighed.

"To understand Hansen at all, you have to understand him thoroughly."

"That's why I'm here."

"Let's go back to my office, we'll forget my mail for now."

*   *   *

Deck's office occupied 1,000 square feet of his house's lower level, which was sunk about four feet in the ground so that he had nice window views of the backyard and the forest of Douglas Firs on the hill behind his acreage. The walls were lined with bookcases. A U-shaped computer station sat diagonally across one corner. Behind the desk, Deck faced the middle of the room. Behind him on two walls were eight file cabinets within easy reach of the rolling desk chair. The right-hand extension of the computer station abutted a large walnut desk. Jan sat across the desk from Deck who leaned his left arm on the workstation in front of the keyboard.

Three shelves of one section of bookcase were devoted to plaques awarded to Deck from various civic and church groups. A picture frame held his ordination papers. Jan thought of him as a "Pentecostal with a brain." To which Deck had responded, "You mean I'm an oxymoron?" They had both laughed. Deck wore his religion on his sleeve, but he was warm and good-natured about it. Something about the mix of Evangelical fire tempered by earthiness attracted Jan. Jan understood that Deck had no feeling of superiority over his fellow human travelers. "Paul called himself the chief of sinners," Deck had once said to Jan, "but he never met me!" Another time Jan had asked Deck why he was always so open and self-deprecating—seeming to be so genuinely humble. Deck had simply said, "I know who I'm *not.*"

Now Deck was holding what seemed to be a very thick Bible in his hands.

"This is a 'triple combination,'" Deck said. "It holds three books considered to be scripture by the Mormon Church: The Book of Mormon, the *Doctrine and Covenants*, and the *Pearl of Great Price*. If you want to know Ronald Hansen, you are going to have to start here."

Jan held up a hand.

"You aren't going to tell me that all Mormons are as crazy as Hansen? Most of the Mormons I know are very nice people and model citizens."

"Of course they are good citizens. And of course Hansen is an anomaly. However, you have to understand that Hansen is—in large part—a product of Mormonism."

"I guess I don't understand."

"Let me introduce one other concept and then I'll try to make some sense of this for you."

"OK."

"The other concept that goes to the heart of what Mormons consider to be 'truth' is the idea of the 'Living Prophet.' Mormonism teaches that the head of the Church is the 'Prophet, Seer, and Revelator.' He is the President of the Mormon Church, but he also is, very literally, the mouthpiece of God on earth. When he speaks, and says, 'Thus sayeth the Lord,' his words have the force of Scripture."

"You mean like when the Pope speaks *ex cathedra?*"

"Exactly so. Therefore, when the Prophet speaks it is as if God were speaking. No one argues that. In the minds of the members of the Church of Jesus Christ of Latter-day Saints, God ordered Joseph Smith—the founder of Mormonism—to engage in and promote the practice of polygamy. Not only was it a *practice,* it was a commandment that specifically stated, within the text of the revelation that produced it, that anyone who rejected it would be damned."

"I have come across references to polygamy as 'The Practice.' With a capital 'P,'" Jan said.

"Right, 'The Practice.' That word is used mostly among the Mormon polygamous sects, but some Mormons openly rebelled against the Practice—what Joseph Smith also called 'The New and Everlasting Covenant' or 'Celestial Marriage.' In fact a lot of Mormons, in the first days of polygamy, left Mormonism rather than get involved in it. Joseph Smith's legal wife, who had watched the 'revelation' evolve from her husband's dalliances with young virgin admirers, was so incensed with polygamy that she threatened to leave him. However, Smith said God told him that those who would not receive the revelation of plural marriage would be damned. He even got a special revelation from God for his wife that said she, specifically, would be destroyed if she didn't allow her husband to go forward with polygamy. This is all recorded in the 132nd Section of *The Doctrine and Covenants.*

"Then, in 1852 after Smith's death, his successor, Brigham Young *publicly* unveiled polygamy in Utah. Of course, in so doing he outraged the citizenry of the United States. In fact, the Republican Party built into its platform the steadfast opposition to 'the twin relics of barbarism: slavery and polygamy.' By 1857, United States President Buchanan, convinced that Utah was in rebellion, garrisoned troops in Salt Lake City, under the command of Albert Sidney Johnston. Up to that day, it was the largest military deployment in American history. For a time it looked like war. The Mormons were convinced Judgment Day was at hand. At the last minute Brigham Young capitulated and his bargained surrender included getting himself appointed governor of Utah territory.

"When the Civil War broke out, the nation had bigger fish to fry, taking the focus off polygamy which continued pretty much unchallenged. Except for the Morrill Anti-Bigamy Act, Congress did little. After the war it passed the Edmunds Act and the Edmunds-Tucker Act which prohibited polygamists from voting, sent many

Mormons to prison, and began the confiscation of Church property."

"And," Jan interrupted, "at that point the Mormon Church capitulated and received a revelation reversing the Church's position on polygamy?"

"Close, but no cigar. In 1890 Church President Wilford Woodruff issued an official statement on polygamy, but *never* reversed the Church's position on its *belief* in polygamy. Although he publicly ordered the practice to stop, it is what he did *not* say and what the Church has *never* said that is the key to understanding Hansen. It is the key to understanding polygamy in the western United States, and it is the key to understanding a strange Mormon doctrine, the doctrine of Blood Atonement. The doctrine of Blood Atonement is the key to understanding Ronald Hansen."

"Blood Atonement?"

Deck waved his hand. "One subject at a time, Jan. Right now we are midstream in discussing polygamy. Bear with me."

Deck drew a breath.

"See, most people think the Mormon Church outlawed polygamy…"

"That's what I thought."

"As I say, most people think that—they think the Church renounced polygamy. Not so. If you look at the official declaration itself—the Woodruff Manifesto—that becomes clear."

Deck opened the book he called the Triple Combination. "This is the 'Official Declaration—1.' It is the statement President Wilford Woodruff put into the official Mormon record at a General Conference of the Church in 1890. But you have to read it closely; it's carefully constructed to satisfy the federal government in order to prevent them from seizing the property of the Mormon Church. But it does not abandon the theology or philosophy of polygamy. It simply denies that they were *at that moment* "sealing" polygamous marriages."

Deck leaned forward holding the book in one hand and tracing lines in it with his right index finger. He continued. "Woodruff told the gathered Saints that he must submit to the pressure of the United States government or three things would happen: one, he would go to jail; two, the temples would be closed; and, three, Mormon property would fall into the hands of the government. Woodruff pondered that information from on high. Then he went before the people and asked them, in effect, 'Which is wiser: to continue to practice polygamy and have those things happen, or to cease its practice and remain out of jail, with the temples open, and the property intact?'"

"So," Jan said, "Everybody understood that they were playing a word game with the government. Polygamy was still God's plan for mankind, but the United States government forced it underground?"

"Absolutely. The Manifesto is—in a very real sense— a form of thumbing the nose at authority. And so, what *really* happened?"

Jan furrowed his brows. "It went underground?"

"Of course," Deck said. Do you think that all those men suddenly sent all their wives out into the streets? Of course not! High profile Mormons took action designed to give that appearance, but what happened was that it all became clandestine. Mormon patriarchs split their families up and housed them in several different locations, then moved among the families freely. Many members of the Church fled to Mexico—where, by the way, polygamy was *not* officially illegal and certainly not prosecuted. The Mexican government has never taken an interest in making monogamists of the many Mormon sects there. Others went to the deserts of southern and western Utah and into neighboring states."

"So in effect," Jan mused, "the truest Mormons continued

the practice?"

"Bingo!"

"And in some way," Jan continued, "even the 'regular Mormons,' for lack of a better word, still believe in polygamy."

"Certainly, when they think of it at all. Polygamy, as a command from God is under temporary suspension—*in practice.* But it will certainly be resumed in heaven. It *has* to be. A recent billboard in Salt Lake City promoted a book about polygamy calling it 'Our sacred pioneer heritage.' Polygamy is still sacred to regular Mormons who believe it will one day be reinstated—either here on earth or in heaven. Tens of thousands practice polygamy in Utah and the state has no idea how to stop it. As a matter of fact, the ACLU and certain Mormon groups are attempting to get the courts to protect polygamy under the First Amendment."

Jan looked quickly at Deck who seemed to be waiting for himto ask a question.

"OK," Jan said slowly, "why do you say it *has* to be practiced in heaven?"

"Because the most central and distinguishing doctrine of Mormonism is the Mormon teaching of Eternal Progression."

"That's the idea that Mormon men who attain godhood will create and populate their own planets? Or something like that?" Jan asked.

"That's right. See, the central teaching of Mormonism is that men and angels and God are all the same kind of beings. God is further 'progressed' than you and I. But He is not a unique, totally 'other' being as—Christians, Jews, and Muslims teach. The most famous couplet in Mormonism, upon which all Mormon theology turns, was coined by the Prophet Lorenzo Snow, who said, *As man now is, God once was; as God now is, man may become.*"

"Well, even I can recognize that is pure nonsense." Jan said.

"Yes, of course it is, but it is a central theme of Mormonism—the Law of Eternal Progression. According to that theology people just keep getting better and better until they become gods."

"Well, OK." Jan was puzzled. "But what has that to do with polygamy?"

"Well, Eternal Progression could also be called Eternal Procreation."

"Say that again?"

"Well," Deck continued, "Mormonism's God procreates *spirit children* in heaven. Elohim and one of his plural wives procreated you, and me, and even Jesus Christ. Not to mention Lucifer, and Hitler, and Bill Clinton..."

"OK, I get it," Jan said through a sickly smile.

"OK, so then our spirits—procreated by a polygamous God in heaven are sent to earth and implanted into a *human* embryo created by human sexual intercourse."

"Wait a minute. Wait a minute! So we do not begin our existence at conception—I mean *human* conception?"

"Nope. We are simply *transferred*. Our spirits, which were *previously* created, have been waiting for the right couple to create a human body for them on earth. They are then transported to earth in order to—as Mormonism teaches—'get a body.'"

Jan scowled.

"Back up, Deck. You said everyone on earth was created spiritually by the god Elohim and one of his polygamous wives?"

"Yep."

"But there are six *billion* people on the earth. Somebody has said that maybe as many as *fifteen times* that many more have lived and are now dead. You're talking about a hundred billion people!"

"Don't you think I look at the World Population Clock on the Internet?" Deck joked.

"When you say *spiritual offspring*, what do you mean? You don't mean that this god..."

"A god by the name of Elohim, actually," Deck said.

"Yeah, but…you are saying that this Elohim was individually involved in some kind of…of…"

"Some kind of sexual act with his polygamous wives? I'm afraid so."

"Oh, come on!"

"Would you like a copy of my monograph 'Was the Virgin Mary Really a Virgin?'"

"Holy Toledo!"

"Precisely."

Deck sat quietly.

"Help me out here," Jan said.

"Just keep processing."

After a couple minutes Jan said, "You gotta be kidding!"

"Do I see the light of revelation in your eyes?"

"Polygamy!"

"Bingo! How else will a man destined for godhood create a world and, as Joseph Smith said, 'people it,' without polygamy?"

"This sounds like one of those impossible math problems. A hundred billion procreations at the rate of x per day equals y number of years of celestial sex."

"Quite a picture isn't it, Jan? One of my zealous acquaintances told me Elohim would have to have procreated 50,000 times a day for six thousand years."

Jan was slumped down in the big chair across the desk from Deck. He steepled his hands in front of his face and squeezed his eyes tightly shut. He thought his brain might explode. He sighed deeply. Finally he spoke.

"So Hansen is not a rebel—an outsider…" he paused, chewing his lip… *"He's the True Mormon."*

Deck nodded his head slowly. "From his perspective? Absolutely!"

CHAPTER EIGHT

S aturday Jan awakened steeped in foreboding. He was headed for a clandestine meeting with someone who would probably turn out to be a weird Sherlock wannabe *(maidenform for heaven's sake)*. Besides that, he had been forced to change his plans. His Saturday afternoon flight would put him into Billings at 6:00 p.m. He had planned to make the drive to Basin in daylight, but his conversation with Deck changed that.

He had asked Deck to elaborate on the Mormon doctrine of Blood Atonement, but Deck had instead made an appointment for him to meet a retired Utah State Investigator who now lived near Billings. Deck said Chuck Black had worked the polygamy clans for nearly 30 years and had recently retired to the town of his youth. In this case the town was Hardin, Montana, an hour from Billings. Deck had arranged for Jan to meet Black for dinner at the Northern Hotel in Billings.

Jan had told Monster he would be safe driving back alone from Billings to Basin. Hansen could track his movements in and around Basin, he had argued, but he couldn't watch the Billings airport twenty-four-seven, could he? Monster had frowned, but finally shrugged his massive shoulders and moved the conversation to something else.

But now, the meeting with Chuck Black would put Jan on Highway 310 after 9:00 p.m.—after sundown. Jan disliked *that* idea, but he had agreed to meet Black anyway.

After a breakfast over *USA Today* in the Seattle Hilton, Jan moved to the bank of pay phones in the lobby and waited. At 10:00 a.m. one rang and he answered it.

"Walk west on Pike, turn left on 5ᵗʰ Avenue and walk south two blocks. On the west side of the street, on the corner of 5ᵗʰ and University is the Chamber of Commerce. Wait out front. A cab will pull up. Get in the back." The line went dead.

"Brother!" Jan said.

Outside the Hilton, cumulous clouds punctuated what Perry Como had (for whatever reason) called the bluest skies he'd ever seen. This morning a brisk wind swept off Puget Sound and whipped Jan's jacket as he stood on the curb in front of the Seattle Chamber of Commerce. He stood there for 10 minutes. He found himself grinding his teeth as he watched a dozen cabs go by without slowing.

Eventually one slowed and stopped. Jan looked in the front passenger window but the driver jerked his thumb toward the back seat.

The cab started down 5ᵗʰ Avenue, it was one-way south. The driver, who had a beret pulled down over his eyes, watched Jan in the mirror. Neither spoke. They turned right on James and drove four blocks, gliding to a stop at Pioneer Square.

"Get out," a raspy voice said.

Outside the cab Jan was surprised to see that the driver was a painfully skinny man with translucent skin. Small dark eyes peered out from under the lip of the beret. The man sort of rocked back and forth from one foot to the other and exhaled heavily through his nose. Jan decided his best course of action was to remain patient and wait for Ichabod Crane in hippie clothes to speak.

Finally the man said, "Follow me." He walked toward a park bench.

"Sit down," Ichabod said, blowing a couple more breaths through his nose. But *he* didn't sit down himself. He stood before Jan making weird circular movements with his shoulders while peering at Jan. Finally, he pulled a small electronic device out of his breast pocket. Jan noticed that his nails were immaculately manicured. He deftly passed the device over Jan's body.

"OK, man, the gun is copacetic. I just want to be sure you ain't wired."

"Am I?"

"Nope, you're clean, man. I called our boy in Wyoming."

Jan assumed he meant George Olson, but said nothing.

"He really didn't give me much to work with," Ichabod said.

To break the image that was imprinting itself into his brain, Jan said, "What should I call you?"

"Granny."

"Granny?"

"My dad named me Granville. I guess he had never heard of 'A Boy Named Sue.'" Granny snorted.

"Oh." Jan waited.

"Here's what I know," Granny said, "…and I'll call you Mr. Smith if that's OK?"

Jan shrugged. He hoped he hadn't rolled his eyes.

"What I understand, Mr. Smith, is that you want to snag some microwave info."

"Well…"

"You want to intercept certain transmissions and relay them to another location. Let me tell you what that takes.

"First, you have to put an antenna roughly between the transmitter and the receiver. Depending upon the configuration of the equipment—the frequency employed by the transmitter—you may have difficulty getting an antenna in the right spot. It's fairly tricky. Secondly, you will need to spend some serious cash."

"How much?"

"Depends. The equipment, plus my fee."

"Which is?"

"Depends. If I just provide you with equipment, might only be 25 percent of the cost of the stuff. If I get involved in further consultation or installation it could get expensive. And I don't put myself in harm's way. If it's dangerous, I can get you the electronics, but you'll have to install it yourself. Before I can be precise about the bread, I'll have to have more specific information. Some of that I can get, some of it you have to get."

"You seem to be rather thorough."

Granny didn't react except to exhale sharply through his nose.

"Anyway, Mr. Smith, I'll need to know what equipment is being used by our friends and where their relay stations are. Once we know *that*, we'll know where we can intercept their signal. Then I'll need to know where you want to send the signal. That's why I can't be more specific on the price of the equipment. Stock electronics will give us relay links of about 40 miles max per link. You can probably figure an equipment cost of 10 grand per link site."

Jan said, "Let me be frank. I have no idea how to answer any of your questions. This whole idea is very new to me."

"Well, you come to me on a pretty good recommendation, so I am willing to work with you."

Granny abruptly sat down on the bench and then jumped back up.

"Let's start at the beginning," he said. "The first thing you should do is fax me all the known corporate entities involved—all the probable company names and the names of likely corporate officers. Then I can search FCC license records. I can probably find out the location and frequency of the transmitters if I know who to look for. When I have that information, I can be more exact on the equipment costs, but there is still the hook-up cost."

"Well, it's possible that I might be able to hook up the equipment. I do have some electronic background…"

"I know."

Jan raised an eyebrow.

"I pulled your military records."

"You really are thorough."

Another snort. "Mr. Smith, I learned my trade from Barney F. White."

"Should I know him?"

"Nope, I'm sure you never heard of him. But he taught me everything I know. The last job he was on tapped two phones belonging to a connected gangster here in Seattle. A week later a guy at a loading dock down on the Pike opened what he thought was a barrel of pickles and found Barney upside down. Drowned in pickle vinegar. So, you'll pardon me if I'm—as you say—'thorough.'"

Granny handed Jan a card.

"Do you know how to get ahold of *me?*" Jan asked.

Granny stared at him.

Jan smiled. "Sorry to insult you."

Granny displayed what might have been an embryonic smile and said, "Can I drop you at your hotel?"

*   *   *

At the hotel Jan retrieved his car from the parking garage. He had checked out and stowed his bags in the trunk of the car before meeting Granny.

Driving to the airport he replayed the encounter with the tall, strange, electronics wizard. Jan wondered if he had already become involved in felony conspiracy. Where was all this leading? If successful, what information would they capture from Hansen? Foreboding hovered like a Seattle fog.

*   *   *

The one-hour flight to Billings was uneventful. After deplaning Jan did the bathroom arming routine, picked up his rental car and headed for the Northern Hotel to meet Chuck Black, the supposed expert on Blood Atonement. Even the words "Blood Atonement" made Jan uncomfortable. The foreboding he felt that morning returned in force. He drove from the airport along the rimrock bluff skirting the northern edge of downtown Billings. He turned down 27th Street passing Saint Vincent Hospital where his friend Freddy Johnson spent six months during the winter of 1958 after shattering his leg in a football accident. Jan had hitchhiked up to see him every weekend. Monster came on one of those trips. They got very drunk on tequila in Freddy's room, sneaking in after lights out, thinking the nursing staff didn't have a clue.

Jan turned right on 1st Avenue, went a block, turned left on 28th Street, and pulled into the parking garage.

He had 20 minutes before Black arrived so he went into the Golden Belle Lounge and ordered a plain Coke. Suddenly he felt tired.

"And old," he said aloud to his face in the mirror.

The bartender, leaning against the back bar, his apron doubled over and tied neatly around his waist, smiled. "I hear ya, brother. I hear ya."

Jan smiled back, sipped his drink, and watched as the bartender walked to the end of the bar to talk to a petite blonde in a smart business suit. A few serious drinkers occupied the lounge, which was quiet for an early Saturday night. One guy in a cowboy hat sat alone and motionless at a table. A couple in a corner booth held cigarettes stylishly. The blonde smiled at him and winked. Jan shuddered at the thought of the complications of dating. He hoped he would be smart enough to remain single.

"Jan Kucera?" a voice said at his elbow.

Turning on the stool, Jan looked into the brightest blue eyes he had ever seen.

"Chuck Black," the man said and stuck out his hand.

Jan looked at him with surprise.

"Chuck…uh…Chuck, nice to meet you. Thanks for coming."

Chuck laughed. "You were not expecting a Latino."

Jan colored.

"Forget about it, my friend," Chuck said. "I have this effect on everybody. It worked to my advantage when I was on the force. Nobody ever expected to see a Chicano cop in Utah with blue eyes. 'Berry berry' effective for undercover work," he said with a grin. "And the 'Chuck' part. That grew out of the fact that my Christian name is Armando. When I first got into the cop business, my lieutenant said, "You are going to have to chuck that name. So I have been Chuck ever since."

Jan surveyed the tall, nattily dressed, copper-skinned man with bright blue eyes. Chuck's hair was slicked back, reminding Jan of Pat Riley, the basketball coach.

"Thanks for meeting with me, Chuck."

Chuck spoke with the slightest trace of a Latino accent. "I do whatever Deck Edwards asks," he said in a soft, melodious voice. The "Edwards" sounded a little like "Ade-words."

"Don't we all?" Jan replied. "How did you recognize me? Deck must have given you a good description of me."

"Actually I had a picture in my files."

"Of me? Really? Why?"

"I caught your *New York Times* story on the Hansen Cult and looked up your bio on the Internet. When Deck set this up I went to the site and printed your picture." Chuck smiled. "Once a cop always a cop. No?"

Jan thought about all the information Granny had known about him when he met him in Seattle. He wondered if he needed to rethink his libertarian position on electronic privacy.

"Well," Jan asked, "Ready for dinner?"

"If you don't mind, I'll join you for a drink first."

"Great. What's your pleasure?"

"Clarence has some Crown Royal. Is that not so, Clarence?"

Clarence—apparently the barman—materialized with two fingers of Crown Royal. The saloon was old and high-ceilinged, with ornate scroll trim. It was dimly lit and cool and quiet.

Chuck motioned Jan to a table across the room. Seated, he sipped the drink.

"*Si, Señor!* My father told me no evening should ever start without something to warm the guts and, if possible, no evening should end without something to warm the heart."

"Your father sounds like he had a positive outlook."

"My father came up here after World War II from Chihuahua. One of the original wetbacks. Worked as a farm laborer. Eventually wound up owning a small farm near Hardin. It's my place now. I went to school in Hardin."

"You explained the 'Chuck,' but I don't get the 'Black.'"

My father's name was del Negro. He just made it easier for the locals by going to Black. My birth certificate says 'Black.'"

They were silent for a moment. "Deck tells me you are hooking up with Ronnie Hansen."

"Yeah, well I guess he is hooking up with *me*."

Chuck was silent, engaging Jan with eyes so blue the pupils seemed almost to float above the irises. Even in the dim light of the bar they were remarkable.

"I was very sorry to read about the loss of your wife." Chuck said.

Jan continued to be locked onto Chuck's eyes. Finally he dropped his gaze to his own glass and said, "Thanks Chuck."

Chuck continued. "Mr. Ronnie Hansen is a piece of work."

Jan nodded. "I grew up with him. Well, at least we went to school together. He didn't really have any friends. His family was pretty self-contained."

"Was his father the classic Mormon patriarch?"

"I didn't ever speak to his dad. I remember he was very aloof. I even saw the grandfather once when I was very young."

"Ronald, Sr.?"

"Yeah. Actually, Ronnie is the third generation in the Big Horn Basin. Ronnie's grandfather came to the Basin in the 1890's," Jan said.

"Fleeing Utah and The Manifesto on polygamy, no doubt."

"Well, I suppose, but I don't know for sure. In fact the Church may have sent him to the Big Horn Basin to *practice* polygamy. Fact is, I don't know as much as I need to about that history. I'm hoping you can help me out."

"A little, maybe," Chuck said, "but I think I probably can serve you better with more recent history."

"Anything I can get will be appreciated. You were with the Utah State Police?"

Chuck looked away. "I was 28 years with the Utah Department of Public Safety. For about 20 of those years I was plain clothes. Sometimes undercover, as I said earlier."

"You specialized in the polygamous groups."

"You could say that. There was no such official position. But I worked those groups."

"The LeBarons for example?"

"Yes. I became quite close with Ervil and his clan." Chuck smiled.

"He died in prison, I recall."

"Yes, he did at that. He was 56. He lived one year for every kid he had. Actually, I think he only had 54 kids, but no one knows for sure, even the family."

Jan chewed his lower lip. "I saw Brian Dennehy in 'Prophet of Evil.'"

"Very realistic account."

"Dennehy is the best. Who was it played your part in that movie."

Chuck shrugged. "I don't remember."

Jan raised his eyebrows at Chuck's apparent humility, then added, "It's a very difficult story to believe. LeBaron was behind some 20 murders?"

"At least. Probably as many as 30," Chuck said softly. "Nobody will ever know for sure. Ervil never fired a shot. His wives, sons, and disciples pulled the triggers, or strangled the victims. He had one of his own daughters strangled. One of his wives and several of his children are doing life in prison. I saw a picture of one of Ervil's daughters recently on *America's Most Wanted*. She is sought in connection with the 'Four O'clock Murders' in Houston."

Chuck's voice trailed off and he looked past Jan, apparently lost in thought. Finally Chuck spoke. "But about *evil...*"

"Chuck, LeBaron *was* evil, was he not?"

Chuck laughed without mirth.

"Sure. Of course! It's just that...Well, I don know how to

explain it. I have worked a lot of bad-guy cases. Guys like Gary Gilmore. The Lafferty brothers. The Laffertys slit the throat of their brother Allen's wife and that of her 15-month-old daughter because the wife refused to accept polygamy. The Laffertys, they used as their defense that they were acting on a direct revelation from God. Not that it helped them at their trial."

Jan waited. Chuck's voice hadn't changed. But the words came slower and the blue eyes seemed to deepen even more. Jan felt as though Chuck had left the room while his body remained. He had seen this in police officers before. And in criminals. And in Monster. And who was Monster really, Jan wondered, cop or criminal? Jan felt as though the room temperature had dropped.

"Well, Jan, I don't want to get philosophical. You are interested in facts."

"I want to know whatever I need to know to understand Ronnie Hansen."

"Well," Chuck sighed, "then I guess you need to hear a little philosophy."

"Shoot."

"Remember, my friend, you asked for it." Chuck smiled a plastic smile. "As to evil, well that characteristic, I have concluded, is not so much resident in people as it is in ideas."

"Interesting. Explain."

"Whenever one gets close to the bad boys, like I have been close to them, you spend a lot of time with them, interviewing them, trying to understand them. Trying to discern their motives. Something funny starts to happen to you. You kind of have trouble figuring out how they are different from yourself."

"God, Chuck! That's a strange thing for a lawman to say."

"Former lawman, my friend. Citizen Black now."

"I still don't understand…"

"Perhaps I can illustrate it with a story."

"Sure."

"The newsman, Mike Wallace, was doing a *60 Minutes* piece about the Nazi war criminal Adolph Eichmann. You will remember him. He was one of the central players in the Holocaust. Mike Wallace posed a question at the program's outset: 'How is it possible…,'" he asked his audience "for a man to act as Eichmann acted? … Was he a monster? A madman? Or was he perhaps something even more terrifying: was he *normal?*'"

"What a strange thought," Jan said.

"Yes, sir, it is. Anyway, Wallace interviewed Yehiel Dinur, a concentration camp survivor who testified against Eichmann at the trial. Mr. Dinur, while a prisoner at Auschwitz, had seen Eichmann. At Eichmann's trial, in 1961, Mr. Dinur walked into the courtroom, seeing Eichmann for the first time in 18 years. A film clip shows Mr. Dinur as he began sobbing, then he collapsed—he fainted."

Chuck took a sip of his drink, rolled his shoulders, and continued. "So Mike Wallace asks him about that. What was going through Mr. Dinur's mind when he saw Eichmann? Was he overcome with hatred, with fear? No, not that, Mr. Dinur explained. When he saw Eichmann he realized the Nazi was just an ordinary man. 'I was afraid about myself,' Mr. Dinur said. He saw he was capable of doing what Eichmann did if he had been in his place. He said, 'I am exactly like he is!'"

"But that's ridiculous, Chuck!"

"Is it? I don't know." The soft voice had taken on a steely edge.

They were both silent, sipping their drinks. Jan found himself becoming uneasy. What was Chuck saying? *Am I really no different from Ronald Hansen?*

"All I know, Chuck continued, "is that there exists a connection between what a person believes and what he does. When he believes—really believes—fantastic things, he seems to be capable of fantastic acts."

Chuck shook his head quickly as though throwing off something unseen, then he continued, "Anyway, ol Ervil was an interesting man. I met him in the summer of 1979 at the Salt Lake County jail. He obviously was a man with a brilliant mind, but he had lived with unreasonable ideas for so long he was not easy to follow verbally. His language was flowery. He could speak nonstop for hours—and he often did. The ideas were rich and confusing."

Chuck laughed softly, apparently lost in a momentary thought. Then he said, "Ervil had been arrested in Mexico and turned over to the FBI in connection with the murder of Dr. Rulon Allred, another polygamous leader from Utah. Allred was a naturopathic healer with an office in Murray, Utah. Ervil sent his youngest wife, Rena, along with one of his daughters, to put the hit on Allred. I interviewed Ervil regularly. He was finally sentenced to life in prison for the death of Allred. Did you know that his first hit was on his own brother, Joel? Anyway, he died in prioson—Draper— in August of '81, just a year or so after he was convicted of Dr. Allred's murder."

Chuck stopped, scanned the room, then continued. "Anyway, Ervil eventually went down for Allred. Even after his death, his followers continued to wipe out other polygamous leaders. His own clan split into four factions. I interviewed his son, Heber, who is doing four life sentences. At that time he was in Florence, Colorado. Heber killed as many as a dozen rival clan members. He went down for the infamous 'Four O'clock Murders' in Houston."

"So," Jan interrupted, "sounds pretty evil to me."

"My point is that as I got to know these criminals during my service in Utah, in every case, they seemed to be forced into their roles by their theology. So, I always came away angry at the *ideas*.

"See, Ervil, for whatever else he was, was a true believer in Mormonism. First, he believed that Mormonism was actually the 'One True Church.' He believed that God's only channel of communication with mankind is through the Mormon Church. So then he looked around and saw that Mormonism had radically changed since its inception—namely by dropping polygamy. Like so many of the Fundamentalists he went back and carefully read the history of Utah Mormonism and discovered that God supposedly had said that polygamy was to be practiced forever. But he saw that Mormon leaders had jettisoned it when the going got tough."

Jan interrupted, "So he decided the True Church wasn't true anymore, or something like that?"

"Exactly. He was deeply sincere about Mormonism. And, like the other Fundamentalists, what he did was appeal directly to God for a vision, and—like so many others—he got one! He believed God told him to be the Restorer of true Mormonism."

"The One Mighty and Strong?"

"Yes, sir. The One Mighty and Strong."

Jan looked around the room.

"Chuck," he said, "this is going somewhere. It is important. I am making a mental connection to what you said with some material I read on the psychology of mind control. But, I'm *famished!* Can we eat?"

Chuck laughed. "Certainly, my friend, certainly. But why don't you let me walk you a few blocks to the only genuine Tex-Mex food in Montana."

"Now you *really* have my attention."

CHAPTER NINE

S aturday night at the compound was temple night. Now, early
in the afternoon, Prophet Hansen sat outside the door of his
office on the deck surrounding the second story of the Lion House.
To his left a door opened into the master bedroom. His viewpoint
presented him with and unobstructed dazzling view of the west
face of the Bighorn Mountains. The Prophet believed no one—
anywhere—viewed such panoramic majesty from his doorway. He
knew the Grand Tetons and their startling awe, but he guessed this
view was even more grand. The master bedroom had an angled
glass roof. From his bed on a moonless night he and his wife *du
jour*—as he playfully called her—would watch the starry dome of
the universe move silently overhead.

The June afternoon heat invigorated the Prophet. The Bighorns, five miles to the east, rose more than a mile straight up from
the valley floor to an elevation of 10,000 feet. From this distance
they were lush green and granite; from five miles further away
they appeared blue.

On Saturday afternoons an uncharacteristic quiet fell over

the compound. Some of the leaders took their families to Billings or Sheridan or Worland for shopping, dinner, and sometimes a movie. Hansen fasted Saturdays and in the afternoon he read the Scriptures and prayed, preparing for his Sunday church meeting. This afternoon he sipped an herb tea and studied, once more, Section 85, verse 7, of the *Doctrine and Covenants*:

And it shall come to pass that I, the Lord God, will send one mighty and strong, holding the scepter of power in his hand, clothed with light for a covering, whose mouth shall utter words, eternal words; while his bowels shall be a fountain of truth, to set in order the house of God...

There was no doubt in the Prophet's mind that he was—of a certainty—The One Mighty and Strong predicted in Section 85. Others before him had thought *they* were that prophesied leader God would raise up to restore order in the House of Mormonism. Noble but mistaken men were among them. Men like Joel LeBaron who made a reasonable case for *his* claim to be The One. On the other hand, there were usurpers, like Joel's brother Ervil LeBaron. Dozens of others had arisen to claim the title since 1890.

Hansen remembered the pitiful spectacle Ervil LeBaron made of himself when he came to the Hansen clan and demanded they tithe to him. Hansen's father had stared the imposing Ervil down and sent him packing. Before Ervil died in prison he wrote his own book of scripture. It contained a hit list which initiated a blood bath that captured national headlines for several years. Hansen had been on the list and had taken special security precautions until Ervil's vengeful sons were behind bars.

Hansen considered the challenge before him. The One Mighty and Strong was God's chosen vessel to restore the Kingdom of God on the earth. Utah Mormonism, to Hansen's mind, was as corrupt as hell itself. Brigham Young had been a true Prophet. So was Young's successor, President John Taylor. The

United States government hated both Young and Taylor and pressured them to give up polygamy. Neither of them did. When Young finally died, the United States government redoubled its efforts against Taylor. He steadfastly refused to sign an anti-polygamy manifesto saying, "I would suffer my right hand to be severed from my body first!"

Then Taylor, knowing it was only a matter of time before the United States had its way in Utah, secretly commissioned a select society of trusted followers to continue polygamy clandestinely while the Church *outwardly* succumbed. In Centerville, Utah, in 1886, Taylor received a revelation from God ordering him to designate men who would carry on polygamy at all costs.

But Wilford Woodruff, who followed Taylor, didn't have that kind of backbone. Woodruff sold out the Church of God to the gentiles. He capitulated in the face of anti-polygamy sentiment. He didn't have the courage to stand up for his beliefs. When he sold out he dishonored the Priesthood. Of course, he continued to keep his wives secretly and sanctioned more clandestine plural marriages. The Church carried them on—underground—for 20 more years. Nevertheless, eventually the mainstream Utah Church stopped solemnizing plural marriages. Polygamy was driven fully underground to be continued only by the bravest men and women— the truest of the true.

It was a mystery to Hansen that Utah Mormonism could go so wrong—could abandon the Practice. Joseph Smith had been chosen by God and given the Holy Melchizedek Priesthood. Three of Christ's original Apostles—Peter, James, and John—had appeared to Joseph Smith on the banks of the Susquehanna River and laid their hands on his head, conferring upon him the Priesthood and the keys to the Latter-day Dispensation—the Dispensation of the Fullness of Times. The Priesthood flowed from Joseph to Brigham and from Brigham to John Taylor. But then men who should have known better betrayed the trust God had placed in them.

Not that factionalizing was new to the history of the Church. Hansen thought of how the young Prophet, Joseph Smith, had lost *most* of his trusted leaders. More than half of all the Apostles Joseph Smith *ever* ordained eventually had to be excommunicated.

The Church, of course, was never at peace with the gentile world. Joseph Smith had run for President of the United States in 1844. Not a truly serious candidacy, Hansen thought, but perhaps a statement—a foreshadowing—of Hansen's own time. The Saints had been driven from Missouri to Illinois, their leaders tarred and feathered, and dozens of the Saints murdered. Joseph Smith himself had been murdered in the summer of 1844 in the Carthage, Illinois, jail where he was being held on a trumped-up charge of treason. Illinois Governor Thomas Ford had come to Carthage to accept Smith's surrender. Ford had guaranteed him protection. But he withdrew and left the Prophet in the hands of a crowd of gentiles.

When Smith died a dozen Church leaders clamored to succeed the fallen prophet. The Church splintered into factions and fled Illinois in a dozen directions—to the East Coast, to Michigan, to Texas. Others within the Church believed that Joseph Smith had prophesied that his own son—Joseph Smith III—would succeed him. That faction became The Reorganized Church of Jesus Christ of Latter-day Saints, headquartered in Independence, Missouri. It was second in size only to the main Utah Mormon Church.

Hansen shook his head and exhaled deeply at the painful memory of the bitter divisions that marked his beloved Church. After Joseph's martyrdom Brigham Young led his flock to Utah. Young established a new nation in the Utah Territory. After the Church capitulated to the United States government on polygamy under Wilford Woodruff, scores of further factions were birthed.

As Hansen continued in his reverie, Bill Campbell walked up to him and waited silently. A full five minutes passed before the Prophet stirred.

The Prophet looked at Campbell and said, "Bill?"

"Yes, President."

"Can I help you?"

Campbell cleared his throat.

"Well, President, you asked me to meet you here this afternoon."

Hansen stared blankly at him. Eventually he spoke.

"Of course I did, didn't I?"

"Yes, sir."

More staring.

"You said you wanted to discuss some 'broad plans.'"

Hansen closed his eyes. He slowly nodded his head.

"Bill," he said, "I have been thinking about our destiny here."

"Yes, sir."

"Sit down, please."

"Thank you, President."

"Bill, things are beginning to move fast."

"Uh huh."

"I mean. Well, there is the Jan Kucera thing. The stuff will hit the fan after we deal with him tonight."

"I'm afraid so, President."

"Also, we are attracting a lot of attention among the scattered brethren."

"It would appear so, President. There seems to be a stream of leadership coming to see you."

"Well, all the Fundamentalists cling to the hope of the rise of The One Mighty and Strong. Thank God that Joseph has given us the 85th Section. You know, Bill, there is one thing I'll never understand."

"What's that, President."

"Why in God's name, when Wilford Woodruff sold out, did not *all* the members of the Church recognize his sin and stand up for the truth?"

"I don't know. I don't think too theoretically, as you know." Hansen, laughed at the joke.

"And, thank God you don't, Bill. Thank God you know how to obey and leave the philosophizing to me. But seriously, the reason the Church as a whole never understood the obvious disobedience of Woodruff and others is that 'many are called, but few are chosen.' Few have the ability to think critically and fewer still have the courage to defend their convictions. But, Bill, a faithful remnant, like the faithful remnant of Israel in the Old Testament, always remains. The mindless sheep scatter. Only the truest of the true can maintain the faith."

Campbell said nothing. Then, he glanced up at the Prophet and said quickly, "Well, I thank God he gave you the light of revelation, President."

Hansen looked closely at him. "Do you, Bill? Do you really?" He paused. "Anyway, Bill. I'm grateful that the Fundamentalists await the coming of The One Mighty and Strong, and are beginning to recognize him. So many have pinned their hopes on false prophets. The claims of the pretenders are, of course, meaningless drivel. Unfortunately, the largest groups, it seems, have given up the hope, wearied of waiting for The One. They seem content to practice polygamy in the canyons and deserts, like bats and moles.

"But now as things are coming together, we are arriving at a critical mass. I can't believe the federal government will wait much longer before trying to shut us down. So, that means several things."

The Prophet rose to his feet and began to pace. Campbell stared at the ground.

"Obviously, Bill, we can't go to war with the United States. Not at this time. Not at this moment. Bottom line? We are going to have to leave."

Campbell looked up. "South America?"

The Prophet nodded. "And soon. But we have a lot of…a lot of …loose ends to tie up first."

"Like Kucera."

"Exactly."

Hansen took his eyes off Campbell and examined the Big-horns. The sun had moved far enough to reveal the letters J-I-R-P formed by the light and shadows of the forest growth, letters that gave the name to the JIRP Ranch at the foot of the mountains. God, he would miss this place. Joseph Smith had named Nauvoo, Illinois, *Nauvoo,* because he said it meant "beautiful place." But brother Joseph had never sunned himself on the west side of the Bighorns. He had never fished the willow banks of Shell Creek, nor ridden through the red desert hills and along the foot of the Five Sisters rock fortress. Hansen had hoped he and his people would be safe in Wyoming forever. Nothing angered him more than having to trade this compound for a steamy jungle.

The Restored Gospel was the only hope for America, the only hope for the world. But now Hansen was forced to leave America temporarily—in order to save her. Look at how the mighty nation of liberty has fallen. Divorce and sodomy rampant. Filth and AIDS and drug addiction. A recent president of the United States with his hands up the skirts of a young woman in the Oval Office.

Hansen nodded to himself. Judgment had come upon the land. He had traveled throughout the country, seeing with his own eyes the debauchery and godlessness turning cities into sewers. He monitored the television drivel sucked up by the mindless citizenry who watched inane programming—complete with canned laugh tracks!

The national educational system was, of course, a joke. High school graduates couldn't read and college students were fed pap—the Great Books jettisoned in favor of touchy-feely nonsense. Professor Alan Bloom was right—the American Mind had closed. Bloom—and him a Jew—so accurately described the sodomized state of America, the death of reason, and the rise of the modern barbarian. Bloom had said it right, "I'm afraid the intellectual soil is now too thin to sustain the taller growths."

"Excuse me?" Campbell said.

The Prophet colored. "Sorry, Bill, I must have been thinking out loud. Anyway, Bill, at least I'm thankful that a few pockets of patriots resist the barbarians at the gates. Some of the Patriot Movement—the Bo Gritzes, the Randy Weavers—and some of the Christian Identity Movement—the Gordon Kahls and men like the fallen Pastor Richard Butler—for all their shortcomings—especially in the shadow of the 9-11 Trade Center bombing—they see what is happening. And without the help of men like Gerry Spence—the world's greatest trial lawyer and a man committed to individual liberty—without help of his caliber a secular America would have crushed the patriots long ago. Of course the patriots are powerless to stop the destruction of America. For all their *sturm and drang* they are simply rearranging deck chairs on the Titanic.

"But God has foreseen the decadence which will destroy the moral fabric of the United States. He has seen that even the Restored Gospel would suffer at the hands of weak leaders. He has prophesied that the Restored Church will *itself* have to be restored by The One Mighty and Strong."

Hansen stopped short. He sucked in his breath.

"Bill, my grandfather was ordained and commissioned to continue the Principle. Commissioned through the very hand of President John Taylor. My father, Ronald Hansen, Sr., ordained me. I am the Anointed One."

Again Campbell hesitated then said, "Yes you are, President."

"But, Bill?"

"Sir?"

"I have never told anyone this, but sometimes I fear that I am not up to the calling. You have no idea how many times I have awakened in damp sheets haunted by the thought that I am not strong *enough!* I know all great men of God go through periods of self-doubt. Many times during seasons of fasting and prayer I have cried out to Elohim, father of Jehovah, using the same words Jesus used when he was in the earth, 'Father, if it be possible, let this cup pass from me.' But God will not remove the mandate nor the mantle. After the doubts, when I am refreshed by fasting and prayer, do you know what I say to myself?"

"No, sir."

"I say—again with Jesus—'If this cup may not pass away from me, except I will drink it, thy will be done.'"

Campbell remained still.

"I also realize that—again like Jesus—I have enemies on every side. Federal agents crawling like worms through the Big-horn Mountains, sneaking and peeping and reporting to fat bureaucrats in Washington. Probably even now arming themselves to enter the compound. *Let them come!* I don't want a fight, but—with the help of God—I am ready if it comes."

Hansen shook his head, his long blonde hair a mane adorning an indignant beast. "But, do you know what troubles me most, Bill?"

"No, sir."

"What troubles me most is that sometimes I am misunderstood even among my own people. There are double-dealing sycophants who would sell their own Prophet for 30 pieces of silver. They are worse than gentile meddlers like Jan Kucera. Kucera, a professional snoop who cares nothing for the things of God, but only for writing titillating stories for the yellow press.

"Bill, I tried to contain my rage when Kucera published pictures of *my wives* in the *New York Times. My wives!* I tried but failed. The unmitigated humiliation! Who is Kucera but a godless wretch of questionable pedigree?

"As you know, Bill, I do not accept the most radical Aryan theology. Nevertheless, I can't shake the feeling that some of the Southern European nations should really be considered of less than pure Adamic descent. While they don't display the black skin of Cain, they obviously are mongrelized. Do you know I heard that Kucera's father had immigrated to the United States from Bohemia before the First World War? In the 1920's, the word 'bohemian' came to designate the unorthodox, anti-God crowd. Wasn't Bohemian Czechoslovakia populated by Gypsies and other mixed-blood peasants?"

Hansen paused, then laughed, "Kucera, the bad Czech."

Campbell looked up at him and smiled.

"Men like Kucera can't be allowed to interfere with the unfolding of holy history. I knew from the time I saw the first filthy newspaper story Kucera penned that I would have to cancel that Czech."

Hansen stopped. He was smiling broadly. Campbell looked up. He returned the smile.

"Cancel that Czech," Campbell said.

Hansen took his eyes off Campbell and studied the intricate face of Shell Canyon's walls in the distance. He thought of the other Fundamentalist leaders who had recently trudged through the compound to acknowledge him. Many, he knew, were petrified of him. They knew the Prophet did not shrink from his calling. He did not even shrink from the practice of Blood Atonement, the holiest of all sacraments. The secondary polygamous leaders knew of men who had resisted him. Men who were now missing.

In the last 24 months a dozen such groups had accepted Hansen's claim of *Doctrine and Covenants* 85. During that same time Hansen had also met with another very interesting Fundamentalist. Not a Mormon Fundamentalist to be sure. Not even a Christian Fundamentalist—but a Muslim Fundamentalist. Even thinking about it now, the Prophet felt a sense of awe. He had traveled to Libya to consult with the polygamist Muslim, Col. Muammar al-Qaddafi. That was before Qaddafi lost courage and capitulated to President Bush after the conquest of Iraq. Hansen had discussed Islamic polygamy with the Arab, exploring the necessary qualities of strength of character in a ruling Prince. They had also discussed money and chemical and nuclear weapons. One of the colonel's aides gave Hansen a crash course in terrorism. The Prophet had been particularly moved by the discussion of torture: "First, you must make them beg you to kill them. Then they will tell you whatever you want to know…"

Suddenly Hansen addressed Bill once more.

"Bill, there is one matter of utmost delicacy…"

"Sir?"

"It's Melissa."

*　　*　　*

After a supper of tea and unleavened bread, which he allowed himself during the 24 hours he fasted before Sunday service, Hansen went to the temple. It was a plain frame building inside of which a room measuring 88-feet-two-inches long and 28-feet-nine-inches wide was constructed. These were the exact dimensions of the upper floor of the Nauvoo, Illinois, temple where Brigham Young conducted ceremonies after the martyrdom of the Prophet Joseph Smith. Nauvoo was the first real temple where the ceremony was conducted. To the best of his knowledge, Hansen's own version of it was identical to the one performed in Nauvoo in 1845.

Saturday nights the temple was reserved for Prophet Hansen and special guests. Tonight he would be taking a new wife, Maggie Balsom. She would be going through the temple ceremony for the first time to receive her own Endowments. Then she would be sealed to him for "time and eternity." Bill Campbell had told Hoyt Akers about the marriage and stood before Akers until the pilot told him he was OK with it. Campbell told the Prophet he thought Akers wanted to say something negative, but finally had just nodded slowly and walked away. Campbell said he was less than happy with Akers' reaction.

The Prophet would really have preferred not to marry Maggie right now, but after Akers had approached him with the idea of marrying Maggie himself, Hansen realized it was better to seal her to himself right away. Akers was out of the question for her. Maggie was a fine, strongly spiritual young woman. She would produce choice babies to be inhabited by the most noble of Elohim's spirits—spirits held back for the very last of the Latter days. And, as a plural wife, she would produce spiritual offspring for Hansen's kingdom.

Bill Campbell was waiting for the Prophet in the reception area, along with Maggie, her parents and other adult members of her extended family. Hansen embraced Maggie's mother and shook her father's hand. The Balsoms were obviously thrilled that their daughter had been chosen as the wife of the Prophet.

"Will you folks excuse me for just a moment, please?" Hansen said. "I need to see Apostle Campbell on a matter of some urgency. Bill?"

Campbell followed the Prophet into the men's dressing room. The Prophet closed the door and motioned him back into the washing and anointing room and closed that door as well.

"Couple of matters, Bill. One, I understand our friend is arriving in Billings tonight. I assume you have that covered. The second thing is the Casper connection."

"Yeah, I'm headed toward Billings as soon as you release me here. I'm in contact with people on the scene there. The two in the Casper jail will be a little more difficult."

Hansen cocked his head and raised an eyebrow. Campbell continued.

"A little more difficult is not the same as impossible, President."

Hansen smiled. "You do good work brother Campbell. I have no one like you."

"Thank you, President. I know that is true."

They both laughed and headed back out to the wedding party. Campbell nodded at the guests and left the building.

*   *   *

The temple ceremony, as always, rejuvenated the Prophet. Tonight, however, he couldn't help watching Maggie, who was going through the ceremony for the first time. Dressed in white and seated between her mother and an older sister, Maggie looked radiant. She was wide-eyed as the endowment ceremony unfolded. Hansen drank in her youth with his eyes. Her auburn hair, her smooth dark complexion. He remembered dandling her on his knees in her parents' living room when she was only four or five years old. Then watching her grow through the awkward years. Only a very few years ago had the Prophet begun to see her as a young woman. That was when she was working out in the gymnasium on the compound. He had gone in to work out on the speed bag when he watched her in leotards stretching.

As the temple ceremony began, Hansen wondered what

Maggie would think of the endowment ceremony. Certainly it would all be new to her. By the time the ceremony began, she had, of course, been washed and anointed by the sisters after taking off her clothes and donning the temple garment. He knew the language of the temple might surprise or even shock her.

Two hours later, in the Celestial Room, Hansen approached Maggie. She had tears in her eyes. He wasn't sure if they were tears of joy, but he didn't ask. He put his arm around her shoulder and drew her close. "Maggie," he said, "sometimes it takes a while to get used to the temple ceremony. I know it is very different from anything you expected. But I testify to you that one day you will come to view it as one of the most spiritual experiences of your life. I encourage you to come here to the temple regularly until you get the spirit of it."

Maggie only nodded her head and pressed a handkerchief to her eyes.

Hansen and the Balsom family entered a small sealing room. In the center of the room was a white altar. The walls of the room were mirrors. The prophet knelt on one side of the altar and Maggie knelt on the other. The President of the Temple approached, joined their hands together across the altar and sealed them for time and eternity. It took less than a minute.

Hansen noted that tonight was the last quarter of the moon and that it wouldn't rise before midnight. He would open the curtains of the master bedroom and show Maggie the glorious celestial display over the Bighorns. Of course Maggie would show him a heavenly display as well. He chuckled, surprised at his own "earthiness."

CHAPTER TEN

J an and Chuck Black left the Northern Hotel and walked north along 28ᵗʰ Street, the warm air brushing their cheeks. The evening traffic was light, still too early for the Saturday night crowds. Jan glanced across the street to where he used to play poker. The card room was closed, and he wondered why. Chuck saw him looking and said, "They closed it last week—prostitution."

They walked to Second Avenue where Cadillacs and Audis discharged passengers at the Alberta Bair Theater for the Performing Arts. A signboard advertised *hors d'oeuvres* and fine wines at 6:00 p.m., celebrating the 20th anniversary of the theater. Jan had heard the announcement on the radio in the rental car coming from the airport. The musical *Chicago* was playing. For $125 you could get the *hors d'oeuvres*, wine, the show, and dinner and dancing at the Billings Sheraton afterward. They turned and headed east toward the train depot.

"I hope you have a big appetite, my friend," Chuck said. "Lizard Leo's is run by a compatriot, Jose del Toro. No relation to the movie actor. But Jose was trained by Stephen Piles of the Star Canyon in Dallas, and also by Robert del Grande at Café Annie in Houston. He's famous for his yellow-tomato salsa."

"My mouth is watering."

Inside the old sandstone building they were greeted by a Mexican in full gentleman-rancho attire. "Señor del Negro! What a pleasant surprise that you visit us on this early Saturday evening. Are you in town for the show, *Chicago*?"

"No, Antonio, no. I am entertaining *mi amigo,* Jan Kucera. Treat us well, my friend. Señor Kucera comes a hundred miles just for Jose's salsa and *pollo con mole.*"

"We shall warm the peanut butter!"

Antonio led them through the dining room. Cacti stood in planters and hung from the 12-foot ceilings. A huge barrel cactus marked the center of the dining room and two giant saguaros touched the ceiling at the rear of the room. Cages of colorful birds hung from the ceiling. Antonio showed the two men to a small table against the east wall so both of them could observe the door. Starched white cloths covered a table adorned with linen napkins and crystal wine goblets. Antonio took their drink orders, cleared the goblets, then left them with menus.

"OK," Jan said at last, "Tell me about Blood Atonement."

Chuck hesitated. He leaned back in his chair and closed his eyes. Finally he leaned forward and said, "How much do you know about the Mormon Priesthood?"

"Not much, I'm afraid."

"Well, let's start there. In Mormonism there is a power— what they call the Priesthood—which is sort of like electricity. It is 'passed on,' as they say, through 'the laying on of hands.' The head of the Church—in this case Ronald Hansen—holds what they call The Keys of the Priesthood. This allows the Prophet to institute *any* doctrinal practice—and no one can challenge him.

"Back during Brigham Young's time," Chuck continued, "the Mormon Church went through a period known as The Reformation. During this time, Young and other Priesthood leaders whipped the Saints into a fearsome lather. People were coming forward publicly confessing their sins. For example, one old woman confessed she had stolen a radish and asked to be rebaptized. The rhetoric in the Tabernacle in Salt Lake City grew more and more gruesome.

"It was at this time that Young laid a theological foundation for Blood Atonement. Addressing the Saints in the Tabernacle, he preached what he had been practicing. He told the faithful that, while it was true that Jesus Christ shed his blood for sins, nevertheless some sins require the shedding of a man's *own* blood. And he was serious. That same day another leader, Jedediah Grant, suggested that some of the congregation should go to Young and have him appoint a committee to shed their blood so they could go to heaven."

Jan shuddered. "Can you imagine sitting in the pew listening to that stuff? But, Chuck, is there any evidence, any hard evidence, that this practice actually occurred? I mean really..."

"Yes, of course they practiced Blood Atonement. Not only *did* they, but they still *do*. Not the mainline Mormon Church, but many of the polygamous sects still teach and practice the doctrine. But did Brigham Young practice it? Certainly, no question about it. Lots of deathbed confessions and witnesses document the crimes of the Priesthood in Utah Territory. John D. Lee, for example, told the grisly story of his part in the Mountain Meadows Massacre.

"I'm familiar with that event."

"Yeah, The Mountain Meadows Massacre stood as the greatest massacre of Americans *by* Americans in the history of the United States. That is, until Timothy McVeigh bombed the Murrah Federal Building in Oklahoma City. On September 11, 1857, at least

127 men, women, and children, traveling in a wagon train from Arkansas, were massacred by order of Brigham Young. McVeigh killed only 39 more in Oklahoma City.

"Is it really true," Jan asked, "that at Mountain Meadows the Mormon militia gunned down women and children?"

"Yes, it is. Lee, had enlisted American Indians—or Mormons dressed as Indians, that is up for debate—to surround the train. Then Lee rode in under a flag of truce and convinced the settlers to lay down their arms and he—Lee—would escort them through the Indians. Of course, instead, he and his men executed all of them."

Jan shook his head.

Chuck smiled thinly. "Lee had been a personal bodyguard of Brigham Young. He was eventually tried and executed for the Mountain Meadows Massacre. Of course he elected to be Blood Atoned. He was shot as he sat on the edge of his coffin at Mountain Meadows itself. In his memoirs, written in the weeks before his execution, he said Young had made him the scapegoat.

"Other Mormon hitmen, whom Joseph Smith and Brigham Young called Destroying Angels or Danites, wrote of similar crimes—Wild Bill Hickman, for example. Hickman told of murders he carried out under the direct orders of Brigham Young. These henchmen first did the bidding of Joseph Smith when the Church was embattled in Missouri. One of the most notable of these guys was Orrin Porter Rockwell, who allegedly shot the governor of Missouri on Joseph Smith's orders. People eventually were Blood Atoned for crimes of adultery, incest, and speaking against Church leadership."

Just then Antonio returned with their drinks, tortilla chips and yellow-tomato salsa.

"Antonio, we really do want to have two orders of *pollo con mole.*"

"Señor del Negro, the order is already in."

"Thank you, Antonio."

"Will there be anything else just now."

"No, sir. These refreshments will make us very happy until the main course arrives. Thank you very much."

"My pleasure. Gentlemen."

Antonio bowed. He vanished almost as unobtrusively as he had arrived. Jan thought he moved like a shadow, almost teletransporting through the room.

Jan selected a triangle of fried tortilla, thin and crisp and golden brown. He scooped some salsa. Chuck's blue eyes followed his movements. With the first bite the flavor seemed to rise like smoke from Jan's palate into his nose. His eyes watered and he inhaled deeply.

"Well, Jan?" Chuck asked.

Jan shook his head, searching for words.

"It's wonderful! If my father were alive he would say, 'This is so good it would make you slap your mother.' I never figured out what it meant, but he always said that about good food."

"Your father, was he born in this country?"

"No he came here as a boy at the age of 10, just before World War I. His family emigrated from what was Bohemia then, Czechoslovakia now. From near Prague."

"So he brought some of the Czech idioms into English. My father did that as well. They never seem to work."

Jan laughed. "You got that right. My dad, if he got irritated with you would say, 'You talk like a man with a paper hat!' I never got that either!"

They ate in silence for a few minutes. Jan's sinuses opened up and his eyes watered. He sipped his diet Coke.

After a while Chuck said, "Here comes Antonio and our chicken with a hint of peanut butter sauce. If you like what you've tasted so far, hang on to your paper hat!"

They both laughed and Antonio set the plates before them. Jan again was struck by the fresh pungency of the food.

Jan was so absorbed in the meal that his mind drifted from their conversation. He found himself thinking about Mexico. He and Emma often traveled there from Los Angeles. Now he was remembering their first trip to Mexico. They had gone to Ensenada for a weekend where they ate wonderful lobster thermadors for seven dollars a plate. He remembered how they had sat on a balcony overlooking the Pacific. It had been a warm summer evening, the sun just setting. He could still see little brown children running on the beach. He could still smell the acrid aroma of the bay floating up to the balcony. He could still taste the tequila and salt and lemon. He saw the highlights in Emma's soft hair, heard her hoarse chuckle, saw the setting sun reflecting from her sunglasses. She didn't remove them—even during dinner—until the sun was completely set. Though he never said it to her, Jan thought she believed the sunglasses made her look mysterious.

"Did I interrupt you?" Chuck was saying.

"What?"

"I asked you if you knew that every person who serves on a jury in a capital case in Utah is *voir dired* on his beliefs on the doctrine of Blood Atonement?"

"Amazing!"

"Yes, every juror will be questioned about Blood Atonement and asked how he feels about that doctrine. I know that's true because I testified in a death penalty appeal case in Utah where a killer was told by his bishop that he ought to plead guilty to a murder so he could save his soul through the firing squad."

"You're kidding! Well, Chuck, as I said, it all sounds pretty evil to me."

"I agree, but I repeat, the evil is in the ideas. Every Fundamentalist who participates in Blood Atonement is a product of the madness initiated by Joseph Smith. Smith's lust, his traumatic youth, his charismatic personality all came together in the twin doctrines of polygamy and Blood Atonement. He doubtless possessed, like all serial killers, a psychotic personality—more specifically what we call a dissociated personality. His imagination was law.

"And then Brigham Young. I believe he was a stony killer. Obviously he had a great sexual appetite. Who can say about the others who followed him? They were generally eclipsed by Smith and Young. But they had this in common with them: They believed—with all their hearts—that they heard directly from God on these matters."

Chuck stopped speaking, speared a piece of chicken breast in *mole* sauce, put it in his mouth, and chewed. Swallowing, he touched his napkin to his lips and continued. "Smith gave us polygamy and Blood Atonement; Young amplified those practices. John Taylor saw the handwriting on the wall—that the United States was going to hold the Church's feet to the fire on polygamy—he got a visit from God telling him to secretly commission men to continue polygamy after the public renunciation. In time Ervil LeBaron, Ronald Hansen, and numerous others came forth with their own visions about restoration. All of them, to a man, believe that God visited them in fiery visions and gave them the keys and commission to save the Church."

Jan interrupted. "And these guys all refer to the Smith prophecy about the One Mighty and Strong—the restorer of polygamy."

"Exactly."

Jan leaned back and rubbed his eyes with his fist. Chuck continued.

"So, my friend, to the conclusion: I don't really care where the evil originated. The bottom line is that it keeps women in bondage and murders all who try to fight it. It has killed hundreds in the past and many, many in our day."

"Including my Emma," Jan said.

"I'm afraid so."

They sat in silence for a few moments. Jan stared at his food; suddenly it held little interest for him.

"So," he said, "Hansen can't stop himself?"

Chuck spread his hands.

"Then who will stop him?" Jan asked. "Will you stop him?"

"Jan…" Chuck said slowly. "Look, I'm a lawman. A retired lawman, true, but still a lawman. I can't ride into Hansen's domain and blow him away. I'm bound by the law."

"I'm not a lawman," Jan said.

"I know."

They looked at each other for a few moments. Those blue eyes becoming a veil. Jan had no idea what was behind them.

"Oh," Chuck said. "There's one more thing."

"Yes?"

"One of Hansen's relay stations is on the Crow Indian Reservation just a few miles from my house."

"How did you know about that?"

Old Blue Eyes didn't blink.

"When and if you need more information on that, give me a call," Chuck said. "And one *more* thing."

Jan waited.

"Are you planning to drive the 310 tonight?"

"Yeah, I am."

"Is that wise?"

"Well, Chuck, I'm armed."

"Not well enough."

CHAPTER ELEVEN

It was past 9:00 p.m. when Jan left Chuck Black at the Northern Hotel, drove 15 blocks to Interstate 90, then 15 miles southeast to the Laurel, Montana, junction, to pick up U.S. Highway 310. He stopped at a Circle K for a cup of coffee. He glanced wistfully as he passed Paula's Poker Palace where a great holdem game was doubtless in full swing.

He watched his mirror intently as he left Billings, but saw nothing unusual. Nevertheless, the SIG-Sauer lay on the seat beside him. He cinched his seatbelt and shoulder harness tighter.

Jan dialed in KOMA—AM 1520, the Clear Channel station out of Oklahoma City still spreading its wings over the Mountain West as it had when he was a teenager. Ironically, 40 years later the station still played the exact song list it did then, but now they were golden oldies. Back then Marilee Smith's head lolled on his shoulder in the sagebrush-scented night under the same astounding starlit sky, her slender body nestled beside him and her valentine face and violet eyes sparkling into his. A saccharin wave of nostalgia swept over him. Where was she today? She married

Johnny Dexter from Manderson; the last he heard she was living in Casper. She was Jan's first love and the trial run that led him soon thereafter to his three-year high school relationship with Ginny. Why had he and Ginny not married?

He drifted down the 310, passing through the sleepy Sunday night hamlets of Fromberg, Bridger, and Warren—towns of 200-300 people. Less than an hour after leaving Billings he crossed the Wyoming border two miles north of Frannie. Ten more miles took him through Cowley, a typical Mormon village. As he crossed the Shoshone River and entered Lovell, he could feel fear rising in him like a cold wave. Leaving Lovell would put him on the 25-mile deserted stretch as the clock approached midnight. If there were to be trouble it would be within the next 30 minutes.

On the main street of Lovell, Jan parked across from the Hyart Theatre. He remembered when it was built in the 50s and how it attracted people from a hundred miles because of its spacious modernity. The tall paintbrush marquee still clung to the front of the building. Jan didn't recognize the movie that was playing. He was sweating, even though the chill night air drifted through the rolled-down window.

"Brother!" he said and dug his cell phone out of his briefcase. He dialed Monster's home number.

"Yo."

"John. Jan Kucera."

"Where are you?"

"Parked across the street from the Hyart in Lovell."

"Any problems?"

"Just my nerves."

"I'll be there in less than an hour."

"I hate to ask you…"

"I know you do, but I'm glad you did."

"Listen, why don't I go ahead and start through the desert.

I'll meet you halfway. Blink your headlights three times at all approaching cars—which won't be many."

"I don't like it."

"Look," Jan said, "I'll wait 15 minutes—that is if you are ready to roll—then you should meet me about half-way. I just don't want you to drive 40 miles at this late hour."

"I still don't like it, cowboy. But I guess if you are going to have company, it wouldn't be at the city limits of Lovell."

Jan stepped out of the rental car and leaned back against the automobile, looking over the darkened shops toward the sugar beet processing plant at the far west end of town. Less than a mile further east, the highway turned south and cut through 900 square miles of alkaline desert populated by sagebrush and sedges, and the large wild horse herd.

Jan remembered that once he had come upon a portion of the herd grazing uncharacteristically close to the 310. A huge sorrel stallion jerked his head up and ran for the hills, 20 mares and a few yearlings in tow. "He looked so *awesome!*" The sound of Jan's own voice in the deserted Lovell street startled him. But he continued to visualize the sorrel—actually more of a true roan coat—but mainly he was a dirty old cocklebur-infested beggar. Jan began to hum lines from "Strawberry Roan."

> *Down in the horse corral standin alone*
> *Is an old Caballo, a Strawberry Roan*
> *His legs are all spavined, he's got pigeon toes*
> *Little pig eyes and a big Roman nose*
> *Little pin ears that touched at the tip*
> *A big 44 brand was on his left hip*
> *U-necked and old, with a long, lower jaw*
> *I could see with one eye, he's a regular outlaw.*

Jan felt about as busted up as that old U-necked roan. He got back in the car.

He swung the rental back into the street and headed out of town. As the road climbed up onto the flat and eased south, for some reason KOMA would not come in. He slapped the dashboard and clicked the radio off and on, but all he got was static and noise flashes; he knew lightning was striking somewhere in the Rocky Mountain West. He watched steadily down the road hoping that Monster would be early.

What he saw in the distance, however, was what appeared to be a vehicle stopped on the shoulder of the road with its taillights flashing. He didn't like it. Then, in his rear view mirror he saw a set of headlights. *Where had they come from?*

The parked vehicle was about a mile ahead of him. Checking the rear view mirror he saw that the headlights were now about a mile behind him. With his right hand, he picked up the SIG-Sauer and began slowing. As he approached the parked car, he could see that it was a Chevy Suburban. Standing beside it was a short, stocky man. He was smiling and waving with his left hand, looking very much like someone who was hoping Jan would stop and offer him some help with his stalled vehicle.

Jan could not see the man's right hand. Out of the corner of his eye he thought he detected movement in the shadows on the off-road side of the Suburban. The lights in the vehicle behind him were coming up fast.

Jan rolled down the driver's side window and steering with the hand holding the pistol, held his left hand out of the window in a gesture of greeting. The man stepped away from his vehicle, crossing the centerline in the road, expecting Jan to slow to a stop. Jan continued to wave and he smiled himself, although he doubted that the man could see his face. He slowed to about 30 miles an hour, hoping that it looked like he was preparing to stop.

As the car behind him closed in, Jan shoved the gas pedal to the floor, the V6 engine caught and Jan heard a short squeal of rubber on the warm blacktop. The man, whom Jan now recognized as Bill Campbell, jumped backward and nearly fell to the ground. As Jan hurtled past, he saw Campbell raise his right arm while another man came around the front of the Suburban, also pointing at him.

Jan heard glass breaking and felt a burning sensation in his throat. He continued to keep the pedal on the floor and although he was feeling dizzy, held the car in the middle of the highway. He glanced at the accelerator and noticed he was doing 90.

*   *   *

Monster Broadbeck saw a vehicle careening toward him. Monster flashed his lights three times but the approaching car didn't slow down. He watched as the vehicle began to drift toward the barrow pit. The car was half a mile ahead of him when its right front tire left the blacktop and hit the soft roadbed extension. The rear of the car lazily drifted in an arc coming nearly perpendicular to the highway when the driver apparently tried to correct the spin by yanking the wheel hard to the left.

For a moment Monster thought the car was going to cross over into his lane. Instead, it rolled over three times down into the barrow pit. By the time it came to rest, Monster had braked to a stop and flipped on the cruiser's red lights. Up the road he could see two vehicles turning around on the highway and heading away from the accident site.

As he heaved himself from the cruiser, he pointed his spotlight at the vehicle in the ditch. "This is gonna be Jan," he said. He leaned inside the cruiser to grab the radio mike. He keyed it and barked into it at the dispatcher who handled calls not only for the county, but for all the city police and fire departments within the county, and the medical emergency team from county hospital.

"Donna, this is Sheriff Broadbeck. I'm about 10 miles south of Lovell on the 310. I need you to get the ambulance out here pronto!"

He didn't wait for a reply, but threw the mike down and ran across the highway.

Jan's car had come to rest upright on its wheels—nose pointed toward the highway—about 50 feet off the road itself. The lights were on and the motor was racing. When Monster looked in the driver's side window he was surprised to find it was rolled down. Jan was slumped over the wheel unconscious. The windshield had popped out upon impact and the rear window was shattered. Monster reached inside and switched the motor off. He did a quick survey of the vehicle to see if it were in danger of bursting into flame and he noticed bullet holes in the front passenger window.

"Bad news." he said.

The driver's door, he was happy to discover, opened. Monster knelt down and shined a flashlight on Jan's face. He was unconscious and, as he breathed, blood sputtered from a hole in his neck.

"Oh, no! Jan! Can you hear me?" he yelled.

Monster ran back up the embankment to his car and grabbed the mike again. "Donna, forget the ambulance. Get Saint Vincent's in Billings on the horn and tell them to scramble life flight. Tell them I have a patient with a gunshot wound to the throat. Tell them I will shoot the pilot if he isn't here in 20 minutes."

Back at Jan's side Monster pulled the hunting knife from inside his boot and sliced the seat belts. He dragged Jan out of the car, carried him up to the roadway, and stretched him out on the warm edge of the blacktop 20 feet in front of the cruiser, his head away from the vehicle. Monster figured Jan would be out of the way of any possible traffic from either direction, not that he expected traffic on this road at this time of night. He directed the beam of the spotlight onto Jan's chest and face.

Monster leaned over Jan and put his ear to his chest. He could detect a strong heartbeat. Blood was gurgling from the neck wound. Monster knew Jan was in danger of drowning in his own blood. As he thrust his meaty fingers into the neck wound his mind went to a similar scene in Vietnam: a medic bending over a wounded soldier doing an emergency tracheotomy on him. It had saved the man's life.

Monster raced to the trunk of the cruiser and grabbed the blister-packed "Spill Saver," a $5 item he required all the county vehicles to carry. It was made out of two six-foot lengths of half-inch surgical tubing connected to each other by a rubber bulb. Monster's patrolmen used these devices to siphon gasoline to aid stalled motorists. Monster did not want jugs of gasoline rolling around in the cruiser trunks.

Tearing open the blister pack, he cut off an eight-inch length of tubing. He removed his jacket, rolled it up and shoved it under Jan's neck so that his head tilted back and his throat was fully exposed. Then Monster placed the tip of the hunting knife blade in the notch of Jan's sternum and punched through the trachea. He twisted the blade to spread the incision wide enough to insert the surgical tube. Immediately the gurgling noise stopped and Monster could hear the sound of air entering and leaving his lungs as Jan inhaled and exhaled.

"Dear God," Monster said. "If I ever needed a miracle, it's now."

The night was dead quiet. The red flashers on the sheriff's cruiser pumped eerily in the dark night. Jan's face was haloed by the spotlight. Monster continued to hold the tube with his left hand while he cradled Jan's head in his right hand.

"Where's the freaking chopper?" he yelled into the night.

CHAPTER TWELVE

Alcohol and Listerine. Those two odors enveloped Jan in the darkness. He lay still and drifted within the cloud of aroma without opening his eyes. Faint whirring sounds and a rhythmic beeping fascinated him. He imagined he was under water or otherwise isolated from the world around him. He wondered if this was how a fetus felt.

Suddenly he heard a door open, heard the soft padding of footsteps, then a voice—not directed at him—asked, "How's our boy doing?"

Monster's voice answered. "He hasn't moved a muscle or uttered a peep."

The other voice was that of a woman. A pleasant voice, tinged with a sort of merry quality. "Well, it's time we got his attention."

Monster laughed. "Well, you have *my* attention. Does that mean anything?"

"Probably, but I don't want to discuss it."

The soft voice spoke to Jan. "Mr. Kucera. Can you hear

me?"

Jan wanted to answer but it seemed like too much trouble.

A hand was gently tapping him on his lower arm. "How about opening just one eye?"

Jan struggled. He managed to raise both eyebrows, but neither eyelid opened.

"Nice try, Mr. Kucera. Once more. This time with gusto."

Jan tried again. By squeezing his right eye tighter shut, he managed to pop the left eyelid open.

Standing before him in lime green scrubs was an angelic face framed by short blonde hair. Green eyes peered at him.

"Atta boy! Welcome to the land of the living!"

"Have you made contact?" Monster said from across the room. Jan heard Monster exhale, apparently rising out of a chair. Monster's face appeared behind the angel's.

"Jan, my man!" Monster said. "How you doin?"

Jan's eyelid fluttered and closed as he tried to absorb their presence.

"Stick with us, Mr. Kucera." A little more authoritative.

Jan flicked his eye back open.

"My name is Dr. Sasser. My friends call me Randi."

"Goodness!" Monster said, "That's what my friends call *me!*"

Jan saw the angel roll her eyes and smile.

Now Monster had maneuvered in front of the angel.

"Jan. No kidding. How you feeling?"

Nobody spoke so Jan figured he was going to have to rise to the occasion.

"Great," he whispered hoarsely.

"Say it like you mean it, bro."

"OK, Mr. Broadbeck...Sheriff. Would you mind giving me a little room to maneuver here?"

"I'll give you all the room to maneuver you need, doc."

Dr. Sasser ignored that.

"Mr. Kucera…"

"Mmmm."

"Mr. Kucera, you have been here since Saturday night. It is Monday afternoon. Welcome back from wherever. I want to discuss your condition if you're up to it."

She waited. Jan guessed she was waiting for him to say something, but he couldn't think of anything to say.

Finally he whispered, "Could we do this tomorrow?"

Dr. Sasser laughed.

"Tell you what, Mr. Kucera, we *will* do it tomorrow."

"Jan," he breathed.

"What?" she asked, leaning closer.

"My name is Jan."

*   *   *

Tuesday Jan was awake for 15 minutes before a nurse came in to look at him. He spent the time trying to orient himself. He was in a hospital. How did he get here? He had lots of pain in his throat. What was that all about? Had he talked to a doctor a few minutes or hours or days ago? And was Monster with the doctor?

The nurse said, "Oh! You're awake. Your friend the sheriff is in the cafeteria. He should be back in 10 minutes. I'll tell Dr. Sasser you're awake."

Ten minutes later, when the doctor and Monster walked through the door, Jan had the feeling they had been to lunch together. Dr. Sasser touched Jan's arm.

"Let me introduce myself again. I'm Dr. Randi Sasser."

She told him again that he had been in the hospital for nearly three days.

"Mr. Kucera…Jan, do you even know what happened to

you?"

"Not a clue," Jan whispered.

"You received a gunshot wound and you were in a car wreck."

"In what order?"

Monster laughed.

"You were shot in the throat. That wound caused you to lose control of your car and you rolled it. You suffered a broken clavicle—collarbone. You also suffered a concussion. All in all you were very fortunate. Your condition—now that you are conscious and talking—I'm upgrading you to 'good.'

"I want to talk to you about your throat wound, but I'll have to do that in about 10 minutes. I have a critical patient I need to get back to, but when I return, if you are still awake, I'll talk to you in some detail. But, for the record, you are going to be just fine."

She smiled, brushed a wisp of hair back, turned and walked out of the room.

Jan spoke in a hoarse whisper. "Where am I, John?" Pain seared his throat when he talked.

"Saint Vincent's in Billings," Monster answered.

"How did I get here? What the heck is going on?"

"You were life-flighted here from the 310."

"Oh, man!"

"What do you remember?"

Jan stared at the ceiling. He remembered pulling his car out into the street in Lovell and heading east. He knew that he was headed home from Billings. He remembered talking to Chuck Black and the drive to Lovell. But that was as far as he could go. Forcing himself, he remembered making the turn south and heading up the hill into the 310 desert.

"I was in Lovell. I headed south on the 310." He paused. "Do I have some water here?"

Monster held a glass of ice water with a straw in it. Jan

sucked a little fluid into his mouth. When he swallowed pain shot through his throat and he moaned.

"Smarts, eh?" Monster said.

"Man!"

"You remember heading out of Lovell on the 310. What else?"

"That's it."

"You made it 10 miles south on the 310."

"Then what happened?" Jan asked.

"That's what I'm hoping you can tell me, buddy. You were bushwhacked. Do you remember calling me from Lovell?"

Jan was silent, staring at the ceiling.

"Sort of," he croaked.

"You said you were going to wait 15 minutes and then start across the desert. You must have done exactly that. When I showed up you were racing south from what looked like a two-car road-block. You apparently thought the rental car could fly."

"Bill Campbell."

"What?" Monster's voice grew sharp.

"Bill Campbell was at the roadblock."

"Are you sure?"

He signaled for another sip. He drank and groaned.

"A Suburban was pulled off the road," he whispered, "and a guy was flagging me down. Looked like he had car trouble. I wasn't about to stop for anyone or anything. So I slowed down like I was gonna stop, but at the last second I gunned it. As I went by I remember looking into the steely dead eyes of Campbell."

"Son-of-a-gun!" Monster said. "Was he the one who shot you?"

"I don't know."

"Where was he standing when you went by?"

"Middle of the road. He passed by my driver's side window."

"You were shot in the right side of your throat."

"Yeah, sort of feels that way."

"Whoever did it was on that side of the road. Probably put a round through the windshield or through the passenger window."

"Shot in the throat? Man!"

"You're one lucky cowpoke."

"You ever been shot in the throat?"

Monster laughed out loud. "Well, maybe lucky isn't the right word. The hot Doctor girl used the word 'fortunate.'"

"What is my prognosis?"

"Beats me. She says you'll live and I believe anything she says."

*　　*　　*

The door swung open and Dr. Sasser walked into the room, accompanied by a male nurse with a clipboard. "This is Jack," she said. "He is the charge nurse this shift. He's well up to speed on your condition. You are in great hands here at Saint Vincent's.

"Now to your condition. Your clavicle will heal without any intervention on our part. You will have your arm in a sling for a week or two. Your concussion is history; I don't expect any problems from it at all.

"As for your throat injury, well, what can I say? You are very fortunate. The bullet passed through the thyrohyoid membrane and chipped the hyoid bone. Basically, we were able to repair the membrane in surgery. The danger from the injury was that the bullet severed a vein—the superior thyroid vein. The blood from that vein was flowing through the wound into the trachea. You were initially in danger of drowning in your own blood. Are you following this?"

Jan swallowed—gingerly—and nodded.

"Had you not received immediate attention you would have been in danger of suffocation. Fortunately, Sheriff Broadbeck—our hero here—saved your life."

She shot Monster a look. He smiled, feigned humility, and shrugged his shoulders. Her look lingered a fraction of a second and she turned back to Jan.

"Sheriff Broadbeck performed an emergency tracheotomy on you in the middle of the highway."

"Side of the highway," Monster interrupted.

"Side of the highway…"

Jan looked at Monster and raised his eyebrows.

Dr. Sasser said, "He performed the operation with a hunting knife and a hose that I think he said he uses to steal gasoline."

"Heh. Heh. Nice one, there doc." Monster said. "Glad to see you loosening up a little."

"A *hunting knife* and a *gas hose?*" Jan whispered.

"However," Dr. Sasser continued, "the sheriff did puncture a pretracheal lymph node and severed one of the two inferior thyroid veins."

"Well, heck," Monster said, "the operating conditions were less than perfect."

"But, he did not touch the thyroid gland itself. A beautiful incision…under the circumstances."

Jan crooked a finger at the doctor. She leaned closer.

He whispered, "When can I get out of here?"

The doctor looked irritated. "What is *with* you guys, anyway?" She sighed—a sort of huff. "Well, you'll need to be here for a week, *at least!* Your throat wound is still a very nasty affair. The fact that you are able to talk *at all* is encouraging. The wound was very clean. I'm not sure what that means ballistically, I'll leave that to the expert lawmen. It is possible you will have to have some skin grafts eventually. I'm afraid your throat will bear the marks of this event for life. But your larynx was not damaged at all. You can thank whatever God you pray to. However, the main reason you are able to talk at all is that you are on a strong morphine regimen. You will be very sore for some time. And you will doubtless be somewhat hoarse for the rest of your life."

"May not be long," he whispered, attempting humor.

"I don't know what problems you are facing. I don't really want to know. But you are safe here. Sheriff Broadbeck seems to have a very personal interest in you. I'm sure you are in very capable hands." She colored slightly as she said that.

"I'll know more by tomorrow, but steel yourself for a week's stay. I doubt if I'll let you go any sooner than that."

Monster looked at Jan, spread his hands out palms up, and shrugged his shoulders.

Dr. Sasser turned and left the room, followed by the charge nurse.

After she was outside Monster said, "Whoa, dude! She is one sophisticated chick! These authoritarians drive me nuts. Now, if she only wore glasses."

Jan was shaking his head and chuckling—very gingerly.

"Is she married?"

"She's divorced. Can you imagine? Woman like that, tough, *and* knocking down 250 large a year. What a deal. But I'm not making any sudden moves on her because I filter every woman through my Special Theory of Female Relativity."

Again Jan raised his eyebrows.

"No matter how beautiful a woman is," Monster explained, "somebody—somewhere—is sick of her."

Jan smiled, then immediately grimaced.

Monster stood silent and looked at Jan for a moment.

"I really thought you bought the farm, man."

"You actually performed a tracheotomy on me?"

"Yeah. No one is more surprised than me. Something just sort of took over. I stuck you in the neck with a hunting knife." Monster paused. "I'm going to take Bill Campbell down."

Jan shook his head—gently. "No, forget Campbell."

"No way!"

"Campbell isn't important. Hansen is the one we're after. We have to keep our eyes on the prize."

Monster glared at him for a full 30 seconds. Then he said, "OK, I can buy that."

"Thanks, I know it's not easy."

"Well, first things first. You'll have a deputy from Yellowstone County outside your door as long as you're here."

Jan nodded.

"I have a present for you," Monster said.

He walked over to the chair where he had been sitting and picked up a briefcase. He opened it and pulled a large black book out of it.

Jan looked at him quizzically. It was a Bible.

"I know," Monster said, "But this is a very *special* Bible. And it's a heavy one."

Monster laid the book on Jan's stomach.

It *was* heavy.

Opening the cover, Jan was staring at the SIG-Sauer resting in the hollowed out Bible.

"I think the Good Book can be a real comfort in times of stress," Monster said.

CHAPTER THIRTEEN

A knock on her door disturbed Melissa. It was not the Prophet's customary knock, but something subdued and tentative. She laid the *Times* aside, frowned, walked to the door, and opened it. Maggie Balsom, now Maggie Hansen, stood outside on the wooden veranda hugging her shoulders and shivering.

"C-c-can I talk to you, sister Melissa? I know it's early and…"

"Of course, Maggie. Come on in."

"I'm sorry…"

"Maggie, please, don't worry about it. You are welcome here. Is something wrong?" Melissa waved the young woman to a chair. "Sit down, Maggie."

"Thank you, ma'am."

"Call me Melissa."

"OK. Sister Melissa. Thank you for seeing me."

"Have you been crying?"

With that Maggie broke down and sobbed. She held her face in her hands. "I'm s-s-sorry," she sobbed.

Melissa knelt by the young girl's chair and put her arm around her shoulder, hugging her to herself. Maggie had a fragrant smell of green apples, probably from her shampoo. She turned and let herself be wrapped in Melissa's arms.

"Thank you…I'm s-s-sorry. …"

"There, there, Maggie. There, there."

Finally, as the sobbing abated, Melissa stood and walked to her small kitchenette, poured a glass of water from a pitcher in the refrigerator, returned and handed it to Maggie.

"Take a drink," she said.

Melissa pulled a fuzzy, pink afghan off a loveseat and draped it around Maggie's shoulders and handed her a tissue. Maggie smiled up at her, dabbed at her eyes, then blew her nose.

"Just what has upset you, Maggie?"

"Oh, sister Melissa. Oh. …" Now she was crying again.

Melissa steepled her fingers in front of her face. *I don't know if I can go through this with this child!*

"Now, honey, does this have something to do with your recent marriage?"

Maggie nodded and commenced sobbing again. Melissa began to experience a familiar numbness. She felt herself shrinking inside herself. But she drew a deep breath and squared her shoulders.

"Maggie, I think I know what you are going through."

"Do you? Do you really, sister? I don't think so." The words were spilling out. "I don't think so at all. You *chose* this life. I *didn't*!"

"I know, Maggie, I know. It has been forced on you. It has been forced on a lot of people."

"I wish I was dead!"

"Now, Maggie, that won't help. You have to pull yourself together."

"I have no options."

"We all have options. They're just not always pretty." Melissa struggled to sound upbeat, but felt her own spirit sink. Watching Maggie was painful.

"Anyway," Melissa continued, "what exactly is troubling you at this moment?"

"Everything!"

"Has the Prophet been unkind to you?"

"Oh, no. Not unkind if you mean has he harmed me or said hurtful things. It's just that…"

"It's just that you didn't want to be in this position?"

"What could I do?" She sobbed again.

"Perhaps nothing. But what can you do *now*?"

"Probably *nothing!*"

"Yes, probably nothing. But *maybe*. But let's not start there. Let's start with your biggest problem at the moment. What is making you the most unhappy? Is it sex with the Prophet?"

"Well, he's *old*! It just isn't right."

"No it isn't."

Maggie looked sharply at Melissa, obviously surprised by her remark.

"Do you mean that, sister Melissa?"

"Yes I do," Melissa said evenly. Her eyes rested softly on the young girl. "It really isn't right."

"But…but, I mean…you are part of the system here. You are a believer in this whole insanity!"

"Am I? Maybe. Maybe I *was*, but no longer am."

"Oh, Melissa! I was right to come here! I knew I was!"

"Well, sweetie, I'm not sure you were right at all. I'm not sure I can help you."

"But at least you can help me try to understand the thing that is bothering me most."

"The temple ceremony?"

"Yes! How did you know? Oh, I see. It bothers you too!"

"Very much so. And, truth be told, we are not the only ones the temple ceremony has bothered over the years. Some of those whom it bothered are no longer with us."

"You mean they escaped?" Fear registered in Maggie's eyes.

Melissa frowned. "Escaped? Yes, you could put it that way. Let's just say they are no longer among us."

Maggie began to sob again.

"Maggie, you are going to have to pull yourself together. If there is any hope for you at all, you will have to pull yourself together."

"But what *is* that mumbo-jumbo in the temple? God, it was *awful*!"

"It is *supposed* to be awful, Maggie. It's supposed to bind you to the Prophet and to the Church. To bind you with fear."

"I'm so afraid," Maggie said. "It was so shocking. It was so…so…"

"So evil?"

Maggie stared at Melissa. Her mouth was open. She closed it and swallowed. Then she nodded. "What is it all about?" she cried. "What does it mean?"

"Well, Maggie, I can only tell you what they *say* it means."

"I mean those women touched my body—all over!"

"The washing and anointing ceremony?"

"I guess that's what they call it. And it was just the beginning of the really weird stuff."

"Well, Maggie, they say they are washing you to make you pure from 'the blood and sins of this generation'—as they put it. And the anointing with oil on your face and breasts and abdomen and loins—that is to anoint your body for holiness."

"Holiness? What's so holy about what the Prophet did to me later that night? And why did I—*do I*—have to wear this weird underwear—these garments? Can't I ever take them off?"

Melissa sighed. "Well, again Maggie, they say that is so you will continue to be reminded that you are special to God. And the garments are to protect you..."

"But they say I can *never* take them off. Only the Prophet, he took them off of me. I just don't get it. Do you wear these things?"

"I did. For years."

"But you don't now? How do you get away with it?"

"Well, I have gotten away with it so far, but..." Melissa smiled grimly.

"Oh, sister Melissa! Oh, no!"

Melissa interrupted. "Let's talk about *you* and *your experience,* Maggie."

"Well, then all those stupid plays in the temple. Adam and Eve and the devil. The devil said some scary things. He said, 'If you don't remember and keep all the vows you make in this temple today you will be in my power!' And the devil, that was Sam Rapp in that disguise. I recognized him."

"Yes, Sam plays the devil."

"But the bloody oaths...I have a question about them."

"Yes?"

"They said that if I reveal what goes on in the temple, I could...I could..." She stopped and shuddered.

"Go on, Maggie. Get it out. It's part of dealing with what you have seen."

Maggie was sobbing. Her face in her hands. Then she spoke quietly.

"They said if I revealed the silly handshakes they would cut my tongue out and slit my throat and rip my guts out...and..."

"Yes, Maggie, that's what they said."

"But they don't really *do* those things do they?"

Melissa was silent. Maggie resumed sobbing. Finally she spoke.

"L-L-et me ask you a question. I don't even know why I want to know this. B-b-but I do. Is this something that is unique to Prophet Hansen. Is our group the only one with this kind of temple ceremony? I mean, did Joseph Smith really teach this, like the Prophet told me? Or did Prophet Hansen think it up?"

Melissa smiled at that. "Oh, no. Prophet Hansen has a lot of gifts, but he isn't particularly inventive. The temple ceremony came from Joseph Smith. Actually he stole it from the Freemasons and *said* God gave it to him."

"The Freemasons?" Maggie shook her head. "I don't even know who they are. But, sister Melissa, what about other Mormons? Do *they* do these same things?"

"Well, yes and no. Prophet Hansen probably practices the temple ceremony in its purest form. By *pure* I mean in the form closest to the form that Joseph Smith and Brigham Young used. It is almost unchanged since Nauvoo. The mainline Utah church removed some of the grisly language in 1911. But they did not stop signifying the blood oaths such as slitting the throat until 1990. Now they just give the handshakes, do the plays, take the vows. But they don't draw their thumbs across their throats signifying the penalty for revealing the secrets. Not for more than 10 years now."

Maggie was sitting silently. To Melissa she looked washed out, like her life had been drained out of her. Eventually she asked one more question.

"I wondered about the veil of the temple and all that."

"OK, honey. Well, the veil represents the entrance into the Celestial Kingdom. The holes in the veil are the same ones that are in your garments. The square, the compass, the little slit representing the mason's rule. When you reach your hands through the veil and are embraced by the actor playing the part of the Lord, and when you say the long paragraph about 'health in your navel and marrow in your bones,' and when you give the Lord the secret handshakes, you are using what you learned in the temple—symbolically—to enter heaven. This is all practice, Brigham Young said, so we will know how to pass by angel sentries in order to get into heaven…"

"Stop it! Stop it, sister. I can't hear any more…"

Maggie jumped up and hugged herself tightly. She stared at Melissa, tears streaming down her face. Her eyes were wide and streaked with red.

"Sister Melissa," she said through lips tinged with foam, "What is to become of us?"

Melissa could think of no answer.

CHAPTER FOURTEEN

Jan gingerly extracted himself from the passenger seat of Monster's champagne Porsche, leaned against the car, and looked at the house where he had spent his teenage years—814 South 5th Street. By an ironic series of events, the house was now owned by Ginny Hollingsworth. She and her ex-husband had purchased it from the retired schoolteacher who had originally bought it from Jan's mother in 1961, when it was near new. Jan's father had built it, or at least had done the masonry work and some of the framing and drywall.

The dozen houses lining the block faced east. An open field lay across the street. Beyond the field was Highway 20 entering town from the south. Across the highway further east the drive-in movie screen still stood, though now Jan could see daylight through the holes in it. Next to the abandoned theater a crew of Mexicans worked on one of the fairground buildings, preparing for the Big Horn County Fair in August. Yet *further* east lay the CB&Q railway track, and beyond that the river. Across the river and beyond the badlands Jan could see the Bighorn Mountains, blue with touches of snow even in July. Cloud Peak, the highest in the state, rose in the distance.

The row of houses—during the late 1950's and early 1960's—embodied post-war modernism reaching all the way to Wyoming. Now the string of little houses looked somehow pitiful to Jan. A huge cottonwood tree towered above the rooftop from the back yard. Jan felt himself transported back in time 40 years. He half expected to see his dog, Lady, race out the front door.

A lark trilled across the road in the empty field in which Jan had replaced the engine in the 1941 Plymouth he had bought from his older brother, Buzz. Eventually, Jan sold the Plymouth to Bobby Caines who drove it into an embankment along the Greybull River and died, impaled on the steering wheel. Bobby had stopped Jan on the street that fateful afternoon and asked him if he wanted to ride to Greybull.

The warm, uncharacteristically humid air felt heavy in Jan's lungs and bore the smell of fresh-cut grass and the promise of rain, portending a break in the heat. For a moment Jan stood lost in memories, silently drinking in the air, glad to be alive.

Ginny was standing on the steps in a white blouse and jeans. "Tight jeans," Monster had said as they pulled up. She had her arms crossed under her breasts and was leaning back on her heels the same way she did as a teenager when she was waiting for Jan to pick her up—usually late—for a date. But this time there was no scowl, rather a half smile. The two stared at each other for a few moments, Jan leaning on the Porsche, she leaning against the door. Monster stood next to the front fender of the Porsche studying the horizon.

Finally Ginny said softly, "You coming in Jan?" Her voice had a trace of cigarette huskiness. She had told Jan she smoked for 20 years, but had quit nearly that long ago.

Jan shuffled up the sidewalk, his left arm in a sling. It was

Tuesday, exactly a week since he came-to in the hospital in Billings and 10 days since the attack on the 310. Dr. Sasser had released him early, but not without misgivings.

Ginny wrapped her arms around him and held him for a few seconds, careful to avoid the injured arm and mindful of the gauze collar around his neck. Then she stepped back and looked into his eyes.

"How you doing, Jan?"

"I'm OK, Ginny."

She looked at his face for a few more seconds then said, "Well, come on in. I know John wants a cup of coffee. Right, John?" she asked, turning to Monster, then disappearing into the house.

Inside she seated Jan in a La-Z-Boy, levered the footrest up and disappeared into the kitchen.

Monster spoke to Jan. "Me and Harold and the boys are going to guard the house twenty-four-seven. We've made up a cot in the garage. We have three concealed low-light cameras trained on the house from power poles. We will monitor every approach to this place from our CRTs in the garage. You and Ginny will not be alone here for the next few days or weeks, whatever it takes to get you back up to speed."

"Is that because you don't trust me to be alone with Ginny?" Jan asked smiling.

"Frankly no. But I figure she's old enough to take care of herself. Actually, I'm really hoping I *can't* trust you with her. Nobody is more ready for a woman's comforts than you are, partner. I'm hoping something gets cooking between you two."

"John, you know I only have eyes for you," Ginny said as she returned from the kitchen carrying a tray with a carafe of coffee, three cups, and some shortbread cookies. No cream or sugar was on the tray.

Monster snorted. "Thanks, Ginny. I'm going to bring our boy's bags in before I have my coffee."

*   *   *

While Monster was outside Ginny poured Jan's coffee and set it on a coaster on a small cherrywood end table by the La-Z-Boy. "My grandfather made this table," she said. "He gave it to my grandmother on their 20th wedding anniversary."

"How long have you lived here?" Jan asked.

"Ten years. Five married and five alone."

"You were married for more than 20 years, what went wrong?"

Ginny looked out the picture window. "What *ever* goes wrong?" she said wistfully. "Who knows? People grow apart. Larry was drinking heavily, but of course he *always* drank heavily. I drank a lot myself in the early years after you and I broke up." She stopped abruptly and looked at Jan. "I didn't mean that the way it sounded."

"I know," Jan said. "Hey, we all drank too much in our salad days."

"Anyway, we drifted apart. After Larry retired from the Army and we moved back here, it seemed to just ... just end. I have given up trying to make sense of it. Larry was—Larry *is*—a great guy. We just lost our way."

They were silent.

"Look, Jan. I'll be straight with you. I have the same feelings for you I've always had. I've never lost them. But I know you totally gave yourself to Emma, and I know you are not over her. I don't need you to be. I don't need anything at all. I'm here. Whatever."

"Ginny..."

"Shut up," she said gently and smiled. "I think John is about to make his entrance."

Monster came through the door with the three bags he and Jan had packed at the ranch.

"Down the hall," Ginny said. Last bedroom on the right."

Then to Jan she said, "That was your room as a teenager. I remember."

Jan colored slightly. He remembered as well. He also remembered the room cluttered with his electrical equipment, much of it on the makeshift workbench he had constructed out of a door and two sawhorses against the north wall. Cigar boxes and the "silks" of his magician hobby were always strewn about. A cage with a couple of mice in the corner.

Monster disappeared down the hallway. When he came back he sat on the couch in front of the picture window. Ginny handed him his coffee.

"Jan, I have a couple of things to talk to you about," he said.

"Want me to leave the room?" Ginny asked.

"Of course not, Ginny. We have no secrets from you. In fact, I need to deputize you if you're up for it, and issue you a side arm."

"John!" Jan snapped. "If that is necessary, I want to leave here right now. I'm not going to put Ginny in any kind of danger…"

Ginny said, "Enough, Jan." Then to Monster, "I have a 357 Magnum Colt Python and I know how to use it. You forget; Larry was an Army officer."

"My, my, my," Monster said, smiling broadly. "What a woman! Good thing for you Jan is here. Nothing excites me more than a good looking woman with a gun in her hand."

Jan stared at the two of them.

Ginny turned to Jan. "Look," she said, "we're all adults here and we're all in this together. You need a place to recuperate and that place is here! If I have chosen to put myself in danger, that's my business."

Monster beamed.

"Jan," the sheriff said, "I hate to interrupt this entertaining display of Ginny busting your chops, but Harold is relieving me in about 30 minutes and I need to fill you in on some of Hansen's latest activities."

Jan's face was white and drawn, but he managed to stammer, "Go ahead."

"The first thing you should know is that the two young studs you captured at the ranch are dead."

"*What*?"

"They were poisoned in the Natrona County jail in Casper. Just a couple of days after you were attacked on the 310. Somebody put arsenic in their stew. They were both in solitary for security reasons. There's a real stink in the Casper papers. The Feds are totally disgusted with the county mounties, as you would expect."

"Good grief!" Jan said. "Just when you think Hansen can't sink any lower, he does." Jan held up his hand. He steepled his fingers and closed his eyes. After a moment he opened his eyes reached over and picked up his coffee cup from the end table and took a sip.

"Anyway," Monster continued. "That's life in your local cult. But there is something else that you will be very, very interested in.

"Two nights ago we had a woman admitted to County Hospital. She was worked over thoroughly. Had been left for dead, but she managed to get to Highway 14 and a rancher took her to the hospital. One of Hansen's wives."

"Dear God!" Ginny exclaimed.

Monster looked at Ginny. "Could you find me a refill, my dear? Gotta tell ya, that is better than what you give me at the café."

Ginny brought the carafe to Monster and filled his cup.

"Got any more of those tasty little nibblers?"

Ginny headed back to the kitchen for more cookies, shaking her head as she went. Monster reached over and thumbed through the magazines on the coffee table. Jan leaned back and sipped his coffee.

When Ginny returned, Monster said, "So this gal in the hospital—pretty little thing, no doubt! Tall brunette, forty-something. Hansen has impeccable taste, you gotta give him that. So I interview her at the hospital. This kid is as cool as they come. Seems like a sweet woman but she looks at you real hard. I mean she doesn't seem to trust men." Monster bit into another cookie. "Is *that* a surprise? Anyway, it took me a couple a hours last night to get her to open up.

"The story is that she has been married to Hansen for about ten years. Her name is Melissa and she is, I think, a woman of high moral principle. Side note, she said that Bill Campbell had fallen for her. She thinks Bill's feelings for her caused a rift between him and Hansen. However, she sort of thinks Campbell is the one who abducted her from the Prophet's harem or whatever they call it. Thinks Hansen may have been testing Campbell by sending him to kill her. Said nobody had access to her room without the Prophet's knowledge. She *didn't* mention that she had been raped and I didn't tell her I knew. The physician who examined her told me."

Ginny stood and wrapped her arms across her stomach.

"The problem is," Monster continued, "Melissa apparently never follows blindly. She began to see that polygamy is simply a way for men to manipulate women. Think of it, 13 wives competing for the affection of one husband. Even *I* know that won't fly.

According to Melissa, polygamy not only doesn't work, it is a miserable lifestyle—for the women that is. Melissa says polygamy creates monsters. To quote her, 'Of course polygamy can't work! How could it work?' Basically, she's saying it's manipulation of the highest order.

"Anyway, for five years now, she's been thinking for herself. She finally thought herself out of the cult. Actually out of Mormonism itself."

Ginny interrupted. "How in the world did she do that?"

Monster smiled and shook his head. "Well, that part is *very* interesting. She told me she concluded that if Joseph Smith and Brigham Young were prophets, then polygamy is true. I mean, after all, they said it was from *God*. So, if they are prophets, then polygamy, *ergo*, is true. But, then she said, 'Well, the converse must be true.' Said if polygamy is *not* from God—and she concluded it *can't* be from God because it destroys women—then Joseph and Brigham were *not* prophets."

Monster looked up at the ceiling and closed his eyes. "She actually used those words, 'The converse must be true.' Melt your heart in a nanosecond, a beautiful woman postulating logically like that."

"John," Ginny said impatiently.

"Oh, sorry. OK, so she says it took her about five years to work all this out. And she concludes, of course, that *Hansen* isn't a prophet either."

Monster continued, "So our lovely Melissa finds herself, as she says, 'On the horns of a dilemma.' No kidding, Jan, she talks like that. I'm not making fun of her. She is as serious and straight as any woman I have ever met, but she talks with this sort of contrived lingo."

Jan said, "Deck Edwards tells me that there is a whole Mormon language. Says once you know it you can be in a coffee shop and tell who is a Mormon by listening to the language."

"Man, after being with Melissa, I can believe that. Spooky."

"Yeah, well, as much as I respect Deck, I think he is probably stretching there," Jan said. "But, anyway, finish the story."

Monster went on, "So Melissa tells me that she finally—about six months ago—tells Hansen she will 'no longer honor the marriage bed.' No kidding, where do you think she learned to talk like that? Rings my bell."

"John," Ginny said, "spare us the sidebars. This is an interesting story in its own right. Not that you aren't entertaining as usual, but stick to the story."

"There you go, Ginny, that's what I'm talking about. Women like you and Melissa, with your golden phrases…OK, anyway, Melissa says Hansen got steely cold when she refused him. Comes to her and says, 'Do you know who I am, Melissa?' And, get this, Hansen *cries!* No, *really,* he cries these huge tears. He says, 'Do you know who I am?' and then he walks out of the room and never says another word to her—ever! Then Sunday night, a week after he orders the hit on you, two men come into her bedroom, take her into the hills outside the compound—'outside the camp'—in Melissa's words, like there's something significant in the phrase—and beat her to a pulp. And as I said, they raped her and left her for dead."

"Good Lord!" Ginny said. "How did she get to the highway?"

"Says she woke up in a ditch and walked to the highway. Anyway, Jan, I want you to meet her. I think she is going to be able, and more importantly *willing,* to give us a lot of good inside dope that may help us penetrate Hansen's little love compound." Monster paused and appeared to be appreciating his phrasing.

"Who's guarding her?" Ginny asked.

"Ah, Ginny, the mind of a true investigator. I have deputized a couple of friends, Ron and Jack Russell."

"Good choices," Ginny said, "the Terrier Twins."

"Or the Terror Twins, as I like to call them. Anyway, I promise you she will be safe at County Hospital with the Russell boys at the door. Those guys will do anything for me and they are capable of doing *anything*.

"However, Ginny, that brings us to another question. What do I do with her two days from now when she gets out of the hospital?"

Ginny smiled. "Well, Sheriff, you have made such an investment in security in this place, it would be a shame to have to duplicate it somewhere else. And, I have yet one more bedroom."

"Ginny, Ginny, Ginny," Monster said in his best Cary Grant.

CHAPTER FIFTEEN

The Big Horn County Courthouse was built in the 1930s, a sandstone structure with tall concrete columns along the top of 25 wide steps. Originally, three architecturally similar buildings were spread along a thousand feet of C Street, stretching two blocks west from Main Street. The trinity of buildings formed a beautiful promenade lining the north side of C Street: first the post office on the corner at Main, then the courthouse, then, at the far west end of the block, the library. The original library, a Carnegie, had been torn down in the 1950s and replaced with a larger, modern facility still flanked by two Civil War cannon. Since the end of World War II the city fathers—during the Christmas season—ordered colored lights strung from the courthouse to the other two buildings and the street. It made for a remarkable display for a small town.

Before any of the county buildings had been constructed, Jan's grandfather had built a two-story sandstone building on Main Street kitty-corner from what would become the post office lot. His building housed the first bank and first mercantile store in Basin.

Jan's family had lived in the upper story for a while after World War II when he was in grammar school after they moved to town from the ranch. His mother had sublet several rooms on the second floor as apartments for oil patch workers. The building currently housed the Fraternal Order of Eagles on street level; the upper floor was now condemned.

Inside the courthouse, marble floors led to two oak-paneled courtrooms upstairs and the sheriff's office in the basement. On Monday—six days after he had taken up residence at Ginny's—Jan sat, with Monster and George Olson, around Monster's desk, sipping coffee from paper cups. Jan wore his shirt buttoned to the top, in spite of the heat, attempting to obscure the bandages on his neck. Monster leaned back in his chair, his lizard boots on the desk. In the middle of the desk a box of donuts from the bakery in Wheeler's Market gave off a light maple aroma. Beside the box of donuts a speakerphone emitted the voice of Granny, from Seattle, describing the microwave system used by the Church of the One Mighty and Strong. Chuck Black, at his home in Hardin, Montana, was also part of the conference call.

"The first thing is that there are no FCC licenses issued to C1MS or any of its officers, and I've discovered they are broadcasting on Spread Spectrum transmitters…"

Monster interrupted, "Talk English, Granny."

"OK. Spread Spectrum is a coding protocol that allows very secure transmissions over low power transmitters that are supposedly good up to 30 miles, but they can be boosted to near double that. Under Title 47 of the FCC rules these transmissions are unlicensed."

George Olson interrupted. "They are probably Lynx transmitters using a fast chip rate and a code 127 bits long. We eat that stuff for lunch."

"I imagined that, my man," Granny said. "You won't have

any trouble decoding the stuff if we can figure out how to intercept it. But I can't figure that out from here."

Monster said, "We know where the transmitters are. The signal goes from the compound to Heart Mountain north of Cody, then back to the Medicine Wheel. That's because Medicine Wheel is not line-of-sight from the compound. From Medicine Wheel it goes almost into Chuck Black's backyard on the Crow Reservation and then to Billings. We do not have the Billings location pinpointed, but I'm sure it's on the north rim somewhere."

Granny whistled. "I guess I'm going to have to reevaluate my opinion of the sagebrush coalition, Sheriff. Sounds like you folks can do some good detective work from the back of a horse. So where will you want to intercept?"

"Well," George Olson answered, "the sheriff and I agree that the signal needs to be shot to an antenna here on the roof of the Big Horn County Courthouse. The only possible single link would be from the Medicine Wheel location. It's 30 miles exactly line-of-sight and downhill all the way."

"Downhill doesn't make any difference..."

"I think George is joking, Granny," Jan said.

"Oh," Granny said, "I get it."

"So, Granny," Jan asked, "I guess you know what equipment we need and can get it. Big question: What about installation?"

"What is the layout of the site?"

"John," Jan said, "Why don't you cover that?"

"OK," Monster said, "This is a 50-foot tower and a cabin. The cabin houses a watchman who keeps the generator running and maintains two-way radio contact with the compound which is less than 20 miles south at the foot of the mountain. The microwave transmitter is located in a small enclosure at the base of the antenna. There are two 27-by-31 inch directional grid antennas on the top of the tower, one pointed at Heart Mountain, one pointed at the Crow Reservation."

"Hmmm. How far is the cabin from the tower?"

"Adjacent."

"Well, you have a problem."

"I'm sure we have lots of problems," Monster said. "What's the first one?"

"Well," Granny said, "We can probably tap into the signal at the transmitter ... but how are you going to rebroadcast it? If the tower is adjacent to the building you'll have a problem doing *anything* undetected. Then you have the problem of stringing a coax cable through the woods to another tower with your own transmitter."

"No way we can do that," George Olson said. "The cabin site is a tiny plot of private land surrounded by Forest Service land. Nobody is going to erect a tower anywhere near there without clipping through a ton of red tape. Even if we could do that, we can't have a wire running off through the grass. That would look way too suspicious."

Everyone was silent.

Jan finally spoke up. "Granny, how big are these transmitters?"

"Small. Some of them actually can attach to the back of the antenna."

More silence.

"Granny, there are two antennas on the tower..." Jan paused. "Ummm...How noticeable would a third antenna be?"

"Whoa, dude!" Granny said. "Of course! Sure. That would work!"

"What are you talking about?" Monster asked.

"They are suggesting," George Olson said, "that we climb the tower and bolt another antenna on. And I suppose," he said to no one in particular, "that we would use their generator to power our transmitter."

"Certainly," Granny said. "They're low voltage—draw only milliamps off the generator. You would have to string a low-voltage line up the antenna. It could be done."

"Would *you* do it?" Jan asked.

"Never! This is a job for some big bad cop who wants to shoot it out with the guard at the cabin. That ain't me, man!"

"What would it take to get the job done?" Jan asked. "And can you talk the right man through the process?"

"Technically it's a piece of cake. A guy who knows how to climb the tower could make a connection to a power lead inside their transmitter housing, run a very small low-power cable up the tower and clamp the antenna on. He'd then disconnect the coax off their receiving antenna, stick in a splitter, and connect it to your own antenna. The work at the top of the tower would take five minutes max, mainly tightening the clamps. There are some other technical considerations. I would need a little more information. I would have to either get a visual of the site or some good photographs and I also need the model numbers off their gear so I know *exactly* what we are looking at. Then I can take a man through a couple of dry runs and he would be able to make the connections— if he didn't get shot that is. The odds are that nobody would notice three antennas instead of two—50 feet off the ground. At least until they have to do some maintenance on the equipment. Then a tech guy would immediately ask questions."

George Olson spoke up. "Granny, we know what you want. We can get it. Let us put our heads together here and when we come up with an operational plan we'll get you down here to look things over. No. On second thought get the gear and get on a plane with it. Don't forget to bring what we will need at the courthouse. I'm assuming you won't need the information you are asking for in order to select our transmitter."

"That's correct. I won't need that until we're ready to wire into it."

"OK. We'll get what you want. We need to get this thing going before Hansen goes nuts and blows somebody up."

"Gotcha, chief. I'll be in Billings tomorrow night. I'll get you the flight information."

"Granny, this is Sheriff Broadbeck. Get *me* the flight information; I'll have a man meet your plane. You got my number?"

"*Puh-leeze.*"

"Sorry, Granny. And, Chuck, thanks for sitting in. Looks like we won't need the Indian connection right now."

Monster reached over and punched the line buttons on the phone and the speaker went dead. Everyone sat in silence and stared at the walls.

Finally Monster spoke. "Obviously one-wing-Willie," he said nodding at Jan, "can't climb the tower. I could climb it but it would bend over and the antennas would point at the ground..."

"I'm your man," George Olson said. "I have an electronics background and I can climb the tower. And I can shoot the guard if it comes to that."

"No, I'll shoot the guard from the ground," Monster said.

"Anyway," George said, "I am half-way there with Granny. I know what he's talking about."

"So how should we proceed?" Jan asked.

"I'll gather together what stuff we have on file," Olson said. "Tonight we'll penetrate the transmitter housing and get the numbers Granny wants. Sheriff, when Granny gets here tomorrow night call me at home and I'll come down. I think you should get him within binocular range of the Medicine Wheel site so he can look at the tower and the transmitter housing."

"You got it, coach."

"I just have one question," Jan said. "How are we going to get up the tower without arousing the guard who is sleeping at the foot of it?"

"Well," Monster said, "You remember what Teddy Kennedy said to Mary Jo Kopeckne when she asked him 'What happens if I get pregnant?'"

Jan raised one eyebrow. "Do I really want to hear this?"

"Teddy said, 'Mary Jo, we'll cross that bridge when we come to it.'"

CHAPTER SIXTEEN

Tell me about life with Ronnie Hansen," Monster said over the rumble of the Porsche.

"What's to tell?" Melissa said. "He's a man with fifteen wives over whom he exercises total dominance—just like he does everyone else."

"Fifteen? I thought he had thirteen."

"He probably has many more than that. I feel certain that he takes wives in isolated communities and swears them to silence. Even the Prophet is sensitive to the charge of extravagance. He travels to meetings of the faithful throughout the West—throughout the whole country for that matter. He doesn't marry them all in the temple, I know that. He didn't marry me there although we were "sealed" there later. His word is law—or, more correctly, scripture. He can do anything he wants."

"Not *anything*." Monster said.

"So you say."

Monster looked at her. She was wearing a loose-fitting skirt of light material that showed the outline of her long legs, and a white blouse that now hung slightly open. Monster did his best to avoid staring. He was taking her from the hospital to Ginny's house. Tonight he would meet with his fellow conspirators and Granny to plan their incursion into the Medicine Wheel camp.

Monster felt slightly uncomfortable around Melissa. What kind of a woman is this? Tough, he thought. Tough, but soft as well. Nevertheless, he felt a strange foreboding as he talked to her; there was a glaze to her eyes that worried him. She looked like a girl who had seen too much. He had seen such women before. He knew she was in danger, not only from without, but from within.

Monster punched the accelerator and passed a truck ferrying calves to the Worland stockyards. U.S. Highway 20 was a short, straight four miles from the hospital to Basin.

"Ronnie Hansen, I'll admit, has been untouchable. But a day of reckoning is coming, I guarantee."

Melissa folded her arms across her chest, laying long slender fingers on her shoulders. "But will that happen before or after he destroys the compound and everyone in it?"

"Would he really do that?"

Melissa laughed softly and shook her head. "Why are men so gullible? How long does it take for them to get the picture? What does Ronald have to do to convince you that he's on a collision course with destiny that will bring about the end of the world— your world or his? It's only a matter of time, I realize, before the great legal power of the United States is brought to bear on him. I know that. But what does he do when he is backed into a corner? Just take a look at me. I told you what he said to me the last time I refused his...his sexual advances? He said, 'Melissa, do you know who I am?' As I told you before, he had tears in his eyes when he said it. I knew my life was over at that moment."

"But *why*, for heaven's sake?"

Melissa was silent. She looked out the window at the alfalfa fields ready for the first cutting. She thought back on her 10 years with Prophet Hansen.

"I was 25 when I married him. I met him in Mexico where I was working in a clinic as a summer volunteer. I had gone down there from Connecticut with a church group that made the trip every summer with outstanding students who wanted to serve humanity before graduating from college and entering the work force. I was a senior nursing student at Boston College.

"Ronald was nearly 25 years older than I, but he was tall, blonde, and handsome. So self-assured. He was visiting the clinic because The Church of the One Mighty and Strong had made a sizeable donation to it. He threw a lot of money around in those days, still does. It took me years to realize that *everything* the Prophet does is calculated to consolidate his power, his authority, his influence, his reputation. The annual donations to the clinic bought good publicity for C1MS in Mexico. And there are lots of polygamous Mormons in Mexico. The Prophet is respected by such groups.

"Of course, in recent years—especially after Jan Kucera's article ran in the *New York Times*—his reputation has sunk. Once he had open doors to the Wyoming governor's mansion; now he is considered a sort of fringe-lunatic. When that happened, something seemed to snap inside Ronald."

"What do you mean?" Monster pulled the car over to the curb on the north end of Basin. The guttural engine rumbled quietly.

"I don't know, suddenly there was a new urgency about him. He changed. I mean, when I met him, he was so charming. He swept me off my feet in Mexico. He took me to Mexico City on the pretext of showing me another clinic. I'm embarrassed to say I was terribly honored. He put me in the then new five-star Camino

Real Hotel. Seven hundred rooms of a luxury I was unaccustomed to, even though my parents in Connecticut are what most people would consider to be well-off. For a week he talked to me of his religion—his call to save the world from poverty and degradation. How could I have been so naïve?

"When he converted me, he bedded me. Married me under the stars in the courtyard, performing the ceremony himself. I bought it all."

"What happened to change all that?"

"Ronald had been good to me—as long as I caused him no trouble. I was, according to everyone, his favorite wife. I excited him like no other, he told me."

"Well..."

Melissa waved him off and continued.

"I *believed* Ronald. I not only believed him, I believed *in* him. Those early years were good. The entire Church treated me with deference. And, I believed, I gave as much as I got. I worked hard on behalf of the other women and the children. I also traveled with Ronald a lot."

She stopped. Drew in her breath. Folded her hands into small fists on her lap.

"But a cloud began to form after the first few years. I discovered I was barren. Not only did I suffer the profound disappointment of realizing that my mothering would be confined to children not my own, but I also discovered that barrenness is the ultimate stigma for a polygamous wife. As much as Ronald cared for me, his theology told him that I was damaged goods. 'Barren' equals 'cursed.' How I have come to hate that word! It's a descriptive you can't escape. Some women are ugly, others are fat, some are stupid. I am *barren*.

"Ronald viewed it as a great irony that his favorite wife would never produce Hansen stock. He viewed my curse as *his* curse.

From that day his admiration changed to simple lust. I was no longer his wife, but his property. It was a subtle change, but it went to the bone. He never recovered from it and neither did I.

"That was when I began to see that for all his 'spirituality,' for all his 'prophetic insight,' he was, in some ways, blind. That knowledge worked into my soul. From there, the unraveling continued."

Melissa fell into silence.

Monster interrupted her reverie.

"I guess I just can't understand what makes him tick, Melissa. Help me understand."

Melissa looked out the window at the park and tennis courts. A father pushed a little girl on the merry-go-round. Faster and faster it turned, causing her hair to stand out straight from her head. She was laughing. So was her father.

"Sheriff…"

"John."

"John, then. John, did you ever read *The Brothers Karamazov*?"

"I'm afraid my cultural attainments wouldn't fill a 44 cartridge casing."

Melissa laughed.

"Well, anyway…John, I read the book during my early estrangement from Ronald. I read a lot then. I was very alone. Anyway, there is a scene in that book that gave me a lot of insight. Jesus Christ has returned to the earth as a peasant in Russia. He has been arrested and put in prison. While he is there, a priest—I think it was a priest, it could have been a city father—came to him. The man says to Jesus something like, 'We know who you are and we know why you have come here. But we can't let you accomplish your mission.'"

"What was his mission?" Monster asked.

"The man tells him 'You want to give people liberty. Free-dom. But they can't handle that. It will ruin them. We have to protect them from you. So, yes, we know who you are and we have to kill you.'"

"Jesus?"

"Yes, they are going to kill Jesus *again*. Anyway, John, Ronald *also* is saving people who can't take care of themselves. If he has to manipulate them to do it, so be it. If he has to kill them to send them to heaven, well…so be that, too."

Monster was now looking at the figures in the park. He was quiet for a while and then asked softly, "What caused you to know Hansen was finished with you and would harm you?"

Melissa looked at him. "The whole community knew that he and I were 'estranged.'"

"And…?"

"No one resists Ronald. No one."

"I still don't understand. You were his wife. *He loved* you."

She laughed. She reached over and touched Monster's arm. "Oh, Sheriff," she said. "You are a throwback, aren't you? You are so full of bluster, but underneath you are a romantic. 'He *loved you!*'" She was laughing harder now. So hard that tears started to form in the corners of her eyes.

Monster looked at her. She was laughing so hard she was sobbing. And then she was only sobbing. Monster reached over and put a beefy hand on her delicate shoulder. Her body shook as she wept.

He pulled her to himself and cradled her face against his chest. She continued to shake and weep. She was moaning.

"There, there," he was saying. "There, there, little girl. It's OK."

CHAPTER SEVENTEEN

Jan and Monster met with Granny and George Olson Tuesday night 10:00 p.m. Granny had been fetched from the Billings airport.

"These are the photographs Darrel Southwick and I got at the Medicine Wheel last night."

"Cool, man!" Granny said, "Was it an exciting procedure?"

"Exciting is an understatement. We waited outside the cabin listening to the guard snore before we got up the nerve to throw a tarp over the transmitter equipment, crawl inside and shoot the flash film. I shot the film, Darrel waited outside. He said every time the flash went off, the tarp lit up like an igloo."

Granny examined the prints. As he looked at them he danced around like a marionette, his long arms sweeping through the air.

"This project is s-o-o-o doable! I need a couple a days to rig the equipment here at the courthouse."

"Yeah," Olson said, "but we have to do it all at night. Nobody here can know what we're up to. I have already run empty plastic electrical conduit from the roof to the storeroom so all you'll have to do is snake the power and coax through it."

"Great, daddy-o, and I'll grill you on the Medicine Wheel hookup. You'll know exactly what you have to know when you get there. I want you to be able to do this in the dark," he said. "Because you will actually be *doing* it in the dark," he added. Then he snickered at his own joke

Jan thought Granny was a strange genius.

*   *   *

After the meeting, when Monster and Jan had arrived at Ginny's, Melissa was stepping into the living room in a bathrobe drying her long, black hair with a towel. Jan didn't escape noticing Monster's reaction at the sight of her.

"Wow," Melissa said, "I am starting to feel like a real woman again."

Ginny smiled. "I don't think you will get any arguments from these two guys on that."

Melissa colored slightly, checked to see that her robe was modestly closed and sat down on the couch. Monster sat beside her.

"Anyone care for a drink?" Ginny asked.

"I'm on duty," Monster said, "coffee for me."

Melissa shook her head. Jan hesitated then also shook his head.

Ginny headed for the kitchen to fix coffee for Monster. When she returned Melissa said, "I have a proposition for you two gentlemen."

Jan and Monster stared at her but said nothing.

She continued, "You were open with me about what you are planning up at the Medicine Wheel camp. I want to help."

"Hold on there, cowgirl," Monster said. "That ain't gonna

happen."

"Please at least hear me out, John," she said, a little sharply Jan thought.

Now Monster colored slightly, but said nothing.

"I know something about the way that operation is run up there. I think I have information you can use."

"Oh," Monster said. "Well, sure...."

Melissa continued. "I also know that every Saturday night, Bill Campbell takes a turn on the hill to give the other boys a break. What you don't know..." She paused..."What you don't know is that Bill has a...a *thing* for me."

She looked at Monster. He rolled his eyes and sipped his coffee.

"Anyway, I won't bore you with the details, but I will say that he...well he 'came on to me,' as they say. It was about four years ago. I was already starting to put Hansen and the group behind me. He approached me one afternoon in the apple orchard on the compound. He was very nice, but very direct. He told me that he sensed something was wrong between Hansen and me and said that although he was dedicated to Ronald, he had very special feelings for me. He told me I could count on him if I ever needed anything."

Silence.

Finally Jan said, "And? ..."

"Well, there's more."

Monster cleared his throat.

"The night I was beaten. I think one of the men who did it was Campbell."

"Why do you think that?" Jan asked.

"I haven't spoken about this to anyone, but I'm sure you know, John, that I was...I was..." Her eyes filled.

"You were raped the night you were beaten," Monster said

flatly.

"Yes. I know that they did lab tests at the hospital and I know you asked me about it repeatedly in the hospital, John, but I just couldn't tell you. I didn't know you, so how could I trust you? And I was certain that no one could ever protect me from either Ronald or Bill Campbell. I thought at that point they were un-touchable."

"But you're not so sure, now," Jan said.

"No, I am convinced that they *are* touchable. I'm convinced your plan will work. I have thought about it a lot ever since you told me about it. But, you guys have a problem."

"Here we go again," Monster said. "Somebody is always telling me we have problems."

"Well you do. A big one. You may have been able to sneak up to the Medicine Wheel cabin and photograph the transmitter, but you will never get a man up the tower carrying an antenna and wrenches without Campbell hearing you."

"I have been thinking about that," Jan said. "But I don't see how you can help."

"Well…" She looked at Monster. She cleared her throat. She brushed her hair away from her face and drew a deep breath.

"Well, as I said a minute ago, Bill Campbell has a thing for me…"

"OK," Monster said. "Hold it right there. Forget it. Just *forget it!*"

"John, listen to me."

"No way. I'm not listening to you because you are not going up to that cabin under any circumstances, even if I have to beat you myself."

"I know you don't mean that, John. And I am very honored that you feel as strongly for my safety as you do, but you don't understand."

"I understand more than you think I do. I understand Campbell is a lecherous killer who attempted to murder you once, and he will try again if he gets the chance."

Melissa looked at Ginny.

Ginny looked back at her evenly.

Melissa looked at Jan.

"The sheriff is right, Melissa," Jan said. You can't be doing what you are thinking. If you are thinking what I think you are thinking."

"I'm going to try to make you all understand something," Melissa said. "I have spent 10 years of my life in a system which has abused me emotionally, mentally, and now physically. I may never be able to live a normal life again. But that isn't the worst of it. There are dozens of other women just like me and hundreds of children who are victims of this mad system. These men *must* be stopped. You guys have the motivation, the power, and the determination to stop them. But, as I understand it, without getting the electronic goods on the organization you are not going to be able to put an end to this nightmare. That is unless Ronald's mental wiring finally totally shorts out and he blows up the compound or some government building—and then it might just be too late. Is that about right?"

Jan said, "Yes, Melissa, it is *exactly* right."

"I can get you up the tower."

"But at what cost? It isn't worth it if you're killed," Jan said.

"I don't think I'll be killed. I think I'll be safe with Campbell."

Monster interrupted, "How can that possibly be?"

Ginny interrupted. "Gentlemen, I see where this is going. Do you mind if I ask Melissa a couple of questions?"

"Please do!" Monster said.

"Melissa?"

Melissa shook her head as if clearing her mind. She looked at the floor for a few seconds, then raised her face to meet Ginny's gaze. Her face was set and cool.

"Melissa," Ginny said. "You are, of course, talking about offering yourself physically to Bill Campbell. I understand your confidence that you will be safe. When you give yourself to him, he has no reason to harm you. *If* you can convince him that you really have loved and wanted him all these years and that you are certain he had nothing to do with your beating. I understand all that. But what I really want to ask you is if you are *really* prepared to do this. To do this with a man who *raped* you?"

"This is ridiculous!" Monster said.

"Hold on, John," Ginny said. "This is *my* interrogation."

"It's still ridiculous!" Monster walked to the kitchen and returned a fresh cup of coffee.

Ginny continued. "Melissa?"

Melissa sighed. "First of all," she said, "I may be able to avoid…to avoid this going all the way. He likes to drink. But…" She turned and faced Monster. Looking into his eyes she said, "Yes, in order to bring down Ronald and Campbell, I would be willing to give them—one more time—what they have already taken from me. I don't expect you to understand."

"Well," Ginny said, "Maybe *I* understand. But, honey, I worry that you will be harmed. I mean I worry you will be beaten and killed. And I worry about your emotional condition, to be honest."

"Ginny, I know you have a good handle on life. And on men. But you don't understand these polygamists."

"That's true," Ginny said.

"Sex for them is…well, it's what they *do*! I don't know how to explain it, but sex is the most important thing in their lives. They've become addicted. Did you know that there are no young men in the Church? Oh, a few "soldiers," but young men can't marry. And do you know why? Because every young woman is spoken for by some old man. The young men wind up leaving the organization. Or they hang around until they are old enough to "deserve" a wife.

"Look, polygamy—for all their high-sounding rhetoric and biblical misinterpretation—polygamy is about lust. Lust drives it. These guys are sex addicts. Oh, they are sophisticated. They drone on about how polygamy 'is not easy.' They say it is a cross they have to bear in order to be obedient to God. And how they wouldn't do it if it weren't a direct command from God. Some of them probably believe their own rhetoric. But, basically, they are steeped in sex. Bill Campbell is not going to kill the golden goose. He is going to take its eggs and do everything in his power to preserve its life."

"That makes a lot of sense to me," Ginny admitted.

"It makes absolutely *no* sense to me," Monster said.

Jan was silent. He looked at the floor. Finally he said, "My God. What have we come to? Not only do I wonder what Hansen and Campbell have come to, I wonder what *I* have come to. I'm about to sign up for Melissa's crazy scheme. Melissa, do you really think it is possible to get Campbell drunk before he rapes you again?"

"I don't know. And I don't want to sound brave, or jaded, or callous, but I don't care. This is a job that needs doing and I can do it. I *insist* on doing it."

Monster headed back toward the kitchen. He turned. "You insist? Well, dang it, don't you people know I am the law here? I can't be party to such a harebrained, dangerous scheme."

Jan said, "John, I don't want to argue with you. And, bottom line, you are probably taking the high road here. However, I will remind you that you are already up to your eyeballs in illegal activities. You and George Olson may well lose your jobs over this.

We may all go to jail. We're breaking and entering, illegally tapping private communications, and maybe even engaging in conspiracy to commit murder."

"So? None of that bothers me. If Hansen shoots me he will probably be doing the world a favor and will doubtless be doing me one…But, Melissa here…"

Ginny smiled at him. She said softly, "John, you are *so* outnumbered here."

Melissa slid out of her chair and knelt in front of Monster who was back on the couch.

"John," she said, "You're such a kind man. You are the missing white knight in any girl's dreams. I deeply appreciate your consideration for me. But I am in full possession of my faculties here. I want to do this. I *need* to do this. Can you understand that?"

Monster did not look at her. He remained silent.

*   *   *

After Harold relieved Monster, Melissa went to bed. Ginny and Jan sat on the couch in the dark. They talked for an hour. They recalled how they had met at Basin High School.

Ginny had just moved to town. Her father was a tool pusher brought in to work a rig in the Torchlight oil field. She was a junior. Jan saw her for the first time in 9:00 a.m. English class. He hated that class. He was bored. He didn't understand grammar. He couldn't diagram sentences. But he could write. It was a natural talent. He said he wrote by ear.

Ginny was wearing a white sweater and a gray wool skirt. He stared at her throughout the period. And in the hall after class he caught up to her.

"Hello, new girl," he had said.

"You stared at me all through class. What's your problem?"

"No problem. I just think you're gorgeous. That's all."

"Gorgeous? Nobody uses that word anymore."

"I do, and you are. By the way, my name is Jan Kucera."

"I'm Virginia. They call me Ginny."

"Hi, Ginny."

"Hi, Jan."

"Hey, Ginny?"

"Yeah?"

"Hey, how about I give you a ride home after school?"

"Well, we live on Orchard Bench. I'm supposed to take the bus."

"I'll get you there before the bus would."

"Well, OK. Why not?"

"Why not, indeed?"

"Indeed? Did you just say indeed?"

"Indeed I did. In-deedy-do."

They did *not* beat the bus home. They drove to Greybull and went to the drive-in for Cokes. They laughed at stupid things until tears came to their eyes. It was nearly 7:00 p.m. when they got to her house and her father was waiting on the porch smoking Chesterfields and looking mean. As it turned out his appearance covered up for a real soft heart—especially where Ginny was concerned. It took about five minutes for Jan to charm him. Jan didn't leave until nearly 10:00 p.m. and he had permission from her dad to pick Ginny up for school the next morning.

That was the spring of 1958. By summer they were seeing each other every night. She shared Jan's total enthusiasm for the dusty Wyoming summer. They spent most summer nights parked on Reservoir Hill listening to Fats Domino singing *Blueberry Hill* on KOMA. They danced on the concrete top of the city reservoir, the little town twinkling below them and the starry host twinkling above them.

*   *   *

Sitting in the dark after Melissa went to bed, Ginny recalled how they had promised themselves to each other forever. They tried to remember why it hadn't worked out. Jan left for the Navy promising to send for her. But he couldn't figure out how to do it. By the time he got out she was married.

They sat in silence for a long time before he reached over and took her hand. He pulled her to himself and kissed her lightly. She laid her head on his shoulder and he stroked her face.

After a while Ginny said. "This is lovely, Jan, but I think I should go to bed before we get ourselves into trouble."

CHAPTER EIGHTEEN

Wednesday Jan, George Olson, and Granny sat on the back steps of the courthouse in the shade of three huge cottonwoods. The morning heat suggested this June day would be a scorcher.

"Wow!" Granny said upon learning of Melissa's determination to be involved, "This gets better and better all the time!"

George Olson turned ashen at the news. "You know, Jan," he said, "I don't mind risking my neck and my retirement to nail Hansen, but I am not willing to risk the life of a civilian. It goes against all my training during 30 years of service. The problem is, I'm already so compromised by my criminal activity that I sure can't be the moral voice here. But, Jan…"

"If it helps," Jan said, "there is absolutely no way you could stop her short of abducting her. She's in."

Olson sighed. "Well, at least Granny says he thinks I can hook this thing up."

"Piece a cake," Granny said.

"Anyway," Jan continued, "this means that we need to hold

off until Saturday night."

"I guess that isn't a problem," Olson said. "Unless Granny has to get back to Seattle…"

"What! And miss the chance to do the nightlife in Basin, Wyoming? Not a chance! I have not yet begun to explore the possibilities for fun and games. I think the Methodist Church has a bingo game planned for this very evening!"

Olson rolled his eyes.

Jan smiled. "Well, OK, Saturday night it is. At least that gives us a little more planning time. How about we meet Thursday night for a dry run?"

"That'll work," Olson said. "I want to bring in my two associates. They'll be running backup for us."

"And I'm sure the sheriff will want to bring Harold in."

"Another thing," Olson said. "Hansen took his chopper to Billings this morning and boarded his jet. He landed in Salt Lake City. I got that info from an FAA buddy. However, we don't have clearance to surveil him in Utah. Seems like he has friends in high places there."

"I'm surprised to hear that. I would think that Utah is one place he would *not* have much authority. I'm sure the main branch of the Mormon Church sees him as a fake, and maybe even a threat."

"Yeah, I don't know the answer to that. Anyway, I thought you'd be interested."

Jan crossed his arms over his chest. He stared into the distance. He wondered what Prophet Hansen was up to.

*   *   *

At 2:00 p.m. St. Andrews Episcopal Church rested among giant cottonwoods, as though hiding from the baking afternoon sun.

Jan parked on the north side and walked around to the west entrance and entered the nave, passing the baptistry on the right. It was the same baptistry from which a priest had dipped water and made the sign of the cross on Jan's forehead when he was five years old. A photograph showed that his father was in attendance in a suit and tie, which Jan remembered as unusual.

Down the aisle of the nave Jan had marched many a Sunday morning as a child, carrying the crucifix, or the brass candle lighter, or the American or church flag, wearing a black cassock and white surplice, looking, his mom said, like a little angel. The smell of the old building was pleasant. Here Jan had sat on polished oak pews listening to Father Sullivan talk about eternity.

Jan slipped into a pew. He remembered solving a conundrum one Sunday in this pew. Every Sunday the congregation repeated a phrase from the prayer book, a phrase that confused him. The phrase was "For Christ's sake." What did that mean he had wondered? Were they swearing? He had never asked anyone. But the prayers were read every Sunday from the Book of Common Prayer. Many of them ended with the phrase "And this we beg for Jesus Christ's sake." The prayer of general confession, for example, ended with "for His sake." These prayers were asking God to forgive men because they were sinners—they had not lived "godly and sober" lives. They asked God to forgive men "for His sake." Evidently for *Christ's* sake! What, Jan had wondered, could that mean? Wouldn't God want men to live good lives for their *own* sakes? Why for *Christ's* sake?

Then one day it had come to him; just came to him in an instant—an epiphany. The revelation was that Christ had sacrificed his life so men could live good, sober, lives. If they did, Christ had not died in vain. Jan suddenly knew *that* was the meaning behind the phrase—*that* was what it meant. By living godly lives, men and women somehow brought fulfillment to Christ's sacrifice. Christ's death was not in vain to the extent that people were changed by it. That was as far as Jan ever went in unraveling the mystery of those words. But they still intrigued him.

Jan was surprised he remembered much of the text of the prayers. He found himself repeating aloud the poetic phrases from the General Confession:

"We have erred and strayed like lost sheep. We have followed too much the devices and desires of our own hearts. We have offended against thy holy laws. We have left undone those thing which we ought to have done. And we have done those things which we ought not to have done..."

"Amen," a voice behind him said. Startled, Jan turned to see Father Sullivan. Not the 30-year-old Father Sullivan that Jan had listened to as a child, but a nearly 80-year-old Father Sullivan who had come back to Basin to finish his years in service to the same tiny congregation he had severed when he was young and full of energy.

Jan had only seen Father Sullivan on two occasions since the priest had returned to Basin five years earlier. He had seen him when he had come to ask the priest to conduct Emma's funeral, then at the funeral itself. Jan had promised he would call on the priest later, but he never did. Today he had arranged to see him here.

Apparently Father Sullivan had seen Jan enter the church from his office window. He must have walked around the outside of the building and followed him into the nave. The priest's once black hair had turned white, but the ruddy complexion and black eyes could not obscure his manly Irish lineage. Father Sullivan's own father had changed the family name from O'Sullivan when he arrived in Hell's Kitchen fresh from Ireland.

Father Sullivan still carried the same broadness in the shoulders and barrel chest that Jan remembered from childhood, the priest's hulk had been ill-concealed even back then by the black robes he wore during Morning Prayer. His voice still had a trace of the Old Country in it the way Jan's father always maintained a trace of Southern Europe.

"Jan, my boy," Father Sullivan said. "I see you still remember the General Confession."

"I'm surprised I do."

"Aye, but not I! Forty-five years ago when you came to see me at your mother's insistence—because she thought you were an atheist—I recognized something special in you."

"I remember the meeting."

"Do you remember what I told you, lad?"

"Yes. You said you weren't worried about me. You said you saw faith in me."

"Indeed I did. I saw it then and I see it now."

"How is it that I can't see it myself?"

"Ah. Good question. Sorry I can't answer it. You see, I don't know nearly as much about faith as I should. People think I do. In truth, I find myself at a loss for much of what I see in the world. However, I catch glimpses of the hiding God—very brief but satisfying glimpses. And I have always seen what theologians call 'fear,' or 'awe,' or 'reverence' for God in your eyes."

"Well, in a way I hope you're right. But honestly Father, I have never had a handle on faith. Not at all. I have almost no spiritual life. And I never have."

The old priest's eyes caught a flash of humor and energy. "Oh! Jan, my lad, I wonder if we are not at a semantic impasse here. The life of the spirit is not always well defined by those who participate in it. But, just now you were praying the General Confession. Why do you suppose you remember it after all these years? I have had priests in my employ who couldn't remember that prayer. I'm sorry, my boy, I hate to mar the profane picture you have of yourself, but I have to stick with my initial judgment of you.

"But, let's leave your delusions of doubt. And, by the way, please call me Aidan. I'm more comfortable with that from you given all our long years of friendship—interrupted though they were by a mere four-and-a-half decades."

The priest leaned forward. "May I inquire, Jan, about your emotional health? How are you dealing with the loss of Emma? It's been two years now, I believe. And, of course, I heard about the most recent attempts on your life."

"How am I dealing with it? I see a shrink, I drink too much, I hang out with John Broadbeck."

Father Sullivan erupted in laughter. "That's an unholy trinity indeed!"

Jan laughed as well. "Which is the chief demon?"

"Oh, the shrink, no doubt!"

They both laughed some more.

"Jan, when you called, you said you had some theological questions to ask me. Would you like to come to my office?"

*   *   *

In the church office a Mr. Coffee dripped its last fresh drops into its carafe. Father Sullivan poured a cup for Jan and one for himself.

"Thank God for a bit of the brew. No amount of prayer can get me through an afternoon like Yuban can."

"Yuban? I didn't know they still made it. That was what my mother drank."

"I remember her well. A tougher congregant I never had. A touch of bitterness in her following your father's fall from grace. She, herself, struggled with faith. And, like you, she seemed almost proud of her doubts. But she was not proud of her *son's* doubts, I believe." The priest laughed. "She passed on about 10 years ago, as I recall."

Jan nodded.

"Father—Aidan—tell me about Atonement."

"Atonement! Well! And you still protesting ignorance in matters of faith?"

"It's not what you think. I'm trying to understand Ronald Hansen."

The priest's face darkened. "Ronnie? Dear Ronnie. Tragic man, tragic family."

Father Sullivan sighed deeply. Leaned back in his chair. He opened a drawer and withdrew a pipe and tobacco pouch.

"Do you mind?" he asked.

"Not at all."

Father Sullivan stoked the pipe. Jan remembered the same ritual when they had met nearly half a century ago. He wondered how the old priest had avoided the consequences of his habit.

Father Sullivan removed the pipe from his mouth. "You, then, are asking rather about the Mormon concept of Blood Atonement, I take it?"

"Yes. That's correct. I think it must be a hybrid of the earlier Christian theology."

"Well, in a sense that is necessarily true. However, the Mormon doctrine may come down to us from a yet more ancient source."

"What do you mean?"

"Let me avoid that answer now. I may return to it later. Let's treat it as you suggest, as an aberration of Christian doctrine. I'm qualified to talk about Christian theology, but I make no pretense of knowing much about Mormonism. My attempt to understand Mormon theology has left me very frustrated."

"How so?"

"It's rather like trying to nail water to a wall. To my mind,

Mormon teaching seems inconsistent. But I must add, I have not studied it deeply. However, it seems that ideas in Mormonism just pop up and are declared to be true by the Mormon leadership whether or not they fit in with anything else in earlier history or practice. As when they declared in the early 1970s that Blacks could hold the Mormon Priesthood, after teaching for a hundred years that they couldn't. When I was here in the 1950s it was common shocking knowledge that Blacks—Negroes then—could never hold office in the Mormon Church. They were considered unfit in some obscure way I can't remember. But then, bingo, it all changes when members of the Western Athletic Conference picket BYU. It seems to me there is no consistent theology, rather a list of beliefs and doctrines which are revised without explanation from time to time. Do you know what I mean?"

"Not exactly, but what you are saying sure sounds like what others are telling me."

"You know, Jan, you probably should talk to a man by the name of Deck Edwards."

Jan laughed. "Deck is a friend of mine. I went to him. He sent me to see a former Utah investigator. I seem to be getting the run-around."

The priest got up and refilled both coffee cups. Today he was wearing his priest's shirt and collar.

"Well, Jan, the problem is that the Mormon doctrine is not out in the open. In fact, the Church leadership denies they ever practiced Blood Atonement—but history tells us they certainly did. So it's rather a closet doctrine. You can patch together ideas and get the drift. But you can't look it up in a book about Mormon theology. That it was practiced and that there *is* such a theory is not in doubt. Mormon scholars and even Mormon Presidents have admitted that in print."

"I guess, Aidan, that I could profit from understanding the

historic Christian position on Atonement."

"With that I can help you. You'll have to bear with me. I might even be able to touch upon the relationship between Mormon Blood Atonement and other religious human sacrifice. But, let's start at the beginning. I hope I don't get too theological or esoteric."

Jan settled back into his chair. He cradled the cup in his hands. He watched as the old man seemed to drift off, drift away to another time and place. He waited for him to speak. Finally he did.

"The life is in the blood." He drew deeply on his pipe. "The life is in the blood."

The words made Jan strangely uneasy. He looked around the old, weathered office where he had sat 45 years earlier. The office was old even then. St. Andrews was a hundred years old. Episcopal missionaries were the first to bring Christianity into Wyoming Territory, establishing churches among the trappers and Indians. As the trading settlements turned into villages, Episcopal churches—their buildings often funded by denominational money from the East—sprang up. Jan's grandparents on both sides—and his maternal and paternal great-grandparents—had been instrumental in the founding of St. Andrews. But now the voice of the old priest talking about life and blood sent a chill through Jan.

"The Bible, Jan, from the first, has taught the interconnectedness between life and death. What living thing survives except through the death of another living thing? That is the principle behind the Jewish kosher laws. The clean animals are slain in order to provide life—as food—to humans. It is, in a sense, a passing on of life. As for the blood, the Book of Genesis tells us that when Cain rose up and slew his brother Abel, God came to him and said, 'The blood of your brother calls to Me from the ground.'

"Of course," the priest continued, "the idea of sacrifice to God was evident from the biblical account of the Garden of Eden. The fruit of the field and the firstlings of the flocks were presented to God as a tithe—a portion returned to Him in thanksgiving for his provision.

"But the idea of sacrifice as an offering for sin, well, we really don't see that in the biblical record until Passover. You remember the story. The Jews are slaves to Egypt's Pharaoh. God sends Moses to tell Pharaoh to let his people go. When Pharaoh won't cooperate, God sends plagues to motivate him. But Pharaoh, the Bible tells us, 'hardened his heart' against the working of God.

"So finally, God tells Moses that an angel of death will stalk the land killing the firstborn of every creature. The Pharaoh's own son is killed and Pharaoh lets the God's people leave."

Sullivan drew on this pipe which had gone out. He produced a kitchen match, struck it on his shoe, and relit it. "God spared the Hebrew firstborn children, by way of a substitute sacrifice."

Jan spoke. "The Passover lamb?"

"The Passover lamb. Now here is where, I believe, the error of Mormonism—as well as the error of other forms of human sacrifice—comes in. It is a mistake to think that the blood of the Passover lamb itself had the power to hide or cleanse sin. It is simply a lamb after all. Much confusion begins here. It is a mistake to think that animal blood somehow pleased or appeased God. Or that it could appease his wrath."

"What?" Jan asked. "Isn't that exactly what we are expected to believe. If not, then why do we have animal sacrifice commanded in the Bible and practiced by pagan cultures throughout the world?"

"Why indeed? That is exactly the point, my friend."

Jan watched the priest purse his lips, working them in and out. Like Nero Wolf solving a crime, Jan thought.

"Jan, let me see if you remember your catechism at all. 'Whom does man sin against?'"

Jan sat in silence and turned his mind back to those chilly afternoons in the basement of the church when he and the future Judge Hartman used to sit at a table while Father Sullivan taught them orthodox Christian doctrine. He could almost hear those words echoing across time. 'Whom does man sin against?'"

"Against his neighbor?" Jan had volunteered back then.

"No!" the priest had said. "No, not against his neighbor, but against God! All sin is against God. Since the neighbor is the property of God, the *creation* of God, when you harm your neighbor you do damage directly to God."

Jan opened his eyes. He looked at Father Sullivan, the 80-year-old priest's eyes aflame with zeal. "Man sins against God," he said.

"Yes, my boy! Yes. The debt is owed to God."

Jan considered that.

"And," the priest continued, "if the debt is owed to God, the debt is really outside the ability of the debtor to pay. Let me return to the blood of Abel, calling out to God from the ground. Whose blood was it anyway? Well, of course, if you had asked Abel, it was *his* blood. But in a larger, more accurate sense, it was *God's* blood. What I mean is the life of Abel belonged to God because He created it. It was a creation of God that Cain spilt upon the ground."

Jan held up a hand. "OK, Aidan. So now Cain owed his own life to God."

"Well, he owed that to Him anyway. It was *God's* life in him."

"Yes, but doesn't the Old Testament teach that a man who

spills blood is to be put to death."

"Oh, indeed it does. But capital punishment was never equated with forgiveness. It is one thing to say that a murderer must be put to death. And we say, in the law, that he 'paid for his crime.' Well, he paid a price all right. But his death does not buy him forgiveness. It prevents him from taking another life. It protects society, that is true. There is a sense of justice in it, but it certainly does not renew the life of his victim. Do you see that, boy?"

"I see that there is no creative power in Cain's blood. Abel will remain dead whether Cain lives or dies."

"Yes, of course. Now take it to the Passover lamb. If there is no redemptive power in a *man's* blood, how much less power is there in the blood of a sheep?"

"Then why? ..."

"Hold on, son. Think for a moment. Where does life come from?"

"God?"

"Then whose life, whose blood, is the only agent able to redeem that which is lost?"

Jan was extremely uncomfortable with the conversation. It was too surreal. Too over the top. What in the world was he doing in a dark office talking to an old priest about blood? He wanted to bolt. He felt like he was watching the end of *The Godfather* or something from *The Exorcist*. Yet, on another level, he felt a strange sense of comfort. Maybe it was what the priest had meant earlier when he talked about a sense of awe.

Jan cleared his throat. "Whose blood is able to substitute for the life of a human?" His mouth was dry. "The blood of God?"

"Yes, Jan. The blood of God! That truth is what Christianity has taught for 2,000 years. Oh, it is a radical and much misunderstood and even much maligned concept. The secular community of today has little interest in the great thinking of the Church. It almost seems sacrilegious even to discuss these matters. The profane world thinks of Christianity as 'a bloody religion.' And, as a matter of fact, it is. But Christendom teaches that Christ is God— God come in human form, making a full identification with humans for the sole purpose of becoming a substitute sacrifice for them."

Jan stared at the priest. He wasn't sure he understood what the old zealot was saying, or that he even *wanted* to understand it.

The priest went on. "The Atonement of Christ is the *real* event, the animal sacrifices of the Old Testament are all simply symbolic shadows of *that* reality—foreshadows of reality."

The priest appeared to struggle. "Look. Take another example. Water baptism is not about 'magic water.' It's a symbolic representation by the participant who engages a faith concept. Pouring water over someone or dipping him in a swimming pool or river only makes him wet. There is no magic in the water and there is no magic in human blood. The sacrifices of the Old Testament were symbolically anticipatory of a real human event that had not yet occurred. Once the *real* sacrifice—the sacrifice of Christ—had occurred there was no reason to continue the anticipatory rite.

"I fear I am waxing a little eloquent here. But I'm trying to make the distinction between Mormon Blood Atonement and the Christian doctrine of Atonement."

"And what *is* that difference?"

"The difference is that, historically, Christians have believed and taught that faith placed in Christ's sacrificial death allows that death to cleanse a man's personal sins. Mormon theology guts the Atonement, robbing it of its true power. It makes the Atonement to be simply *one part* of the process of cleansing a person from sin. Man, according to Mormon theology benefits—to a degree—from the Atonement of Christ, but the blood of Christ—*alone*— is not enough, in Mormonism, to save a sinner from his sins."

Sullivan upturned his pipe, tapped it against an ashtray, and laid it aside. "Mormonism's Blood Atonement doctrine makes that clear. The anchor point for understanding Mormon salvation theology is in the infamous statement of Brigham Young: 'There are some sins which the blood of Christ cannot atone.' In those cases, Young said, a man's own blood must be shed. That is a quantum leap from the orthodox doctrine of Atonement, but a quantum leap backward!"

Now Jan's chin was on his chest. His fingers were steepled over his stomach. His brow was furrowed.

Finally he said to the priest, "So, the difference between Mormon Blood Atonement and Christian Atonement is that Brigham Young taught his people that if murderers—and other gross sinners—would have their own blood spilled they could find forgiveness; and Christian Atonement says that a person simply needs to believe that Christ's death is a substitute for his own sin?"

The priest snorted! "*Just believe?* You say that as though it is an easy thing to do. You, Jan, a man who has spent 40 or more years struggling to believe? And just now you can cavalierly say 'A person simply needs to believe?' As though believing were simple. As if believing were nothing. No, my friend, believing is *everything*! Faith must not only be found, it must be nurtured, protected, and defended!

"The bottom line, Jan, is this. The shedding of mere human blood serves no purpose whatsoever. On the other hand, the shedding of the blood of *God* represents the exchange of the life of God for the sin of mankind. That action *does* have infinite power to make an actual, legitimate claim against sin. It is called substitutionary Atonement—the substitute of life for life, or death for life, if you prefer.

"All I'm saying," the priest continued, "is that *if* there is a God, and *if* that God did atone for sin—as the Christian gospel has proclaimed for 2,000 years—then all attempts to assert the idea that human bloodshed is an agent for the forgiveness of sin are flawed."

"And that is what Mormon Blood Atonement tries to do?" Jan asked.

"As I understand it, yes. But, I have to remind you of what I said earlier, that Mormon doctrine is elusive on this point. This doctrine has been kept hidden since the practice was initiated more than a hundred years ago."

"Do you, Aidan, really believe it was widely practiced by early Mormon Church leaders?"

"It depends, Jan, on what you mean by 'widely.' Do I believe that hundreds have been blood atoned in Mormondom? Yes, I believe that. Just as I believe human sacrifice, which is a demonic rip-off of true Atonement, has been practiced since the dawn of time and is still being practiced on many fronts to this day."

"You actually believe that?"

"I do. All you have to do is read the Utah papers to know that. Clan leaders, like the Laffertys, are proud that God ordered them to kill people in order to save their souls."

"Yeah. I know about them. And, I know Ronald Hansen is a stony murderer. I'm certain he murdered Emma. But all this stuff about religious sacrifice—human sacrifice—it seems so far from the…well…the *real* world."

"Oh, it's real all right. In every age human sacrifice has been practiced. The Mayas, the Incas, the Old World pagans… In fact, I was reminded of that by my recreational reading this week. I'm going back through Winston Churchill's *History of the English Speaking Peoples*. He talks about human sacrifice as a unifying concept."

"What?"

"Oh, I don't mean he condoned it. But he wrote that Julius Caesar in the summer of 55 B.C. stood on the European shoreline of the English Channel and surveyed what Churchill called, 'the heavy island.' Caesar saw the Druids of Britannia as the spiritual headwaters of the Northern Barbarians. He noted their proclivity for human sacrifice. He said, and I quote, 'The unnatural principle of human sacrifice was carried by the British Druids to a ruthless pitch. The mysterious priesthoods of the forests bound themselves and their votaries together by the most deadly sacrament that men can take.'

"Churchill evidently thought that the bloody practice of human sacrifice is what kept the priests in power, kept the clans in subjugation."

"Good Lord!" Jan said, "Are you saying that this is what is at the heart of Mormon Blood Atonement? That the Mormon concept of Blood Atonement is a form of terrorism designed to subjugate the troops?"

The priest was silent.

"Is that what you meant earlier when you said that Mormon Blood Atonement may not be an aberration of Christian Atonement but that 'it may come down to us from a source earlier than that?' Come on, Aidan!"

Again the priest relit his pipe. This time he drew the smoke in and held it deep within his chest, his eyes closed. After a few seconds he expelled it through his nose and looked at Jan.

"How much do you know about the Mormon Temple Ceremony, Jan?" The priest stood, walked over to a bookcase, withdrew a large book, and tossed it onto the desk. He heaved himself into the chair and slowly thumbed through the book. As he thumbed, he said, "You know, Jan, the Mormon Temple Ceremony has evolved over the past 150 years. It hasn't changed, but the wording has been made less and less offensive as the text of the ceremony has gotten out."

"By the way, Aidan, how *does* the text get out of the temple if everyone is sworn to secrecy?"

"In most cases it comes from disaffected members who make notes about the ceremony after they leave. In a few cases, Mormons who were about to depart went to the temple wearing recording devices."

"Wires?"

"Well, I guess that's what you call it. Each one armed with a miniature tape recorder. Pretty bold move. Some of these exiting Mormons are pretty disgruntled and zealous."

The priest continued to trace his finger over the pages of the book.

"This book is a compilation of the changes which have occurred in the Temple Ceremony over the years. A lot of changes took place in 1911 and a lot more in 1990. But listen to some of this language. You know the ceremony is made up of dramatic skits and the taking of secret oaths. In one of the skits, a man playing the part of Lucifer makes a big show out of hiring Protestant preachers and Catholic priests to preach the devil's doctrine to unwary parishioners. But here Lucifer says, 'I will take the treasures of the earth, and with gold and silver I will buy up armies and navies, popes and priests, and reign with blood and horror in this earth!'"

Jan stared. *"Blood and horror?"*

Sullivan continued, "Then when God, in the Mormon temple drama, kicks Satan out of the temple, the devil stops and turns to the people who are watching the drama and says: 'I have a word to say concerning these people. If they do not walk up to every covenant they make at these altars in this temple this day, they will be in my power!'"

"Jan, couple this highly charged drama with bloody oaths in which the participants—at least up until 1990—symbolically slit their throats and are threatened with disembowelment if they reveal some silly handshakes…Well, you tell me if Julius Caesar wasn't right about priests using blood oaths and human sacrifice to subjugate people. These things come from the belly of hell itself!"

Now Jan sat silently. He cleared his throat. He shook his head.

"So, Aidan, I guess you believe in the devil and modern Satanism, and all that?"

The priest looked evenly at Jan. He smiled benignly. "Oh, Jan. *Of course I believe in that!*"

CHAPTER NINETEEN

Prophet Hansen leaned back in the oversized seat of the Gulfstream V. He sipped a daiquiri made to his specifications by Bill Campbell. Like the founder of Mormonism, Joseph Smith, Prophet Hansen believed that the moderate use of alcohol was no sin. He smiled when he remembered that Smith, for expediency, had forbidden his *flock* to drink *any* alcoholic beverages. Hansen also knew that he and Joseph both sometimes expanded the definition of the word "moderation" when it came to their own drinking.

At the Salt Lake City airport Hoyt Akers taxied the jet to a stop and Campbell opened the door. As the Prophet stepped out onto the tarmac, he inhaled the warm, fresh air, a welcome change from the sterile air conditioning of the jet. He smiled at the man approaching him.

"Thanks, Jake, for meeting us."

"My pleasure, President."

Jake Kellog, a giant, pear-shaped man, opened the door to a dark gray Suburban and, when the Prophet was seated, closed it.

Hansen had told him a dozen times he didn't have to hold the door for him, but Kellog, a man of stock phrases, always had the same reply. "I'd rather be a doorkeeper in the house of the Lord," he said, "than a king in the gentile world." Hansen would smile wearily. Akers and Campbell took the middle and back passenger seats so they could stretch out during the two-hour ride to the Manti cabin.

Hansen was quiet during the trip. If he opened a conversation with Kellog, he would be engaged all the way to Manti. So he leaned against the Suburban's door and watched the high desert scenery. At Spanish Fork, south of Provo, they turned east on US Highway 89. At the Thistle Junction the highway turned south, meandering through the sleepy Mormon communities of Fairview, Mt. Pleasant, Spring City, and Ephraim. A haze obscured the long view of the Sanpete Valley.

"Manti Forest is ablaze again," Kellog said. "Fighting four major fires."

Eventually, the Manti Temple rose out of the haze. The Mormon Prophet Lorenzo Snow dedicated the temple in 1888, the third of the Utah Temples. To Hansen it was the most beautiful of all the temples, and he had always hoped that one day he would wrest it from the Utah Mormon Church so he could do the *real* Endowment Ceremony in it. Inside the temple, he knew, two spiral staircases accessed three floors and 86,000 square feet of endowment and sealing rooms. The Utah pioneers had quarried the temple's fine-textured, cream-colored oolite limestone from the hill upon which the building stood.

Hansen had first seen the Manti Temple as a boy of eight when he accompanied his father to a conference at Short Creek, a town on the Utah/Arizona border. That was before the infamous 1950s Short Creek raid in which Arizona state cops descended on the polygamous community and jailed all the men. At the time of

Hansen's visit to Short Creek, some of the houses still rested on timber skids. The polygamist patriarchs, in the earliest days at Short Creek, would hitch teams of horses to the skids to drag the small houses across the state boundary at the approach of lawmen. When Arizona authorities came to harass them, they lived in Utah; when Utah police came, they lived in Arizona. When lawmen mounted motor vehicles instead of horses, the skids became useless. In recent years Short Creek—now named Hilldale, Utah and Colorado City, Arizona—festered, embroiled in a battle with the State of Arizona which sought to break up the polygamous community. A group called "Help the Child Brides," had attempted to rescue young girls who resisted polygamy. Hansen sighed. *What nonsense!*

The sleepy village of Manti, Utah, was known to polygamists as "The Gathering Place." Seeing it now, Hansen again felt a wave of emotion sweep through him. Manti, Hansen believed, was a spiritual vortex; a place central to Mormon history. All the Mormon splinter groups coveted the Manti Temple. For that reason, Manti drew Mormon Fundamentalist leaders—pretenders Hansen called them—like a magnet.

In Manti, Hansen had confronted David Longo and his sword-wielding archangels. That was shortly before the lunatic Longo ordered his wife to toss their seven kids from the eleventh floor of Salt Lake City's International Dunes Hotel and then jump herself. Longo then drove to a canyon outside Salt Lake City and committed suicide. Longo had claimed to be God Himself. Hansen recalled a recent article circulating in the Western press that some of Longo's left-behind followers still remain faithful to his memory, still awaiting his resurrection and return to earth.

The Suburban passed the headquarters of another Latter-day Prophet, Jim Harmston, founder of The True and Living Church of Jesus Christ of the Saints of the Last Days. Harmston had purchased two of the buildings on Main Street in Manti, painted them red and waited for the world to be delivered into his hands. Hansen had viewed a videotape in which Harmston read a prophecy stating that "the name of the Living God is Harmston."

The Suburban turned left, passing along the south side of the temple fronted by a lush green carpet of lawn where the main Utah Church presented the annual Manti Pageant—a depiction of the founding of Mormonism played out by hundreds of actors on the temple hillside after dark. The Manti Pageant was modeled after the one in Palmyra, New York.

Thickening smoke engulfed the Suburban as it began its assent into the Manti National Forest. They passed the turnoff to the hunting camp where Heber LeBaron had assassinated Daniel Ben Jordan in 1987. Jordan had been the number two man to Heber's father, Ervil LeBaron. On written orders from his father, Heber eventually dispatched Jordan, and a dozen other dissidents. Heber had orchestrated the so-called Four O'clock Murders in Houston in 1988; he and his team executing four different people at exactly 4:00 p.m.

The Suburban continued up Manti Canyon, past the Cottonwoods Campground and Milky Falls, and headed north on Skyline Road toward Jet Fox Reservoir. Before reaching the reservoir, they turned onto a logging road. Five minutes later Kellog pulled into a graveled parking lot outside the C1MS cabin on Cove Creek. After Kellog helped the Prophet out of the vehicle, he fetched a bucket of water and began washing the Suburban.

*   *   *

Samuel Pete Marchon loved the drive from San Bernadino, California, to Hansen's Utah cabin. He liked the quarterly business meetings. He liked being with the other Danites and being in the presence of Bill Campbell and especially the Prophet himself. He was proud to be one of the Danites, a group named after the elite guard that had done Brigham Young's bidding. Samuel Pete styled himself after the three Destroying Angels—Bill Hickman, Orin Porter Rockwell, and John D. Lee.

Samuel Pete wished he could have driven the Corvette, but that wouldn't have been prudent. The rental Chevy would be fine. At least it was a full-sized car; he hated to drive short wheelbase cars unless they were power machines like the Corvette. But, the Corvette, of course, would attract too much attention and raise too many questions. The brethren would not like his flashy taste and they certainly would not approve of the way he financed his lifestyle.

Samuel Pete had struggled with the innovations he introduced into his relationship with the Church of the One Mighty and Strong, and his favorite wife, Erin, had warned him that he was on dangerous ground. But he was too loyal and valuable to the Prophet to be very concerned. Not only was he a Danite, he was Bishop of the San Bernadino branch of the Church. And mainly, he brought in nearly $5 million a year in tithes, and profits. Ninety percent or more of the money came from the drug profits.

Samuel Pete prided himself on his inventiveness. He had turned a $1 million-a-year drug business into nearly $5 million annually in less than five years. The Prophet was very proud of him and had given him several bonuses. The first time profits had hit $3 million the Prophet had flown Samuel Pete and his three wives to Cancun for a week at Sandal's. The Prophet had given Samuel Pete a plaque commending him for "bringing the gold of the gentiles into the Kingdom of God." The coke addicts of Riverside County were funding the worldwide operations of the Kingdom. The plan had a certain irony that fascinated Prophet Hansen. He loved the idea of stripping money from reprobate gentiles. Samuel Pete liked the plan because it gave him ample opportunity to exercise his talents as a Destroying Angel. He ruled his domain with what he thought was a brilliant combination of charm and terror.

Occasionally Samuel Pete wondered if Prophet Hansen would overlook the fact that a few hundred thousand dollars a year were channeled into Samuel Pete's private accounts. Actually, the Prophet had been very clear in saying that he would *not* understand skimming. But only a fool would fail to realize that Samuel Pete was a great asset to the Church even if he had a penchant for the good life.

*   *   *

Bill Campbell went inside, checked out the cabin, and then waved the Prophet in. It was 3:00 p.m., the others would be arriving in a couple hours. Hoyt Akers, the pilot, followed.

The front door of the cabin opened into a large room. A 20-foot oak table dominated the center of the room, surrounded by 20 chairs, enough for all the Danites and Hansen with a few left over. Off the common room were four bedrooms, a kitchen and two bathrooms. Jake Kellog kept everything open all winter long, including the last two miles of road which he cleared using the Suburban fitted with a snow blade. Kellog also kept the cabin spotless, although the acrid smell of smoke from the forest fires irritated the Prophet today.

"Hoyt, after you sweep the cabin for electronic bugs," Hansen said, "man your lookout post. I want you in position by 4 o'clock. Bill and I are going to take a walk."

Hansen and Campbell strolled in silence through the pine forest for several minutes until they came upon a stone outcropping that overlooked the Sanpete Valley. Bloodstains were on the stone ledge.

"How many know about this place?" Campbell asked.

"Just you, me, and Charlie Pickens." Hansen smiled. "I mean, of course, we are the only *living* people who know about this place."

* * *

At 4:00 p.m. cars began to arrive. All 20 Danites were invited to this meeting, but Harry Bushnell from Dallas would be briefed later because his first wife was dying of cancer and he was with her at the hospital. Hansen had reluctantly granted Bushnell's request to be excused.

Hansen took each arriving Danite aside as he came in, hugged him, and told him how much his service to the Church was appreciated. He also handed each of them an envelope with 20 crisp $100 bills inside.

When everyone was present, Hansen dismissed Hoyt Akers to join Kellog outside. Bill Campbell called the meeting to order and everyone stood for an opening prayer. The first order of business after they were seated was to sustain Ronald Hansen as Prophet, Seer, and Revelator. This procedure was performed at each official gathering of the Danites. The question was posed and a show of hands confirmed that all the men recognized Hansen's prophetic calling. They also swore allegiance to the Prophet and to the Church. They swore to defend the Prophet with their lives. Campbell then introduced Hansen.

Hansen uncurled from his chair and looked around the table. A white tablecloth covered it, and bottles of water and bowls of nuts were within reach of each man. The nuts, according to Hansen's instructions, were macadamias and pecans, heavily salted—the Prophet's favorite snack.

For an hour, Hansen covered routine matters. Nathan Asay

from Houston complained that the local "Utah" Mormons were making trouble in Texas. Asay's own polygamous family, as well as several other C1MS families had been in the news. Recent bigamy prosecutions in Utah had lured Texas newsmen into sniffing around Asay's family, going so far as to accost one of his daughters at high school.

"So President," Asay asked the Prophet, how far can I go with these guys?"

Hansen didn't hesitate. "You meet the reporter privately. Tell him if he ever intimidates one of your children again he will have purchased a ticket to hell." Then he added, "Make sure he isn't wired when you talk to him. If he doesn't get in line, Silent Bill Campbell will take a vacation to Houston."

Everyone looked at Bill. Campbell acted as if he hadn't heard the remark.

Hansen spent 30 minutes comparing income figures from each of the Danite domains. "Every last one of you shows an increase!" he said with enthusiasm. "I'm proud of you."

The Danites glowed.

After covering several other routine business items, the Prophet discussed the Argentinean plans. This was always of great interest to the Danites, who liked the assurance that in case of emergency there was a haven for them outside the country.

"I want to go over the procedure for a major evacuation," Hansen said. "These are especially dangerous times. All of the normal procedures remain in place. However, I want to review the computer destruction plans. You need to be sure that you have data stored only on your alpha computer. Nowhere else. I want you to wire a plastic explosive charge to the computer. It needs to be enough to destroy the entire room in which the computer is housed. It needs to be set up so you can detonate it from your cell phone. If you are ever going out of cell phone range, be sure the room will explode if anyone gains entrance. If you have any questions as to how to accomplish this, you need to call secretary Satterwhite and have him give you the information you need. Of course, we need to be updated immediately if you change the number of the detonator.

"As far as your electronic reports are concerned, I want you to start sending them daily. Again, I emphasize, we are in critical times. We are vulnerable. We need to be up to date and mobile. Be extremely vigilant." He paused. "Any questions?"

There were none.

"Well, I know you are anxious to get back on the road. There is, however, one more order of business. And I'm afraid it will take a while, so settle in. We will, however, take a fifteen minute recess."

*   *   *

When they reassembled, Bill Campbell was absent. Hansen called the meeting to order.

"Brothers, it is my sad duty to convene a President's court." As he surveyed the group, Hansen saw shock move around the table in a wave. The men looked at each other, their faces registering confusion and fear.

"I'm going to need to ask Samuel Pete Marchon to take the chair at the head of the table."

Samuel Pete went white. "What?" he gasped breathlessly.

"Come now, brother," Hansen said. "You have nothing to fear if your conscience is clear."

Hansen turned to a large man on his left with a Brigham Young beard—a full beard except the upper lip was shaved clean.

"Charlie, would you take a seat beside brother Marchon? I am appointing you his counsel. I want you to make sure that whatever we do here in no way abridges Samuel Pete's God-given right to a fair trial."

Charlie Pickens slid his chair back slowly. Hansen saw Pickens' face cloud. He had been a trusted advisor to Hansen for 20 years. He had followed him down many dangerous paths and had always been totally and absolutely faithful. He was, as he said of himself, "A do-and-die disciple of Ronald Hansen." The Church held him in great respect. There was nothing—*nothing*—Charlie Pickens would not do for Prophet Hansen. Pickens was as well known for his wisdom and honesty as he was for his commitment to duty. But today, the Prophet was picking up something in the face of Pickens he had never seen before. The Danite was a beat too slow in rising from his chair. He looked at the Prophet for a split-second too long.

Pickens moved to the chair that had been pulled alongside Samuel Pete's. Samuel Pete looked at Charlie in a way that said *What's going on here?* Charlie touched his shoulder reassuringly.

Hansen placed a tape recorder on the table and said in an official tone, "Let the record show that this is the President's court, convened to consider the matter of Samuel Pete Marchon, charged by the President with wrongdoing in the discharge of his office."

He looked at Samuel Pete.

"Brother Marchon, I think you know where this is going. Would you like to say anything that would make this easier for all of us?"

Samuel Pete looked around wildly. He finally looked at Hansen, shook his head, and looked down at the table."

"Very well, brother."

Hansen produced a manila folder from a briefcase that was lying open on a chair beside him. "Let the court note that I am offering into evidence copies of bank statements and other financial papers. I will briefly describe what the paperwork reveals.

"First, in violation of Church rules and the direct command of the President, brother Marchon has opened bank accounts in his own name. At least six, as these documents demonstrate. Of course, there can only be one reason for such accounts to exist. That is to deposit monies acquired as a result of brother Marchon's performance of duties in his official capacity as an officer of the Church. He knows full well that all outside income is to be reported to the Church. No such reports exist. We therefore conclude that he has been attempting to hide these funds from the eyes of the brethren. But, of course, he cannot hide anything from the eyes of the Lord."

Hansen paused. He stared off into the distance, then said aloud, almost to himself, "I wonder why our brother thought the Lord would not reveal his activities to the Prophet?"

Then he addressed Samuel Pete, "Brother, I would ask you if we have mistreated you in any way? Have we failed to provide handsomely for you and your three wives and eight children? Have we withheld any blessing from you? Have we failed to appreciate and reward your earnest and devoted service to the Church?"

Samuel Pete, eyes moist, shook his head.

"Brother do you recognize the seriousness of this matter?"

Samuel Pete nodded.

The room was silent.

Hansen said, "The seriousness of these charges is underscored by the fact that the various bank accounts we have discovered contain more than $300,000! And of course there is the matter of your lifestyle. The Corvette convertible, the lavish expenditures for entertainment and personal accouterments for yourself and your wives...

"Brother, it seems as though you left us and went your own way and thought that we would be unaware. As you can see, that is not the case. Do you have anything to say for yourself that will help us understand your behavior?"

"President, I…I…can't think of anything. Except, I am sorry…"

"Really? I expect you are, at this moment. And, I *hope so* for your soul's sake. If anyone was ever in need of repentance, it is you, my dear brother."

Samuel Pete had his head lowered, his nose just inches from the table. Hansen could hear the sounds of the breathing of the other Danites, but no one spoke or even cleared his throat.

Finally, Hansen spoke. "Well, brother Marchon, I think we have no choice but to find you guilty as charged. So let it be recorded.

"Now, brother, I want you to go with brother Campbell while we move into the penalty phase of this trial."

Bill Campbell had materialized at the back of the room. He was wearing a Colt 44 on his hip. Samuel Pete turned to look at him. Campbell smiled and held out his hand in a gesture indicating Samuel Pete should stand up anf accompany him. Samuel Pete did so. They left the room.

Hansen continued.

"I want to introduce a little background law into the proceedings."

He retrieved a well-worn Bible from his briefcase and opened it.

"You are all familiar with the story of Ananias and Sapphira from the Book of Acts. Let me summarize it to refresh our memories."

Several of the brethren were glancing around the table looking from face to face. Others were stoic. Charlie Pickens crossed his arms over his massive chest and stared straight ahead.

"We find," Hansen said, "that the Apostles of Christ were gathered together not long after Jesus had ascended into heaven. They were questioning one of the disciples, Ananias. Peter asked him about a certain piece of property; property he had dedicated to the church, but then sold. He gave some of the money to the church and kept some of it for himself.

"Peter asked him why he had set about to lie to God in the matter. He said that the property belonged to Ananias and that he had been free to do with it as he pleased. But after he gave it to the church, it was pure devilish deception to sell it slyly while pretending that he was a great contributor to the church.

"You may recall that right in the middle of Peter's rebuke, Ananias fell dead at Peter's feet and Peter had him carried out of the room. Shortly thereafter, Sapphira, Ananias' wife came into the room. She was a party to the deception and when Peter asked her about the selling price of the land, she lied to him."

Hansen looked around the table into the eyes of all the gathered men. He put his finger on the text of the Bible before him and read Peter's words to Sapphira: "How is it that ye have agreed together to tempt the Spirit of the Lord? Behold, the feet of them which have buried thy husband are at the door, and shall carry thee out." Hansen looked up from the book, "At that," he said, "Sapphira dropped dead.

"I recount this story to underscore the serious nature of our brother's crime. It goes to the root of trust, does it not? We are the leaders of an organization that God has established to move in these last days in very serious and dangerous enterprises. How can we have traitors in our midst? Need I remind you that at this very moment law enforcement agencies are watching our every move, waiting to pounce? Do we dare trust our lives into the hands of someone who is stealing the Kingdom's money to squander it on his own lusts? Do we dare entrust the welfare of the Church itself into such hands? No, we cannot do so. We dare not do so.

"And, what shall we do with such a person? He has violated the most solemn trust that could ever be given a man in this lifetime. He has been a trusted guardian of the Prophet of God and of God's Church. He has violated that trust. I tell you in the most solemn words that at this moment our brother has prepared a place for himself in hell."

The Prophet looked into each face, one after another. "How then, I ask, can we help our brother?"

Hansen paused and looked around the table once again. Everyone knew what was coming.

"Just to be clear," Hansen said, "let me recall the words of earlier prophets in similar situations. The bottom line is that brother Marchon had placed himself in eternal peril and there is but one way to save his soul."

Hansen paused, reached for a glass, and took a sip of water. "President Brigham Young articulated our theology for us. He told us that—while it is true that the blood of Christ is the atoning agent for sin—there are some sins a man commits that cannot be cleansed by the blood of Christ. For those sins, the only possible remedy is the shedding of the man's own blood. President Young had the courage to follow his convictions in these matters, as you well know.

"I want to read a quote from a passage I just recently came across. This is President Heber C. Kimball recounting, in the Salt Lake City Tabernacle, how the apostles of Christ, as an act of mercy, blood atoned Judas Iscariot. In case anyone wants to look up this reference it is found in the *Journal of Discourses*, Volume six, page 126."

Nobody put pen to paper.

The Prophet continued, "The biblical account incorrectly states that Judas *hanged* himself and that while hanging from a tree, his bowels gushed out. The truth is, according to President Kimball, 'The other apostles *kicked him* until his bowels came out.' Kimball then went on to state publicly, 'I know the day is right at hand when men will forfeit their Priesthood and turn against us and against the covenants they have made, and they will be destroyed *as Judas was.'*

"Now, brethren, I am not suggesting that we handle brother Marchon in *that* way. But we have no choice, if we love him, but to do what is necessary to save his soul.

"I therefore pronounce capital judgment upon him. The responsibility falls to me. I am the Prophet. I accept that responsibility.

"I will not trouble you further in this matter. You have heard the facts. You see what the outcome must be. I ask only one thing of you. By a show of hands, I want all of you to affirm your confidence in me to act according to the Word of God and according to the leading of the Holy Spirit."

Every hand at the table extended in submission to the articulated will of the Prophet.

"Thank you very much brothers. I know this has been a trying day for you all. I want you to be prepared to step forward to receive brother Marchon's kingdom. We will seek God as to whom his wives and children should be given for their protection. We really do not want to break up the fellowship of his three sister wives. So that means that one of you will probably be seeing an increase of 11 in the size of your family. I will dispatch brother Pickens to the wives this afternoon. I remind you that you are under solemn obligation to treat this entire matter with the utmost secrecy. Reveal nothing you have seen or heard here today upon penalty of the sacred oaths you swore in the temple.

"Do not discuss this matter among yourselves. Now, I want you to quietly gather your materials and leave for home at once. As I said, brother Pickens will stay behind with brother Campbell and myself so that all will be done in the presence of responsible witnesses."

*   *   *

Bill Campbell, Charlie Pickens, and Samuel Pete Marchon were gathered at the bloodstained rock. Samuel Pete was white and shaking. His hands were bound in front of his body at the wrists with white cord. The cord was anchored to another cord which went around his waist. He was wearing a white shirt and white pants provided by Campbell. They were a little too large for him because Campbell had been unsure of Samuel Pete's sizes. Samuel Pete tried to hitch the pants up with his elbows. Around his waist a green apron flapped in the mountain breeze. He asked if he could be seated. Campbell helped him down to a sitting position. A mountain bluebird sang in the treetops.

Just then Hansen appeared on the trail. He was dressed in a white gown. On top of his head was a white hat that looked like something a baker would wear, only it was scarcely two inches in height. He wore white shoes. A band of white material stretched from his left shoulder down through a gold-corded belt and around his back to connect at the shoulder where it originated. He, too, wore a green apron. Stuck in his belt was a large jewel-handled knife with a Bowie blade.

Samuel Pete heard his approach but refused to look up. At the prodding of Campbell he did so and gasped. He looked wildly at Pickens and Campbell, but their eyes were dead.

Campbell stood him on his feet. Hansen addressed him formally.

"Brother Marchon, having been duly tried by the President's court and found guilty, it is my responsibility to announce the official penalty ascribed to your crime."

Hansen paused and looked at Samuel Pete with compassion.

"Son," he said quietly, "It is my sad duty to tell you that out of our hearts of love for you we find it absolutely necessary to shed your blood for your crimes."

He waited a moment.

"Son, it would be very important for you if you were able to accept this penalty. I know how hard this is for you, but I assure you there is no escape from what awaits you. The only question is whether this sacrifice will sufficiently appease the anger of God. I believe that whether or not God accepts this sacrifice depends directly upon your attitude in the matter. All of us come eventually to the hour of our death. You, of course, did not expect that moment to come today. I appreciate the misgivings you are experiencing—the dread, the terror."

"But, dear brother, there is no dread or terror for those who approach their deaths with their consciences clear. If this sacrifice is effectual, you will awake in paradise where you will await—with confidence—the resurrection. If this sacrifice is effectual, you will attend the Morning of the First Resurrection, rather than the resurrection of the unjust.

"So, brother, I beg you. Please repent of these crimes and signify that you accept this penalty as just. In doing so, you may earn a better resurrection."

Samuel Pete shook his head and looked at the ground. "What about my family?" he whispered.

"You have lost them—eternally lost them."

After two or three minutes of silence, punctuated only by Samuel Pete's sobs, Hansen spoke again.

"Son, in view of your emotional condition, I think we can accept a nodding of your head as assent and confession. Can you do that, dear boy?"

Finally, Samuel Pete nodded his head almost imperceptibly.

"That will do," the Prophet said.

*   *   *

Bill Campbell, Hoyt Akers, and the Prophet rode from the Manti Forest in silence in the Suburban. The driver, Jake Kellog, who had not been privy to any of the proceedings of the afternoon, whistled tunelessly as he drove. As they pulled out of the parking lot, Kellog asked, "How come Marchon's rental car is still here? Did he ride back with someone else?"

Hansen said, "Don't worry about it."

Hansen was lost in thought. No matter how many Blood Atonements he conducted, he could never get over the solemn sense of destiny which accompanied them. His eyes closed, he recalled the scene: Bill Campbell's strong hands wrapped in Samuel Pete's hair, pinning his head to the rock; Pickens astride Samuel Pete's bound feet; the feel of the Bowie's blade as it penetrated to the neck vertebrae; the round, almost cherubic mouth of Samuel Pete in the long death scream. The procedure—strangely enough—always reminded Hansen of the first time he ate canned salmon and bit into one of the soft vertebrae which crunched between his teeth and sent shivers up his spine. But this time a new emotion rose up within the Prophet, something wild he had never felt before. Only the light touch of Charlie Picken's hand on the Prophet's elbow had caused him to stop sawing with the Bowie blade. The trachea, the jugulars, the carotids had all given way and the neck vertebrae were succumbing. When he stopped, Samuel Pete's head was still attached, but barely, so that carrying the body to the shallow grave required all three men.

Finally, as they approached Salt Lake City, the Prophet spoke.

"Bill, where is that place near the airport where we got that great steak? I'm famished!"

CHAPTER TWENTY

S aturday afternoon, Melissa drove the rental car into the Medicine Wheel relay station. The afternoon sun stood high above the eastern horizon and at 10,000 feet elevation, the view from the relay station encompassed the valley of the Bighorn River. At 5:00 p.m., the valley was a hazy bowl 60 miles wide and a 100 miles long. Bill Campbell was on the porch nailing plywood across the porch rails. As Melissa pulled to a stop, Campbell stood up, looked through the windshield at her, and laid the nail gun down on the steps. Melissa stepped out of the car. She was wearing a print short-sleeved blouse and white shorts. Her legs, unaccustomed to the sun, were white and smooth. She knew that Jan and John were watching her with binoculars from a crest less than 200 yards away. She assumed the sheriff was training a riflescope on Bill Campbell.

"Melissa!" Campbell said, wiping his hands on his jeans, "Where have you been? I have been very worried about you. I heard you had left the compound. Ronald has been worried too...My God! What happened to you? You have bruises all over your arms!"

"Hi, Bill. Good to see you. I'll tell you all about it."

"Come in, come in."

Melissa followed him into the cabin without looking back or hesitating. Inside, Campbell pulled a chair out from the table and said, "Coffee?"

"No thanks, Bill. I was hoping for something a little stronger. But that can wait. I'm really glad to see you."

"And I'm glad to see *you,* Melissa. Honestly, I have been worried about you."

"Well, Bill, I'm so glad to know you don't know what happened to me. That's important to me."

"I have no idea. All I know is that Ronald said you had left in the dead of night…"

"That's not completely accurate. I left in the dead of night, all right, but not by choice. Ronald probably thought I was dead, he tried to kill me. Or, rather, he had others try to kill me."

"Melissa! I can't believe that. Ronald loves you."

"I guess you don't know Ronald as well as you think you do."

Melissa watched Campbell for any sign that might indicate he thought she was lying. "I was dragged from my room at the compound, taken into the hills, raped, and left for dead."

Campbell shook his head. He said nothing.

"I was asleep when they came for me. I awoke with a blanket over my head. They gagged me and covered my eyes with duct tape. I was tied in the blanket, and taken in a car. There were two of them. They never spoke. Then they beat me and raped me. They left me, as I said, for dead."

Campbell spoke. "Are you absolutely positive you have no idea who abducted you?"

"Well, I assume it was one of the Prophet's most trusted. To tell you the truth, Bill, I thought it might even be you. But then I just *knew* you couldn't do anything like that to me. And now, I know I was right because I can tell this is all news to you."

Campbell nodded.

"In fact, Bill, that is why I came to see you. To find that out, and then to ask for your help."

"My help?"

"I'm not sure exactly what I want." She lowered her head, let a small sob escape, and wiped her eyes. Then she looked at Campbell. She thought he believed her story.

"Sure you don't want a cup of coffee?" the Danite asked.

"You know what? I have a box of groceries in the trunk. And I have a bottle of wine. I thought, if you don't mind, I'd fix you dinner."

Campbell raised one eyebrow and looked long at her. A small smile pinched at his lips. "Mind? Of course I don't mind. I would love to have dinner with you."

"Come help me get the groceries. Then I'll tell you everything."

*   *   *

Jan and Monster watched Melissa and Campbell come out of the cabin and go to the trunk of the car and get the box of groceries.

"Thank God!" Monster said.

"Looks like things are going OK so far," Jan said.

"I still hate this whole thing."

"So do I, John, but we're committed now."

"That don't make me like it."

"Nope."

"Jan, do you really think this cockamamie scheme will work? I mean the digital eavesdropping?"

"I don't know, John. All I know is that information is power. If we can actually tap into Hansen's information flow we'll learn a lot. I want to get to him. I want to destroy him."

"You want to *kill* him."

"I guess I do."

"Did you ever think, before Emma's death, you could even consider something like that?"

"I didn't."

"Well, Jan. I hope you are listening, because I need to tell you something."

Jan turned to Monster and looked at him. The big man was staring intently at him. Monster held up a finger and waved it.

"Jan, fact is, I'm afraid you *couldn't* kill Hansen."

Jan eyed him coldly. "What do you mean?"

"Killing isn't so easy. Most people can't do it. Especially a guy like you who is all wound up in moral introspection. I'm not trying to be unkind, Jan. I'm trying to save your life."

"I say again, what do you mean?"

Monster looked at Jan for a few seconds. "When the moment of truth comes," he finally said, "a guy like you has too many conflicting thoughts. Men like Hansen—men like *Campbell*—they don't have those problems. Hansen *knows* God is on his side. He *is* the moral law. And Campbell? Well, Campbell has killed so many men, and probably women, that it is no longer problematic. But you, my friend, by the time you work through all the issues, you'll be the one who is dead. Campbell draws down on you and you are doing some kind of internal Socratic questioning and he blows your heart out."

Jan stared at him for several seconds. Then he dropped his eyes.

"See, *hombre*? You are no killer."

"People do what they have to do."

"Yes, that's true. And you may be able to do it, but you have to 'get there' in your head first. You have to come to the intellectual conclusion that Hansen needs to be removed from the earth, and you have to decide if you're the one to do it. You have to get to the place where you know you *will* do it. You need to go over it in your head. You have to see him as a snake coiled to strike you, and you have to move instinctively. Or he will bite you, my friend. He definitely will bite you."

"Well, isn't there any conflict in your own mind on this?"

"Jan. He killed your wife, he has tried to kill you, and we know he has killed a score of others who have crossed him. No, I'm sorry, I'm as prepared to execute him as I would be if I held a Writ of Execution signed by Governor Hinton."

*   *   *

Melissa swirled the glass of White Zinfandel. Campbell had poured himself a shot of Jim Beam and had a tumbler of water on the small table. The cabin had two rooms. The main area was 20 feet square, with a bed, a combination cook/heating stove, and some storage shelves. A long wooden bar provided a place to hang clothes. A separate room housed electronic equipment and a desk.

"Bill," Melissa, said, "you once told me you cared deeply for me. Do you still?"

Campbell nodded.

"I need help."

"I guess I'd do just about anything for you, Melissa."

"That covers a lot of ground."

"You are very important to me."

"Why?"

"Don't make me tell you that, Melissa. I have wanted you from the day I laid eyes on you?"

.

"Wanted me?"

"Yes."

"Well." She smiled. "I think I like that."

Campbell sipped the drink, but made no move.

"Tell me what happened to you, Melissa."

"I told you about the…the abduction. And the rape." She stopped and looked at Campbell. Nothing in his eyes betrayed what she knew to be true—that he was the one who had raped her, but she wanted to see if he believed her. If he thought she knew he was the rapist, he would never allow her to leave alive. On the other hand, if he believed her and felt safe from entrapment, she thought his lust would make him vulnerable.

"Anyway," she continued, "I woke up in a ditch behind the compound. I suppose someone was going to come to bury me or something the next day. But I walked three miles to the highway and hitched a ride into Greybull. I was taken to the hospital, and after a few days I was released."

"Who talked to you in the hospital?"

"Sheriff Broadbeck."

"That snake."

"Yes, he really is creepy. He thinks he's a ladies' man or something. Nevertheless, he was nice enough to me. He asked me a lot of questions about the compound."

"What did you tell him?"

"As little as possible. I don't trust him."

"That's smart."

"Of course I don't trust Ronald either. I'm sure he ordered me killed."

"Come on, Melissa. I have my problems with Ronald, but really…after all he *is* the Prophet."

"Do you believe that, Bill? Be honest with me."

Campbell looked down at the table. "I used to believe it."

"So did I."

"So what are your plans. Melissa?"

"I don't know yet, Bill. I guess that's why I'm here. The first thing I need to do is take care of myself. I really don't know how to go about that. But I think I need a strong man in my life. And you are about the strongest man I know."

"Melissa, where have you been staying for the past few days?"

This was the question she had been waiting for. She had rehearsed her answer over and over. She knew that Campbell knew very well where she was staying. She knew Hansen's people were watching the house. She couldn't afford to lie to him on this point.

"I have been staying with Ginny Hollingsworth, a waitress at the Basin Café."

"Isn't she a friend of Jan Kucera?"

"Well, she told me they had a thing once. And he is staying at her house, too. I guess he was a victim of an assault by Hansen as well."

"What happened to him?"

"He was shot."

"Who did it?"

"He doesn't know. He assumes it was Hansen. Sheriff Broadbeck thinks you probably did it. I have never talked to Jan Kucera in any depth. Mainly, I just stay in my own room. I have talked to Ginny a lot, though."

Campbell stared at her. "And what about Broadbeck?"

She took a drink of wine.

"What about him?"

"Have you talked to him in any detail?"

"No. Why do you ask?"

Campbell continued to look at her with dead eyes. Melissa stifled a shudder. She had the eerie feeling she was looking into the eyes of a reptile. There seemed to be no life in them at all.

Finally, Campbell broke the gaze. He poured another drink and said, smiling, "Did you say something about dinner?"

CHAPTER TWENTY—ONE

Centuries before any white man set foot in the Bighorn Mountains, the Sheepeaters gathered atop 10,000-foot-high Medicine Wheel Mountain, from which they could see into what is now
three states. The sun dances, ceremonies, and the sacrifices they
performed there remain the secrets of history. Much later—probably around 1700 A.D.—the Shoshones built the Medicine Wheel
on the site. When Jan was a boy, he drove to the wheel and walked
among the cairns. Now it was encircled by a chain-link fence and
visitors had to park their vehicles and walk the last mile-and-a-half
on foot, up a steep grade. Unless, of course, you were with Monster Broadbeck, who drove around the barrier and up the service
road to the Wheel. When Jan was a kid, the Medicine Wheel was
an interesting oddity, now it was a shrine for American Indians and
New Age mystics.

Twenty-eight granite stone spokes—coinciding both with the
number of lunar days and the number of tribes in the original
Shoshone nation—radiate from the center of the wheel. Some of
the spokes terminate in hollowed-out pockets lined with similar

stones. These rock cairns precisely align with the rising sun at the summer solstice. Some investigators speculate that ancients filled the pockets with water to perform a kind of baptism—a view discounted by most anthropologists who consider such a theory an attempt to impose Western culture on a pagan society.

As an adult, the Medicine Wheel infected Jan with a ghostly feeling similar to what he had experienced at the Custer Battlefield, 40 miles to the northeast. Indeed, there was a connection between the Medicine Wheel and the Battle of the Little Bighorn. Some legends say Sitting Bull danced three days at the wheel just before the battle. And, for certain, a contingent of warriors came to the Medicine Wheel immediately after the battle. Sitting Bull, a Hunkpapa Lakota Sioux, wound up in Canada, but a huge band of warriors trekked up into the Bighorns before eventually straggling back to the Black Hills Reservation. The battle on the Little Bighorn occurred on the banks of the stream which took its name from its larger counterpart—the Bighorn River which flowed by Jan's ranch. The Little Bighorn makes its confluence with the main Bighorn a few miles north of the battleground where General Custer died on June 25, 1876.

Mystical types, Jan knew, spoke of the Medicine Wheel as a spiritual vortex—these same folks consider Manti, Utah, and Sedona, Arizona, to be similar vortices. But even dyed-in-the-wool secularists admit to feeling "something" at the Medicine Wheel. Something conjured by the ancient chiefs and maidens who danced and mated under the stars and orbiting moon. Nearly all traces of the Sheepeaters have long since vanished, except for the spiritual residue infusing Medicine Wheel Mountain.

Tonight Jan, Monster, and George Olson parked in the turnaround at the Medichine Wheel. They regarded the wheel silently through the chain link fence. At 2:30 a.m. they pulled equipment bags from the trunk of the county cruiser in the near total darkness—the quarter moon having barely set. They headed across the meadow toward the C1MS relay site.

They walked the mile to the relay site in silence. As they approached the dark and silent cabin, they saw Melissa's car still parked in front. She, of course, had taken the private road which avoided the Medicine Wheel altogether.

"Hope Melissa plied him with booze," Jan said.

"Yeah," Monster said, "I hope that's *all* she plied him with."

"Apparently the generator is off for the night," Olson said. "That's nice because we won't be interrupting any transmission. On the other hand, we won't have its noise for cover and we won't know if we have power to our unit. We'll just have to trust Granny's schematic."

"Well," Monster said, "I guess that is about as sure a bet as we'll get in this operation. If there is one professional in this outfit, it's Granny. No offense."

"You got that right," Olson said. "Granny gets my vote for the 'Most Reliable Criminal Contractor' award."

Olson paused, checked his gear one last time and said, "Well, boys, ready or not, here we go. No more voice communication from here. After we drag the equipment to the tower, you two take up covering positions and I'll skinny up the pole. This whole operation shouldn't take 30 minutes if all goes well."

"Don't worry, George," Monster said. "We won't let you fall into Campbell's hands. If he comes outside, I'll shoot you off the tower."

"Knew I could count on you, John," Olson said.

*   *   *

Getting up the pole had been easy for Olson—much easier than opening the transmitter box and attaching the power leads. Sweat had dripped off his forehead as he worked under the tarp in the beam of a dim penlight Velcroed to his baseball cap. The colors on the wires were nearly imperceptible in the feeble light. That was something Granny had not counted on. Olson *thought* he got the wires right.

He climbed the tower, trailing the light power lead which he taped to the pole every five feet or so. From 50 feet up, he secured himself with the leather safety belt and gently pulled the antenna up. It was tethered on a light line, and he drew it up slowly so it would not bump into the tower.

Holding the antenna in front of him, he pointed it in the general direction of Basin, whose lights were clearly visible 30 miles due south on the valley floor. Olson remembered taking a commercial flight from Chicago to Boise one night years earlier—when he was on his way to testify in the Ruby Ridge trial. From 35,000 feet he had been able to locate the towns of Northern Wyoming—Sheridan to the east of the Bighorns and Cody, Greybull, Basin, Worland, and Thermopolis to the west.

Tonight the panorama was breathtaking. The sky in the east was just beginning to lighten and would, within a couple of hours, extinguish the starry host. Olson had the sensation that he was at the very top of the world. Looking up he was lost in crystal clear heavens with stars so bright and distinct he felt that if he reached out, he could scoop up a handful of them. This must be how astronauts feel on space walks, he thought. It seemed as if he let go he would drift off over the Big Horn Basin like a leaf. To the north he could see outlines of mountains in Montana, and to the east he saw the darkness over the Great Plains—the rolling buffalo hills undulating toward Devil's Tower. He remembered his first visit to Devil's Tower after coming to Wyoming. Driving through the rolling grain fields heading west from Belle Fouche, suddenly the tower appeared in front of him. So remarkable was the sight, his breath caught and he thought he was not going to be able to take another. Indian legend said the scarring of the tower was done by the claws of a giant bear. But the sight of Devil's Tower was every bit as astounding as it had been made to appear in the movie *Close Encounters of the Third Kind*. Olson shook off the thought that he was having some sort of weird psychological—or was it *spiritual*—encounter right now.

He pulled the bolts from the pocket of his jacket and inserted them through the clamps on the antenna. In five minutes he had them cinched down and, sighting along the antenna horn, he guessed he was pointed dead on Basin.

Carefully, he unscrewed the connector on the antenna belonging to C1MS, attached his adapter, and reconnected it. Then he connected the lead to his own antenna and checked the power wires to the small transmitter box at the back of the antenna.

"If that doesn't do it, we ain't gonna get the job done," he said to himself.

Just then, a shaft of light burst through the cabin door and Bill Campbell stepped out. He was dressed entirely in white! Olson's heart leaped into his throat. He held his breath, waiting for Campbell to look up. He hoped Monster had a night vision scope trained on Campbell.

Campbell walked to the edge of the cabin's porch. He didn't look up. Instead, he walked to the edge of the porch and stood very still. Olson now saw the reason. Campbell was relieving himself.

*   *   *

On the ground with Jan and Monster, Olson found he was trembling.

"S'matter, George?" Monster said. "I thought you *federales* never got nervous. You think Campbell was coming up the pole after you?"

"I was worried that you might start shooting at Campbell and blow me off the pole, is all," Olson said.

Monster guffawed at that.

"What the heck was he dressed in white for?" Olson asked. *"That* was spooky!"

"Those were his garments," Jan said. "His temple garments."

"Why was he wearing those?"

"Mormons wear them all the time once they have been through the temple. They have occult markings sewn in them above the breasts, navel and knee."

"Oh, yeah." Olson said. "The holy Mormon underwear."

"That's it."

*   *   *

At the cruiser, they looked back at the cabin which was beginning to become visible in the predawn.

No one mentioned Melissa, but Jan couldn't erase from his mind the picture of her and Campbell alone in the cabin. He held his breath hoping Monster wouldn't bring it up. But Monster was silent in the front seat behind the wheel of the cruiser. Too many wheels in motion here tonight Jan thought: the celestial wheel of the stars, the cycle of love, the grinding wheels of justice. Rocks flew from the cruiser's wheels as it picked up speed down the hill and away from the Medicine Wheel.

CHAPTER TWENTY—TWO

J an, Monster, and Olson met the morning of July 4, a Wednesday, four days after they sabotaged the Medicine Wheel relay site. They met in the sheriff's office, coffee and donuts on the desk, along with Monster's feet in size 14 boots. Olson looked cool in a dark blue suit and narrow tie. Jan wore a Hawaiian shirt Ginny had given him, the shirt hanging over faded Wrangler jeans.

"I hadn't planned to bother you today, Jan," Olson said. "I understand both you and John have dates tonight. How is Melissa anyway, John?"

Monster waved the question off. "Let's just say she survived Campbell Saturday night. But, the word 'survive' is up for discussion."

"Well, anyway," Olson said. "This is moving fast. Washington has been receiving the live data feed. As of this morning, we have collected enough evidence to mount a RICO case against Hansen. The information coming from the Danites through the Medicine Wheel station is fascinating. Hansen's penchant for record keeping has given us more info than we could have hoped for. We should be able to get a conviction."

"Should?" Jan said raising an eyebrow.

Olson returned his gaze. "Jan, with these things there is never a certainty of conviction. At the very least we will keep him busy in court for the next three years if we bust him now. And we *should* be able to get a conviction. I supplied the feed to Washington and they received it without requiring me to divulge how the interception of his information was accomplished—for now at least. I told them I had been tipped off by an anonymous source to erect an antenna on the courthouse and prepare to receive. The suits in Washington assume our source is a disgruntled disciple within the compound."

Jan spoke. "A *possible* conviction is not good enough."

Olson looked at Monster, who smiled back at him.

"What did I tell ya?" Monster said.

Jan spoke. "George, keeping Hansen busy in court is not good enough. If we haven't got enough to put him away for life then we should wait."

"We can't wait," Monster said.

"And why not?" Jan asked.

Olson spoke. "Because this morning all transmission stopped."

"What? What do you mean?"

Olson said, "I can only assume Hansen found out he had been compromised. He must have discovered the antenna."

"Great!" Jan said.

"So," Olson continued, "We have what we have. I think we gotta move quickly." He paused. "And, I also think Hansen will uproot soon and head for South America."

"It isn't that easy," Jan said. "He has several hundred people and lots of hardware to move."

"Well," Olson said, "Maybe he has thought of that."

"I get the impression there is something you are not telling me, George," Jan said.

Olson cleared his throat and looked out the window of the sheriff's office.

"John, I think I will let you take it from here."

"Sure, *amigo*. Well," he said turning to Jan, "We have an informant."

"No kidding?"

"Yeah, he is nearby. I'm going to have you meet him in a minute…"

"He's here?"

"Yeah, he is. In the next room. Anyway, he tells us that Hansen has the compound loaded with ammonium nitrate bomb material. Almost every building is a storehouse. Our informant thinks the compound is being wired so it can be completely destroyed in an instant. He even worries that Hansen may be planning to exterminate part of his loyal followers."

"Come on!" Jan said. "That's insane!"

Olson looked coolly at him. "Yes it is, Jan."

Jan stared at him. He shook his head.

"You are telling me," he said, "that Ronnie Hansen would blow up the whole compound and every man, woman, and child in it?"

Olson said nothing but continued to look evenly at him.

"Look," Jan said, "This is too crazy, even for Hansen. *I went to school with this guy* for heaven's sake! He grew up here. He…"

"Jan!" Monster said. "C'mon, bro, grow up. What's the matter with you? You ever hear of Jonestown? Ever hear of Marshall Applewhite? Hansen doesn't think he would be killing his people, he would simply be giving them an easy ticket to the Celestial Kingdom."

Jan sat down heavily in a chair. Was Hansen actually capable of such an act? Had Jan initiated a chain reaction? He felt as if an atomic pile had just gone critical and there were no control rods. They were headed for a meltdown.

"So what do we do?" he asked Olson.

"You know what?" Olson said, "I'm almost out of the game now. This situation is in red alert in Washington. My life as a private mercenary is nearly over. Don't get me wrong," Olson continued. "I'm in for a pound as well as a penny."

Looking at Monster, Olson continued. "Our brilliant commando colleague has an idea I am very uncomfortable with, but I want you to hear it at least. My career is over even if I survive this. If I'm not drummed out after this operation, I'll retire."

Jan turned to Monster. "Well? Let's hear it."

"OK, buddy, here it is. We don't have much time. No more than two, three days. If we don't do something, Olson says Washington will probably act by Monday or Tuesday. And I have no confidence that they can land our fish."

"So our plan...anyway...how would it serve your purposes if we could get Hanson to abandon the compound, his Church, and everything? Say for 10 years?"

Jan chewed on his lip. "Go on."

Monster gestured to Olson. "Agent Olson, here, has contacts in Iran. He can find a secure home for brother Hansen behind 12-foot walls. He wouldn't be harmed, he would live in comfort, but he would be confined."

"How do you propose to get him there?"

"He goes alone. He abandons all of his wives and kids," Monster said chewing on an unlit Pall Mall.

"What in heaven's name would persuade him to do that?"

"Fear for his life?"

"You know that wouldn't do it," Jan said, "he'd let us rip his eyes out before he'd go willingly into captivity."

"Aha!" Monster said. "Now you're talkin'!" Monster smiled, then continued, "No," "if we can get him in our custody and present him with a life and death choice, maybe he'll be smart."

"And if he isn't, what do we do, execute him?"

Monster raised his eyebrows. "Works for me. But, of course, we won't know about you until you are faced with that decision. I reference my earlier arguments. However, there is a chance that a convincing enough bluff will get him in our control. And that, Jan, is where all your philosophical meanderings may help us." Monster smiled.

"I'm listening, John."

"Well, sir, I see it this way. Hansen would never put himself in my hands. Not for an instant. Even if he saw no way out, he would escape or die, never negotiate. That is because—demonstrating his penetrating insight—he doesn't trust me. He knows if I get him in cuffs in a cruiser, he'll never get to this office alive.

"But you Jan—*because of* your fascination with fairness— you might cause him to become reckless. If we could get him backed into an inescapable corner—with absolutely no way out— *you* he might negotiate with."

Jan continued to chew on his cheek. He inhaled sharply and closed his eyes. Finally he spoke. "So how do we put this all together? How can we draw him into a corner with no windows?"

"George," Monster said, looking at Olson.

George Olson walked over to the doorway of the storage area and opened it. Hoyt Akers stepped into the room. He had a two-day growth of beard and looked like he hadn't slept recently. His eyes were red and watery. Jan looked at him apprehensively.

"Hoyt," Monster said, "meet Jan Kucera. Jan, Hoyt Akers." Akers nodded, but did not speak.

"Jan," Monster continued. "Mr. Akers, here, flies the Prophet's helicopter, *and* his jet. Akers is the man who told us that the compound is a powder keg. And he has also told us that he thinks the Prophet is considering fleeing to Argentina. Finally, he said that the Prophet has ordered him to be ready to fly to Jackson Hole on Saturday."

Akers continued to stand silently before the men. His face was an impassive mask. He never blinked his eyes. Jan thought of Steve Forbes, the publisher and one-time unblinking presidential candidate.

"Mr. Akers," Jan said, "can I ask you why you are willing to assist us?"

Akers pursed his lips and after a moment said, "Let's say I have my reasons and leave it at that."

Jan sat in silence. He looked at the floor, ran his hands through his hair, and shook his head.

"John, give me the rest of the plan, please."

"Certainly!" Monster said. "But first let me say that I think we can trust Mr. Akers. I have known him for a long time. We've never been friendly, but I can say he has a reputation for honesty and loyalty. I don't know what has turned that loyalty, but I have an idea.

"Nevertheless, Hoyt is not only the chopper pilot, he maintains and services the aircraft as well. So when he came to us, I asked myself, 'John, how could we use Hoyt to deliver Hansen to us?' I came up with this idea."

Monster lit his cigarette with a gold Zippo. "Let's say we get Hoyt to plant some plastic explosives in the chopper. We wire it up like a remotely operated bomb. Then when he gets Hansen in the air, we radio him to land the chopper at Dead Horse Gulch. If he refuses, we tell him we will blow him out of the air."

"But, John, we can't do that. What about Akers? This is crazy…"

"Hang on, boy, hang on. Yeah, I knew you wouldn't go for

actually wiring him to explosives. But *he* doesn't know that. If we can get him landed in the gulch, he is in our custody. And, I think we should land him in the gulch on his return trip from Jackson Hole. As I understand it Hoyt thinks they will be coming home around 8:00 p.m."

"Let me get this straight," Jan said. "We plant the explosives—or we pretend to plant the explosives. When he flies back over Basin after going to Jackson, we radio the chopper. Akers puts Hansen on the radio with us and we demand he set down in Dead Horse or we push the button. He lands, we take him into custody and ship him to Iran? You're kidding, right?" Jan paused. "Man! What a world we live in. Am I in Disneyland or have I fallen down a rabbit hole?"

"Well, *kimo sabe,* you got a better idea?" Monster said exhaling a cloud of smoke.

CHAPTER TWENTY—THREE

Jan and Ginny sat on the porch at the ranch, Jan mulling over his earlier conversation with Monter, Olson, and Hoyt Akers. Three bright-faced sunflower plants swayed waist high. The sun was just going down and the moon, now waxing toward full was already high in the eastern sky. In the river bottom, brush deer unfolded from afternoon naps and eyed the meadow at the south end of the ranch.

Ice cubes frosted two glasses of Coke on the overturned half-barrel that served as a table on the porch. Ginny, wearing a long print dress and white sandals, lay against the chair back with her eyes closed. Her hair was pulled back highlighting her high cheekbones, and she was smiling.

Jan had convinced Monster to let them spend the evening at the ranch instead of at Ginny's. Monster insisted that he accompany them to the ranch, inspect the grounds, and then exit while Jan set the perimeter security. Monster was full of misgivings, but Jan told him he was going to spend the 4th of July at the ranch with or without his cooperation. Monster only agreed when Jan condescended to let Monster accompany them to and from the place. He would return at midnight to escort Ginny and Jan back to her home. No way was he going to allow them to be outside the security of Ginny's safe house in the wee hours when Hansen normally sent his goons on secret missions.

"It really is a great way to spend an evening, isn't it?" Jan said.

"She opened her eyes, looked at him, and said, "It's the best, my friend. I haven't felt this—well, this *comfortable* in years."

"I feel peaceful."

"Yes."

"You sure you don't mind missing the fireworks in town?"

"Not at all. You couldn't dynamite me out of here tonight."

*   *   *

Prophet Hansen closed the door to his bedroom as he stepped out onto the porch. Maggie Balsom was asleep in the big bed. Hansen walked to the north end of the compound to the heliport. The sun was fully down now at 10:00 p.m., only a slight hint of twilight remained.

The Sikorsky sat, its massive rotor turning slowly. Bill Campbell was loading plastic milk jugs filled with gasoline into the helicopter as Hoyt Akers checked gauges in the cockpit. Campbell turned a deaf ear to Akers' repeated questions concerning tonight's operation. "You'll know after we are in the air," Campbell had said.

Hansen approached the chopper. "Those are probably the biggest Molotov Cocktails anybody ever constructed."

"Well, that's because we don't have to throw them. We just drop them over the side. From 50 feet the jugs burst on impact," Campbell added. He smiled, "After all, it *is* the Fourth of July."

"So when the target is saturated, how do you ignite it?"

"You're gonna love this, President."

Campbell produced a hunting bow and an arrow wound at the tip with cotton T-shirt material.

"I have three of these soaked in gasoline. I flick my Bic, and fire my shot."

"Geronimo would be proud of you, Bill."

"It *is* a nice touch, isn't it?"

"I'm really hoping this will solve the problem, Bill."

"Well, it won't solve all our problems, but it will rid the earth of Kucera. If he leaves the house I will spray him with 9mm slugs. Spray him until his lifeless body quits jerking. I might even land and take a scalp."

"I'd like that, Bill!"

"On the other hand, if he doesn't exit, he will be roasted like the pig he is."

"You *are* a sweet talker, Bill. You're certain he is at the ranch house?"

"We had him under visual observation until sundown. He and his girlfriend were on the porch until dusk. They went inside 30 minutes ago. No vehicle has left the ranch. So I guess the girl goes also."

"I like that, too. Sounds like you have everything covered, Bill."

"I think so," Campbell said. "We'll hit them half an hour from now, right when the fireworks are peaking at the fairgrounds. That'll give us additional cover.

"All sounds good, Bill."

Campbell hesitated then said, "President, I was wondering…"

"Yes?"

"Well, President," Campbell said slowly. "I was wondering what we are going to do?"

"To do?"

"Well, you know, about the intercepted transmissions."

"Do you trust me, Bill?"

"You know I do, President."

"Well, let's just say that I have the situation under control. Can you go with that?"

Campbell was silent for a moment. He looked at the Prophet, Seer, and Revelator—a man he had served for more than 20 years.

"Sure, President. Sure, I can go with that."

"Good man, Bill. Listen, Saturday I am going to fly to Jackson to visit Charlie Pickens. I don't know if you noticed, but Charlie is not the same man he once was."

Campbell looked up quickly. "What do you mean?"

"Well, during the…the *incident* at Manti. You know, I just got the feeling that he was…wearing thin."

Campbell stared at the Prophet, looking into his eyes longer than he had ever dared to before. Then he cleared his throat.

Finally he said, "Well, we can't let that happen, President."

"No, Bill," Hansen said evenly, "No, we can't. I have received a direct commandment from God regarding Charlie."

Campbell dropped his eyes to the ground.

"One other thing, Bill."

"Yeah?"

"I have contacted the Danites and told them to resume transmission. I have told them to send sanitized information—information that is unimportant and certainly not incriminating. I want our friends who compromised your post the other evening…"

"I just don't know how that could happen," Campbell said quickly.

"I'm not criticizing you, Bill. I'm just hoping that by resuming transmission we can make them think that maybe we're *not* wise to them. Maybe we can buy ourselves some time."

"OK."

"The main thing is that we want everything to look normal here. I need to buy a little more time. I want to continue to man the cabin, so you won't be going with me to Jackson Hole. I want you at the Medicine Wheel just like everything is normal.

"OK, President. I understand."

"You always do, Bill. You always do."

*   *   *

At 10:30 p.m. Jan and Ginny were sitting in the darkened house watching a DVD. Jack Nicholson was throwing a dog down a laundry chute. Jan became aware of a strange drumming sound. The sound was lower-pitched than the bass back-beat from any hot-rod sound system. It reminded him of something from his child-hood. When his dad fired up the old one-cylinder John Deere, it would make a unique popping sound. Jan remembered those trac-tors were called "poppin Johnnys."

But the sound also reminded him of something else. The first summer after being released from the Navy and before going to college, he had worked in Alaska for a company that provided radio location data to oil company ships plying the coastal waters looking for oil. His job was to maintain the radio equipment which provided the ship with an electronic triangulation signal. He had spent the summer on a mountaintop, near Yakutat, overlooking Malespina Glacier. Every two weeks a helicopter would fly from Yakutat 50 miles to the station on the mountaintop. Ten minutes before the chopper came into view you could hear the sound of its blades chopping the air...

Suddenly Jan bolted upright. Chopper! Now the sound was directly overhead. He heard the sound of heavy objects being dropped on the roof of the ranch house. Suddenly he saw the kitchen ceiling burst into flame. Outside he heard the sound of automatic rifle fire.

Ginny was looking at him, her eyes wide with terror.

"Quick," Jan said grabbing her roughly and dragging her off the couch. "Follow me!"

He led her quickly down the hall and into the bedroom. Chunks of flaming ceiling were falling on them. He heard Ginny screaming and turned to see her hair aflame. Grabbing a bath towel off a chair, he wrapped it quickly around her head. Immediately he could smell burning flesh. Ginny tried to touch her hair and began to moan in pain.

Jan grabbed her around the waist and dragged her through the closet door, through the hidden doorway and into the basement. With sweaty hands he grabbed a flashlight and shined it on Ginny's red and blistered forehead.

"Are you OK?" he yelled above the din of the chopper blades, chopper motor, gunfire, explosions, and falling lumber. Immediately the ranch house's floor, which was the ceiling of the old basement house, burst into flame. Smoke began to fill the room.

"C'mon," he yelled, "we've got to get out of here." Grabbing the shotgun which stood in the corner of the basement, he led her to the tunnel exit. At the far end of the tunnel, he boosted Ginny up into the boathouse. Once outside, he helped her into the aluminum boat, released the tether and shoved off into the darkened river.

As they drifted away from the bank he looked back at the inferno which was his home. The Sikorsky still hovered above the house. Bill Campbell was leaning out of the passenger door still spraying the house with an automatic weapon. Jan doubted they would spot the boat, but in the light of a nearly full moon it was possible. He struggled to the stern, climbed gently over Ginny, and pumped the primer on a small outboard. He yanked the rope and the motor caught. Heading downstream in current, motor full bore, he would reach the Basin bridge—and relative safety—in minutes.

Holding the rudder with his left hand, he reached over and touched Ginny. She was lying on her stomach, with her feet in the bow, resting her head in her arms on the center seat. He patted her shoulder.

"I'll be OK," she murmured softly.

CHAPTER TWENTY—FOUR

S aturday morning a breeze blew off Shell Creek and across the compound, rustling the cottonwood leaves above Hansen's head. He sat at a rough-hewn table with his cup of tea, his Bible, and his Triple Combination containing the Book of Mormon, the *Doctrine and Covenants*, and the *Pearl of Great Price*. A yellow legal pad lay next to the books.

Hansen loved the compound. He had personally and carefully overseen the construction of every building within the fenced perimeter, first drawing detailed plans in spiral notebooks. In recent years he had transferred all those plans to computer files. Every electrical and water line, every architectural rendering of every building, the location of every tree and shrub was depicted in the files which he fetched from the off-site computers via microwave and printed out on a large-format printer. Often he would spend hours going through the printouts, penciling in changes and additions which he passed on to construction workers and grounds keepers to implement.

Today as he inspected the compound, he wondered how long

it would stand. The last thing he wanted was to oversee its destruction. In fact, his hesitancy to move to South America was due in large part to his inability to consider leaving the compound behind. But, of course, there was no way he could let it fall into the hands of gentile federal agents. And he sensed that day drawing near.

Recently he had begun to feel closed in. The ultimate insult was the discovery of the new antenna on his Medicine Wheel tower. How stupid, he wondered, did his enemies think he was? How little they understood his attention to detail. He had spotted the antenna the first time he went to the cabin.

Of course, Bill Campbell had *not* noticed the antenna. Not only that, Hansen suspected that it had been placed there on Campbell's watch. But what would account for such carelessness on Campbell's part? What distraction had softened him? Hansen wondered if Melissa had gotten to Bill. Possible. Bill had never been able to conceal his feelings for Melissa. That was why she was still alive, a reality that enraged the Prophet. Bill had been *unable* to kill her. He left her alive. Now, Hansen supposed, she had come back to haunt him.

It made little difference. Campbell would follow Hansen to South America. In spite of his flaws, Campbell was still Hansen's strongest player.

In the meantime, however, the Prophet realized it was time to prepare for instant flight. He gathered his notebook, books, and cup and walked to his office.

Once there, he carefully returned the books to their rightful places. On the back wall of the office, he unlocked a door to a small room. Inside, on a long table against the far wall, sat a two-line telephone and several pieces of electronic equipment. The Prophet pulled up a chair and picked up a cell phone from the table. He dialed a number. On the table an answering machine picked up, and a message in his own voice said, "Dial the access code." He punched in a six-digit number and a yellow light ignited in a panel on a black box on the table.

The light meant that the box was "armed." If he or anyone else dialed a *second* phone number within 30 minutes, a *red* light on the box would light. The Prophet dialed the second number and smiled when the red light glowed.

Hansen had thought and rethought this security arrangement. It seemed sufficient. The advantage to this simple system was that he could—from almost anywhere on the face of the earth—light the red bulb on the box.

Now he unlocked another box on the same table and fed a cable through a hole in its side and jacked the cable into the back of the first box. At that moment, he possessed the ability to destroy the compound with two phone calls. When he lit the red light, a signal would detonate more than 50 ammonium-nitrate bombs with a TNT equivalency greater than what Timothy McVeigh used on the Murrah Federal Building.

One other plan was forming in his mind. Before he left for South America, he would, of necessity, destroy the compound. He now realized he must use that opportunity to purify the membership. Not everyone would go to the new location. When the time came his wives, children, and selected others would be shuttled safely outside the compound and sent to South America. He would send the others to the Celestial Kingdom. To his surviving clan, he would blame the explosion on either the ATF or a rival group. Of course, if he were backed into a corner he would send everyone beyond the veil.

He left the room, locked the door, and headed to the temple, to sanctify himself for his trip to Jackson and the work he had to do there.

*　　*　　*

Melissa walked numbly through the Medicine Wheel cabin. She poured herself a cup of coffee and walked out onto the porch. She looked up at the antennas on the tower. She looked out across the meadow to the crest of Medicine Wheel Mountain. The air was warmer and sweeter than she ever remembered it to be. A chipmunk stood on tiny hind legs and regarded her expectantly.

"I have nothing for you, little man," she said.

She had come to the Medicine Wheel cabin before noon that morning—Saturday morning. Campbell had been surprised to see her, but he had tried to conceal that. She had suggested playing the game he liked to play with the handcuffs. But this time it did not take him where he thought it would. This time she had cuffed both his hands and feet to the bedposts.

The chipmunk, apparently impatient, scurried off. Melissa finished her coffee, stood up, and drew her eyes along the mountain ridge. Wildflowers danced in the breeze and little animals scurried among the grasses and sedges. A hawk seemed paused in flight, doubtless focusing on some potential prey. She heard a helicopter in the valley 10 miles away, the sound of its rotors carrying clearly through the mountain air. She looked at the Bighorn Mountains for the last time and went into the cabin.

She sat down at the table and opened a notebook. She refused to look at the thing in the bed. She took out a pen and wrote a note to Monster. When she finished it she folded it and paperclipped it to a letter addressed to her mother. Then she picked up the 25-caliber pistol on the table.

CHAPTER TWENTY—FIVE

Hansen met Akers at the heliport at 2:00 p.m. The flight to Jackson Hole was never a piece of cake. The chopper had a range of 175 miles and could, theoretically, fly non-stop to Jackson in a straight line directly over the vast wilderness of the Rockies. That would take an hour. But neither Hansen nor Akers wanted to do that. Instead, they flew south along the Bighorn River to the mouth of Wind River Canyon where the Wind River morphed into the Bighorn. They flew above the canyon, across Boysen Reservoir, and refueled at Riverton, then followed U.S. Highway 26 over Togwotee pass into Jackson Hole country, landing at Jackson airport six miles north of the city of Jackson itself.

Charlie Pickens was waiting for them. Akers didn't like this at all. Pickens, he knew, had been in on several "incidents" with the Prophet and Bill Campbell. Akers had never actually been party to any Blood Atonement, but he knew the Church doctrine well, and Bill Campbell had told him enough more. He knew what the Prophet was capable of.

Now Akers was a long way from home and alone with the

Prophet and Pickens. After flying the chopper during the Fourth of July raid, Akers knew things were coming to a head for the Prophet. He also knew that Hansen, in a pinch, could fly the helicopter. Akers wondered if he might not be going back to Basin with the Prophet. The Prophet had been evasive when Akers had asked him what their mission was.

"If Hansen knew Akers had been in contact with Sheriff Broadbeck and Jan Kucera, he was dead! It was as simple as that.

Akers tongue scraped around in his mouth like sandpaper when they slammed the doors on the chopper and met Pickens at his Suburban. Pickens' ranch and six wives were north of Jackson, not far from the airport. Akers didn't know Pickens well, but the huge old guy spooked him big time. This whole thing was really looking bad...

"Charlie!" Hansen said, slapping his disciple on the back. "How are you? How are Martha and the others?"

"Just fine, President. Everybody's doing good." His voice rolled out of his massive chest like a caricature of the voice of God.

"The new wives settling in alright?"

"They're gonna do fine."

"Good, good, good!"

Hoyt Akers said, "Howdy, brother Pickens."

Pickens stuck out his hand and his huge mitt encompassed Akers' hand. His grip was as cold as his eyes.

"I want to take you boys to supper in Jackson," Hansen said. "I think I'll ride in the back. Hoyt, you sit up front with Charlie."

Akers got in on the passenger side, trying to ignore the sweat rolling down his stomach under his shirt. He definitely didn't like the Prophet sitting behind him. He hoped they wouldn't notice his hands were shaking.

As they pulled onto the highway, Hansen said, "Hey, Charlie, let's show Hoyt the *Gros Ventre* Slide. You gotta see this Hoyt.

The world's largest landslide. Just a few miles off the road. Happened in 1925. Dammed the *Gros Ventre* River. Two years later the natural dam broke and flooded the town of Kelly. Killed six people. Viewing the *Gros Ventre is* a once-in-a-lifetime experience," Hansen said and laughed.

Pickens turned up the *Gros Ventre* road. They drove in silence, Hansen whistling tunelessly in the back seat. Six miles down the road they passed the little town of Kelly, and six miles further they came to the massive slide and Lower Slide Lake which had been created by the disaster.

The road was totally deserted. Pickens pulled over into a little stand of quaking aspen.

"Get out boys." Hansen said.

It occurred to Hoyt to try to jump in the driver's seat and take off with the vehicle, but he knew he could never do it fast enough. Surely both Hansen and Pickens were armed. He started to say something to Hansen, but he could think of absolutely nothing to say. He got out.

Hansen was relieving himself at the base of a small white aspen. Pickens was looking at Akers quizzically. They were about three feet apart.

When Hansen turned around he was holding a blue-steel Colt 45 Cowboy. Akers started to scream, but his voice was drowned out by the sound of the firearm as Hansen shot Pickens four times in the chest.

As the shots echoed off the *Gros Ventre* mountains, Hansen looked at Akers.

"Little jumpy aren't you, Hoyt?"

Akers stood frozen looking at Hansen.

"Can you drag Charlie's carcass over in those trees for me? We need to bury him then leave his Suburban at the airport. I think we'll skip supper and head on back. You OK with that?"

CHAPTER TWENTY—SIX

O n the rim of Dead Horse Gulch Jan and Monster heard the
chopper as it flew north along the Bighorn River toward the
compound. They heard it for five minutes before they saw it. The
afternoon heat had subsided and the sun was beginning its descent
into the main chain of the Rockies in the west.

Monster shuffled his feet in the dirt, his hand resting on the
Redhawk 44 in its holster on his hip. He looked across the scrub
prairie to the Bighorn River three miles to the west. On the banks
above the river the outline of Basin lay quietly in the gloaming.
The workers at the grain and bean elevators had already made their
way home to cold beers and suppers on tree-shaded patios.

Monster flicked his Pall Mall into the wash 30 feet below.
Dead Horse Gulch had been carved out of the badlands, centuries
or millennia before. At some point a river must have run through it
to empty into the Bighorn. Now it was as dry as the bones of
whatever dead horses had given it its name.

"Better key-up, boy," he said to Jan.

Jan nodded. They jumped in the county pickup, drove to the

bottom of the gulch, and parked.

Jan picked up a microphone from its cradle on the transmitter in the back of Monster's truck.

"Hansen!" he said into the mike.

* * *

In the cockpit of the Sikorsky, Hoyt Akers turned to the Prophet.

"I have a radio transmission addressed to you, President."

"What? How can that be?"

"I don't know, sir, let me put it on the speaker."

"Hansen!" the voice said.

"Hansen, this is Jan Kucera. Pick up a mike. Make it snappy, your seat is wired with 20 pounds of C4."

Hansen looked at Akers. "What is this?"

Akers shook his head and shrugged his shoulders. Hansen glared at him for a moment. He reached under the seat and felt the package. Looking again suspiciously at Akers he reached up and pulled a microphone from over the windshield. He put it up to his mouth and said, "Kucera? What's going on? Somebody told me you died in a fire."

Hansen instinctively opened his briefcase and took out his cellular phone and punched in the number to arm the compound. He turned fully toward Akers.

The voice coming in over the noisy cockpit answered, "Hansen, this is Kucera. Yeah, you missed—again! Anyway, you need to be concerned for your *own* life. As I said, you're wired and I'm holding a transmitter. If I punch the red button, all that will be left of you and your chopper wouldn't wrap a piece of gum."

Hansen again looked at Akers.

"Hoyt, if you are betraying me you will deeply regret it."

"President, I swear, I have no idea what is going on."

"Hansen, respond," the voice over the speaker said.

"Yeah, yeah. OK, Kucera, get on with your foolishness. I'm already losing patience."

"Don't get impatient, Ronald, that could be disastrous. I want to talk to you one-on-one. Fly that thing over to Dead Horse. You will see the sheriff's truck in the gulch. Land in the wash, we'll join you there. If you don't follow these instructions, the box under your seat will be detonated. I hope you believe me."

Hansen struggled his body into position to look under the seat. He saw the box with wires leading to a plastic package of explosives. He sat up, looked at Akers and nodded. The chopper rolled right and headed toward Dead Horse Gulch.

Instructions continued to issue from the overhead speaker.

"OK, Hansen, good move. Now, when you land in the channel, step out and approach us. No one else is to exit the chopper. We see any guns and you're dead."

Hansen keyed the mike. "Yeah, and what are my options? You gonna kill me if I exit the chopper?"

"Not unless I have to," Jan said. "I hope I can talk some sense into you."

Hansen laughed—with the mike keyed. "Your arrogance knows no bounds, Kucera."

"Probably. Anyway, Ronnie, 'Give Peace a Chance.'"

Hansen laughed—with the mike keyed. "Well, you really do have a way with words."

"Yeah," Jan said, "I should have been a writer."

"You certainly wrote plenty of lies about me…"

"Save it, Hansen, we'll chat when you get down here. Out!"

*   *   *

The chopper stirred the dirt in the wash into a storm. As the blades slowed and the air cleared, Jan could see Hansen exiting. Akers sat motionless in the cockpit.

When Hansen approached within 10 yards, Jan ordered him to stop.

"What's that in your hand?" Monster called out.

"A cell phone."

"Planning to call Mommy?" Monster said and barked a short laugh.

Hansen smiled.

Jan said, "Ronald, the jig is up. We have enough information to put you away, hopefully for the rest of your life. You know about the microwave tap, of course."

"Of course. But you're too optimistic. Your information is extremely tainted. I'm certain the tap wasn't authorized. You probably won't be able to get your information introduced in court. I'll doubtless skate. Won't *that* upset you?"

"Well, Ronald, that's why I want to talk to you. I think we both have something to gain through negotiation. Maybe we can work something out. I believe we can take you to trial and get a conviction. And, as of this moment, you are our prisoner. So I think you had better listen up."

"Don't become overconfident in your apparent position of superiority here," the Prophet said. "You may not hold the upper hand at all." He flipped the cell phone lightly in his palm.

"Well, of course I know you are extremely devious, Ronnie, but anyway, just listen for a moment, will you? I know it isn't what you do best."

A dark look crossed the Prophet's face. "Proceed," he said crisply.

"I'm willing to offer you a way out. I have to tell you that it has taken all my persuasive powers to convince the sheriff and the other officers involved to make this deal with you."

"By 'the other officers' you mean, of course, George Olson," Hansen said. He sounded bored.

"Anyway," Jan continued, "I want to offer you the chance to live in relative freedom."

"In exchange for what?"

"For shutting down your operation in its entirety."

"Explain that in detail, please."

"We have a friendly emirate where you may be given sanctuary for ten years. You will have everything you need except contact with the outside world. At the end of ten years you will be free to do whatever you want to do."

"So I am to be deprived of all contact with my family and imprisoned in a foreign land for ten years?" Hansen snorted. "Unacceptable!"

Jan cleared his throat. "The alternative…"

"The alternative is imprisonment in the United States? No, you're wrong. The alternative is death. The only question is whose death or, rather, whose *deaths.*"

"You do cryptic well," Monster said.

"You fools. Do you think I fear death? And of course you, Kucera, could not pull that off. That is why you have your large, coarse friend here to do your dirty work."

Monster smiled. "I'm here to serve."

"At any rate," Hansen continued. "As I mentioned, you have—as one would expect—overestimated your position. I don't think you have the power over me you think you do."

Hansen held up the cell phone.

"My finger is touching the redial button on this phone. Try to guess what happens if I push it. Be creative, now." He smiled.

Jan stared at him for a full minute. Then he said, "The compound!"

Hansen smiled again. "Very good, Jan. You are receiving

an education today. It will serve you well in the future if you survive this day. I will allow you this one concession—a futile explanation, I'm sure, but..." His voice trailed off. "The *reason* I am willing to sacrifice my flock rather than go into exile is that they would never survive without me, not matter what you think. They *depend* on me. I am not going to turn them over as lambs to be devoured by the degraded nation you boys are so proud of. Wallowing in this social cesspool is not life. The Kuceras and Broadbecks of the world are the walking dead." Hansen paused. "Now I guess it's time for me to give you *my* ultimatum. You ready?"

Monster and Jan were silent.

"No answer? Fine. Let me tell you how it is. First, I am going to return to my helicopter. You stupid imbeciles are going to leave me alone. Oh, I don't care if you proceed with your attempts to nail me in the courts. They will fail. At any rate I am nearly ready to become an expatriate. You know, of course, that I am moving to South America. And I am taking everyone with me."

He smiled and corrected himself, "Well, not *everyone.*"

While Hansen was speaking, Jan observed, out of the corner of his eye, movement in the chopper. Akers exited the cockpit and, keeping the chopper between himself and the negotiators, moved to the wall of the gulch and began to climb up the side.

Hansen continued. "Now, let me tell you what is going to happen here. You, Kucera, are going to hand me the detonator and I am going to return to the helicopter. I do hope you don't try anything foolish."

He looked at Monster. "For example, if you move your hand toward that ostentatious firearm you use to intimidate the populace, I will push *my* button and you will see an enormous cloud arise at the foot of the Bighorns. I'm sure you are not foolish enough to think I am bluffing. And, of course, Kucera here, with his over-developed sense of moral righteousness, could never live with the idea that you forced my hand, and I blew up 200 people." Hansen smiled at Jan. "I guess you are in what some people call 'deep doodoo.'" He chuckled, then his eyes narrowed and he said, "So hand over the detonator.

Jan hesitated, then stepped forward and passed the device to the Prophet.

Hansen pushed open the battery cover and flicked the battery onto the floor of the ancient riverbed. He pocketed the detonator, held up his cell phone for Monster and Jan in a mock salute, and backed toward the chopper. Then he stopped. "One more thing, I have failed in my attempt to put an end to your misery, Kucera, but write it down. I *certainly* will get both you and your stupid friend, the sheriff. Both of you must realize that I have people who will visit you when you least expect it, when you are completely off-guard. By the way, Kucera, I compliment you on your fantastic luck in staying alive. It won't last, I promise. And, I really am sorry about your wife. If you had cooperated with the first attempt on your life she would still be alive. I hoped to wed and bed her. She moved *so* gracefully."

Jan swore under his breath.

Monster said cheerily, "All's well that ends well, *amigo.*"

Startled, Jan turned toward the sheriff as Hansen walked away.

"Jan, did I ever tell you about the time the Brinkerhoff boys got the drop on me and were taking me to Shell Canyon to shove me off the overlook at Shell Falls? No? Anyway, they disarmed me, but didn't realize I had a Smith and Wesson Tactical in my boot. You know that sidearm? It was a Compactor..."

"John! What the heck are you talking about!" Jan was watching Hansen walk toward the chopper.

"My point is, *amigo,* I learned a long time ago to *always* have a backup plan. Anyway, I have another detonator in my pocket. And the chopper actually is wired to explode."

"What! Where's Akers?"

"He has left the building," Monster said. "In a moment Hansen is going to figure that out—when he reaches the chopper, we really do need to detonate it. Question is: Will you do it or will I do it?"

"You told me you wouldn't use real explosives." Then realization dawning, Jan said, "You and Akers planned it this way from the beginning."

"The man has gotta go, Jan."

Jan was silent. He watched Hansen walking, as if in slow motion, yet taking giant strides, toward the chopper. He thought of Emma. He thought of the ammonium nitrate at the compound. He thought of all those Hansen had killed or caused to be killed. And yet, to execute him in cold blood...

Alternatives filled his mind. Could they entrap Hansen again? No. And if they did, what then? Hansen had placed the entire compound on the line. There was no doubt that Hansen would kill his own followers—*al la* Jim Jones—rather than be captured. And he had hinted that when he left for South America, some of his followers would die as he destroyed the compound. But could Jan kill him in cold blood? In cold blood! Cut him down like a frothy-mouthed dog? But wasn't that what Hansen was?

Jan looked at Monster. "John?"

Monster shook his head. "Your move, buddy."

As Hansen backed into the body of the chopper he called over his shoulder, "Hoyt!" Hearing no response he turned and looked into the cockpit. "Hoyt?" He climbed into the chopper.

Jan accepted the backup detonator from Monster. "Can he fly that thing, John?"

"Oh," Monster said, "I'm sure he can. Man like Hansen

always has his own backup plans. And he can't keep his fingers out of any pie. Very interesting guy. Actually, I sort of admire him."

Jan let the last comment go. Monster was goading him. But his decision could not be made at that level. He wished he had five minutes to think. To *think*. But there was no time to think. From nowhere words flooded into his mind—the words from the prayer of General Confession. *We have erred and strayed like lost sheep. We have followed too much the devices and desires of our own hearts. We have offended against thy holy laws. We have left undone those things which we ought to have done...*

The blades of the chopper began to rotate. The pitch of the sound increased with the speed of the blades. Jan felt a dusty breeze start at this knees and work its way up his body. *We have left undone those things which we ought to have done...*

The chopper slowly lifted into the air, ten feet, then wavered, then straightened. Then, oddly, instead of banking left and rising out of the gulch, the chopper pivoted until it was facing directly at Monster and Jan. Suddenly the nose cowl of the chopper exploded and Jan heard the pocka-pocka sound of the chopper's Heckler & Koch 50-caliber machine gun. Slugs ripped into the earth at Jan's feet and the pickup windshield exploded. *We have left undone those things which we ought to have done...* Monster was screaming something at Jan. Jan closed his eyes.

*   *   *

When the chopper exploded it sent a fireball hundreds of feet in the air. The secondary explosion of the fuel tanks showered debris down upon Jan and Monster. Monster was struck by a piece of metal and knocked to the ground.

Jan got up and bent over Monster examining him. The left

side of his shirt was bloody.

"I'm OK," Monster said, struggling to his feet, grimacing in pain. Nodding toward the truck he said, "I got some duct tape in there. Couple broken ribs is all. Let's get 'em taped."

Jan looked at the smoldering wreckage. He had a vision of Hansen's spirit lifting out of his body and sailing—where? He heard the sound of fire consuming chopper fuel. Pops and cracks sounded from the wreckage. The hulk of the machine shuddered in its death throes.

Jan shook his head. Then he sprang into action. In the truck he found the duct tape and wound it around the sheriff's huge chest. A 50-caliber slug had grazed the sheriff's shoulder and it was bleeding lightly. As Jan wrapped the tape, Monster sucked air. When Jan finished taping him, the sheriff slumped against the pickup.

Finally Jan spoke. "We gotta get you out of here. Get you to the hospital."

"That'll keep for a few minutes. If you listen close, you will hear sirens. If I am not mistaken, my ace deputy, Harold, will arrive here momentarily. No offense, but I'd rather have him transport me, than you, in your present shaky condition."

"What about Akers?"

"Yeah, well, he climbed the wall of the gulch while we were engaging Hansen. He had a vehicle parked over there on the ridge."

"And you and he had it planned all along?"

"Jan," Monster sighed. "Look, *compadre,* life is complicated for you. It's just simpler for me that's all. I really wish I could have done it myself, but this is the way it was supposed to be."

"Yeah, maybe so."

Monster pulled a pack of Pall Malls out of his shirt pocket and a lighter out of his pants pocket. He looked at Jan.

"You ever smoke cigarettes?" he asked.

"Just today," Jan said, reaching for the pack.

"Welcome to the killer's club, *amigo*."

"John, once you told me, 'You dance with the devil, you get burned.'"

"Yep. You're a killer now. I wish I could have prevented that."

"You actually could have."

"No, I couldn't."

"But," Jan said, "obviously you *could* have detonated the chopper. You didn't have to let me do it. I'm not saying that's what you *should* have done. I'm just saying you *could* have."

"No, not really."

"Why?"

"Well, Jan. I'm not God. You were convinced you were on the higher moral ground. I'm not insulting you. You *thought* you were standing up for decency and order by refusing to kill Hansen—using your words—'in cold blood.' You had made a date with destiny and I didn't have the right to interfere with it. Besides, honestly, if I had done it, you would have been released, in a way, from your responsibility—your *culpability*. By intervening I would have helped you fail at what you had convinced yourself was your job. Maybe it wasn't your job, but you *made* it your job. Once you did that, I had to let you finish if I could. You can't save a man from himself, partner. I'm sorry for you—that you have become a member of that fraternity of men who have taken other men's lives—but some things are harder on a man than taking a life. Failing to do so when it is the right thing to do is one of those worse things."

"And what if I *had* failed, John?"

"If you had failed I would be driving your failed hulk to Basin, back to a life of regret. Not that you won't regret *this*. Look, partner, if it helps, you just saved a significant part of the population of Big Horn County. Of course the ones you saved are all weird cultists, but, what the heck…and you prevented the biggest fertilizer explosion since Oklahoma City. And, of course, with 50-caliber slugs fired at you by a madman, a judge would have said you acted in self defense. And that is true. But you are still a killer now, and that means you are different than you were before."

Jan shrugged. "Well, when you force an aircraft from the skies with the intent of kidnapping a passenger, you are committing a felony. And when someone is killed in the commission of a felony, courts tend to look upon it as murder. So, was it murder or was it saving my life and the lives of all those Hansen would eventually kill? Did I fall from that higher moral position in the process?"

"Who can answer that? Do I look like a guru with cosmic knowledge of the mystical strings that hold life and death in balance? Hey, I can't even say, for certain, that Hansen wasn't the good guy in all of this. Maybe he is right. Maybe we are the ones wallowing in—what did he say—'a cesspool of degraded civilization?' Who knows who should live or die? Maybe the world would be better off if he blew up the compound and everybody in it. Who knows? I sure don't. But when I was in 'Nam I learned one thing. I learned that a man has to go with his instincts. No guarantee his instincts are right, or if they will save him or get him killed. No guarantees at all. But we deal the hand we are played, or we let people shoot the cards out of our hands. I gave up, long ago, on trying to figure anything out. I just act and react, act and react."

Monster sucked in a big hit from his Pall Mall. "Frankly, I get tired of thinking. That's all. When I see a spider in my house I just step on it. In my book Hansen needed killing and I wouldn't have lost any sleep over doing it. Just my reaction to a bug. But, the spider was in *your* house. And you felt you had to kill it. Time will tell if you did right—maybe. But, buddy, one thing I know for absolute sure."

"What's that?"

"No matter what the movies and popular novels lead you to believe, when a man kills someone, it is an event that stays with him forever. Hansen is bound to you with a short rope now, boy. A man like you, if you live thirty more years, a day won't pass that you won't ask yourself if you did right or wrong.

"For better or worse, you're a killer now. And you can't undo that."

*   *   *

The sound of the sirens grew louder, signaling a response from Basin to the explosion. Harold slid to a stop and unfolded his tall, skinny frame from the cruiser. Jumping out, he surveyed the scene as he walked up to Jan and Monster. His eyes narrowed and he methodically scanned the smoldering chopper, the sheriff's bullet-riddled pickup and, finally, Harold saw Monster's torn and bloody shirt.

"Bet that hurts," he said.

"My, yes," Monster said.

"What should I do, Sheriff?"

"Not much to do, Harold. Seems like Hansen's committed suicide by blowing up his chopper."

"What about the pilot?" Harold asked.

"Well, I believe we will discover that Hansen was alone. I sort of think it will play out this way. Hansen probably picked up some C4 explosive in Jackson, dropped Akers off outside of town, then flew to Dead Horse Gulch and blew himself up. Akers will probably confirm that Hansen was acting real strange."

Harold hesitated.

"Then, Harold, I think George Olson will investigate the scene and report that the wreckage confirms Akers' story. The FAA will doubtless conclude this was a suicide."

"Yeah, but Sheriff, how are you going to explain your presence here."

"Well, Harold, only *you* know I was here."

Harold smiled faintly, looked at the sheriff and shook his head. Then he said, "Gotcha, Sheriff. But what about your wound?"

"I haven't decided yet how I got that."

The chopper continued to burn. It muttered and popped as its contents and structure erupted and collapsed in the heat. Other than that, the canyon was deathly quiet. Jan supposed Dead Horse Gulch would soon forget this event as it doubtless had forgotten other strange occurrences over the centuries or millennia of its existence. The three men stood silently.

After a moment Harold spoke. "John?"

Monster turned to him and waited.

Harold looked at the ground for a few seconds. Then he looked up and caught the sheriff squarely in the eyes. "Got some bad news for you, John."

"Must be bad, indeed, Harold. You never call me John." Monster paused, drew a deep drag, exhaled through his nose.

"I suppose it's Melissa," Monster said.

CHAPTER TWENTY—SEVEN

Harold pulled out of the hospital parking lot and headed toward Greybull. Monster was in the passenger seat and Jan was in the back. Monster had given the emergency people 20 minutes to clean his wound and wrap his chest, although he wouldn't allow them to x-ray him. "I can breathe, so forget it. I'll come in tomorrow and let you do whatever you want."

As the cruiser crossed the Bighorn River in Greybull heading east toward the mountains, Harold told them, again, what he knew.

"One of Olson's men, Franklin James, was watching the cabin. He saw Melissa arrive in the afternoon. Neither she nor Campbell came out of the cabin for a couple of hours. James heard what he thought was a series of gunshots, so he began sneaking up on the cabin. But then Melissa came out on the porch with a cup of coffee and stared at the scenery. Said he didn't know what to do.

"When she went back inside, James heard yet another gunshot so he approached the cabin again. This time he peeked inside the window and he could see Campbell handcuffed to the bed and

Melissa slumped over the table. He entered, confirmed they were both dead, and went to his car to radio Olson. That's all I know, John."

Jan had called Ginny from the hospital to break the news to her. She had taken it badly. Jan realized Ginny was in a rough spot psychologically. They all were.

*   *   *

They stopped briefly at the roadblock set up at the turnoff to the Hansen compound, where a flotilla of government vehicles was parked. Flack-jacketed agents and state troopers milled around.

George Olson came over to the passenger-side door of the cruiser. Monster rolled down his window. "Sorry to hear about Melissa, John," Olson said, noticing the blood on the sheriff's khaki shirt. "You OK?"

"Yeah," Monster said. "What's your estimate of the situation here?"

"Well, I really don't think we are going to have a lot of trouble," Olson said. "Harold radioed me about Hansen while you were in the hospital. With both Hansen and Campbell dead and the compound wired like a fireworks show, I think the folks here will be glad to let us in to disarm the explosives. We really don't have warrants for anyone. We just want some cooperation."

"Yeah, you'll be alright," Monster said. "You don't need me, I'm going to the cabin."

"Absolutely, John," Olson said.

The cruiser pulled away toward Shell Canyon and the Medicine Wheel. Soon they approached the switchbacks that led them up the canyon walls to Shell Falls. The full moon stood overhead. Just a month, Jan thought, after the machine gun attack on his ranch by Hansen's two disciples, both of them now dead along with too

many others. They continued past the turn-off to the ranger station, turning West at Burgess Junction by Bear Lodge. At the
turnoff to the Medicine Wheel they encountered a state trooper
who waved them through to the cabin.

*   *   *

Outside the cabin six vehicles cooled in the thin, mountain
air: Campbell's pickup, Melissa's sedan, two state cruisers, Doc
Albertson's Land Rover, and the county EMT ambulance. The
two EMT's sat outside on the porch smoking, looking away as
Monster mounted the steps.

Inside Doc Albertson studied the scene while one of the troopers photographed it. When he was finished the trooper turned to
the sheriff. "We were first on the scene after the ATF agent. This
is your jurisdiction so, if you don't mind, we'll just turn this over
to you. I'll have these prints on your desk first thing in the morning."

"Thanks, Lee," Monster said to the chisel-faced trooper.
"Yeah, me and Harold have it under control."

Monster walked across the room to where Melissa's body
was slumped over the table. He stroked her hair for a moment. He
picked up the letter and note, turned them over, and laid them back
down on the table.

All eyes eventually made it to the nude body on the bed which
was difficult to recognize as Campbell. He was handcuffed to the
four bedposts. A nail gun lay on the floor.

More than a dozen nails were buried in Campbell's body—
the force of the nail gun had driven them flush to their heads. One
was in his right knee, one in his genitals, one in his navel, and two
in his chest. His right hand and right wrist were penetrated. A nail
had punctured through his mouth to protrude through his throat

just behind his chin. Another penetrated the bridge of his nose. One in each eye, each ear, and one in his forehead.

No one spoke for two full minutes.

Finally agent James said, "The nail gun sounded exactly like gunshots from where I was."

Then Monster said, "Jan, see if you can get Deck Edwards on the phone."

"Sure, John."

* * *

"Well, it's classic," Deck's voice said over the phone. "The nails in the knee, the navel, and chest correspond to the marks in the Mormon temple garment as well as those in the temple veil itself. The wrist and hand correspond to the First and Second Tokens of the Melchizedek Priesthood as revealed in the temple. The genitals and facial nails represent the anointing ceremony in the temple."

"My Lord!" Jan said. "She didn't miss anything."

"Well, as a matter of fact she did. Are you sure there isn't one in his feet?"

Jan said to Monster, "John, move that sheet covering his foot."

"Bingo!" Jan said into the phone. "What is the significance of that one."

"It's also part of the anointing ceremony. So 'you may run and not be weary and walk and not faint.'"

"Well, Campbell won't be running," Jan said, "Listen, Deck, are you going to be around tomorrow? I need to go into this with you in detail."

"I'll be here after church. Call me in the afternoon."

* * *

When Jan hung up, Monster asked if he could be left alone in the cabin for a few minutes. Everybody filed out. Monster opened the note from Melissa and read:

> *Dear John,*
>
> *Wow, that salutation sounds so wrong. But actually it is correct, because this will be my last message to you.*
>
> *Let me tell you that I have come to love you. You are so kind. So hard on the outside, but soft on the inside. So caring toward me. How I wish I would have met you years ago before I became corrupted by this evil. "This present darkness"—you can find that phrase in the Bible.*
>
> *I wish it didn't have to be this way, but it does. I can't go on. I am too deeply damaged, my soul is too weary. I just have seen too much, been used too much, and now after to-day, I've done too much.*
>
> *I hope with all my heart that by the time you read this, you will have dealt with Hansen. I hope if I go to hell, he is there already. Somehow, however, I think he and I will never face each other again. I really do have a hope of a better future. Maybe I'll see you there one day.*
>
> *I leave you Campbell as a gift. I know it looks excessive, but I think his end is just. Does that make me evil? You wouldn't know, poor dear, because you are not evil and you have not lived with evil—not with* real *evil.*
>
> *I guess I am having trouble saying goodbye.*
>
> *The letter accompanying this note is to my Mom in Connecticut. I know you, though, you won't mail it, you'll take it. That isn't necessary, but I can't stop you and I love you for it.*
>
> *You are my one regret.*
>
> > *Your friend,*
> > *Melissa*

*　　*　　*

Outside the two EMT's continued to smoke. Doc Albertson raised his eyebrows at Jan and shrugged his shoulders. Harold sat on the porch and put his elbows on his knees. Jan leaned on the Doc's Land Rover and looked at his feet.

Ten minutes of silence was broken by what sounded like a soft moaning wind coming from inside the cabin. After another five minutes Monster emerged.

"All yours," he said to Doc Albertson. "Harold stay here, secure the cabin after everybody is out. Me and Jan will take the cruiser back and I'll send someone up for you."

"You got it, Sheriff."

CHAPTER TWENTY—EIGHT

I just don't get it!" Ginny said. "This is not the Melissa I knew. I guess I didn't really know her at all. It's all so…so *grizzly*."

Ginny was sitting in her living room. Her head was bandaged and a bandage was on her right forearm where she had tried to deflect a piece of burning wreckage during the fire at the ranch house. Jan had a cup of coffee and was standing in the middle of the room.

I had a long talk with Deck Edwards," Jan said. "He has a theory. It sort of helped me understand."

"Well?"

"Deck says that Melissa was trying to deliver a message…"

"A message to whom? What sort of message?"

"Well obviously, Melissa had come to the end of her rope. She, in her own words, 'had seen too much.' She came to see Mormonism as an elevation of lust and superstition—particularly within the Mormon temple ceremony. She had seen the religion used to turn women into baby-factories while the men were turned into studs."

"OK," Ginny said. "But how does she get from there to...*this?*"

"Melissa came to believe that she had given her life, not just to nonsense, but nonsense which was designed to turn women into sex slaves. So when she came to the end of her rope, she returned to the temple ceremony and drove a nail into the areas of Campbell's body that correspond to the areas where she was 'anointed' in that ceremony. Deck called it an act of repudiation."

Ginny sighed deeply. "What keeps this going, anyway, Jan?"

"Who can say. It's like a bad dream that can't be exorcised. Throughout the West, prophets keep coming forward saying they represent true Mormonism. According to Deck, the problem is that the system was so inbred from the start that it can't be fixed. He says it's doomed to perpetuate, now that it has reached its present size—probably forever. Most of these movements never make it past the first generation or so before they peter out. The genius of Joseph Smith was to get himself martyred. The genius of Brigham Young of course was to isolate the church until it achieved a respectability because of its size and wealth."

"I'm not worried about Campbell," Ginny said, "I'm worried about Melissa."

"Yeah." Jan said. He softened. "And I'm worried about you, kid. How you doin'? You've been through a lot yourself."

"Me? Hmmm. I haven't thought about that."

"Well, it's time you did. In fact, maybe it's time we both thought about taking care of ourselves for awhile."

"I think you're right," she said.

*　　*　　*

Monster was sitting at his desk, feet up, looking at the ceiling, and smoking when Jan came in.

"Isn't this a smoke-free area?" Jan asked lightly.

Monster continued to look at the ceiling, attempting to make smoke rings. Jan put two paper cups of coffee on the desk and a box of donuts. At the rustle of the paper sack, Monster sat upright.

"You sure know how to get my attention," he said.

"Well, you're easy to tempt."

"I am at that," Monster said. "How's Ginny holding up? How's her burn healing?"

"She's OK. At least she'll *be* OK. I know that because she told me so herself."

Monster smiled. "Yeah, she will. Tough girl, Ginny. I feel good about the two of you."

"Yeah?"

Monster chuckled. "Jan, Jan. Time to move ahead, boy."

"Oh, yeah? How about you? You gonna move ahead?"

"Been thinking about retiring."

"Uh huh."

"Yeah, gonna let Harold run this place for six months. My contract with the county commissioners allows me to take a six-month sabbatical and appoint an acting sheriff."

"I suppose you are going to Connecticut?"

"Well, among other places."

"John, what would you do if you didn't chase bad guys?"

"Who says I won't chase bad guys? Don't need a badge to do that. Matter of fact, been thinking about all the little Ronnie Hansens running around here in the Wild West. Also been thinking how handicapped the law is. Look at Olson. Liable to lose his retirement over all the fun we've had."

"Monster Broadbeck, bounty hunter?"

"Has a nice ring to it, doesn't it? But there is no bounty, so I won't be obligated to bring 'em back alive. I kinda like that part."

"John," Jan said, "I think I said this before. Sometimes you scare me—big time!"

Monster laughed loud at that. He crushed out his cigarette. He formed his right hand into a gun, index finger pointing at Jan, thumb cocked like a hammer.

"Pow!" he said and laughed some more.

CHAPTER TWENTY—NINE

Jan and Ginny drove to the ranch from the graveyard, arriving late in the afternoon. Melissa was buried in Jan's family plot next to Emma. The two would lie in silent vigil overlooking the dusty little river town. Melissa's parents were not able, they said, to attend. Jan marveled at that. Father Aidan Sullivan had done the funeral. He had phoned Jan upon hearing of the events at Dead Horse Gulch and the Medicine Wheel, asking how he could help. What about the "little girl—Melissa?" he had asked. At the funeral itself Jan could detect no sense of condemnation from the priest, although Jan's own mind was still deeply troubled.

After the funeral he pulled Sullivan aside.

"Aidan," he said, "I have a friend in Montana who was raised a Catholic. A couple of years ago he went through a catechism to study the foundations of the faith. It didn't work out for him, but it interested me when he spoke of it. I remember I went through a similar kind of class when I was 12. Do you still do that, and is it something I could attend?"

The old priest looked deeply into Jan's eyes as if to say "I wasn't wrong about you." Instead he said, "Would you object to sitting in a class with three or four 12-year-olds?"

"Not if I wouldn't intimidate them."

The priest snorted, "Nobody intimidates 12-year-old catechism students."

*   *   *

The burned-out ranch house looked like a bomb crater. A 36-foot Pace Arrow motorhome was parked next to the building, twin air conditioners humming on its roof.

"You got a big job here, cowboy," Ginny said, eyeing the debris-strewn basement of the former house.

"I thought maybe you'd help me?" Jan said.

"Probably, but we need to talk about it."

Jan looked at her quizzically.

"Look, Jan. You have some decisions to make…"

Jan was silent.

Ginny continued, "You have a lot to think about. Such as how we have been thrown together in all this. I'm glad we have been and I hope it works out. But I just think we need to back off and come at this again in a more…well, *normal* way."

Jan smiled. "You mean we should begin dating?"

Ginny smiled back. "Yeah, I think that *is* what I mean. But, you know what? I think we ought to have a moratorium on that as well. I saw you talking to Father Sullivan. Why don't you work on your foundations for the rest of the summer? Let's see where we are when the pumpkin frosts."

Jan looked down at the ground. Ginny reached out her hand and he took it. Jan looked up again at Ginny, admiration filling his heart.

They walked down to the boathouse. Huge cottonwoods

shielded the sun and a breeze off the river was actually cool.

"Last quarter moon tonight," Jan said.

They sat on the old couch in silence. After a few minutes, Ginny spoke. "How were things at the compound?"

"Well, the Red Cross is helping Hansen's and Campbell's wives cope with their losses. The leadership out there seems to be numb. George Olson told me he thought he could engineer a breakup of the cult. I'm not so sure, however. These things, if my reading is correct, don't ever end. Somebody will step up to the plate, a new leader will emerge."

"Did you say there was some grisly business come to light in Utah?"

"Yeah, seems like Hansen had a cabin down there in the Manti Mountains. Apparently a half mile out in the woods they found a rock with lots of recently spilled human blood. The investigators said the volume of the blood would be consistent with a Blood Atonement."

"There seems to be no bottom to this stuff."

"That's what Monster thinks. And by the way, Monster said that Akers told him Hansen killed one of his lieutenants in Akers' presence in Jackson Saturday afternoon before we met him at Dead Horse Gulch."

"No!"

"Yeah, Monster took that a little hard, because he made the decision to encounter Hansen *after* the Jackson trip."

"How *about* Monster? How's he doing?"

"I worry about him. I think he's a man who could go his own way pretty easily."

"Hasn't he always?"

"To some extent. But this little adventure is like nothing he has encountered before, especially the Melissa part. He blames himself for her, because he allowed her to get involved. Add all this to what he went through in 'Nam…Someday I'll tell you about that. He got sort of confused over there."

"Who didn't?"

"Anyway, now, watching George Olson struggle with his politically correct superiors…I don't know. I think the sheriff is about to retire from law enforcement and go into Monster enforcement. He has amassed a nest-egg that will cover his finances for the rest of his life. He doesn't need a job."

"Scary if you ask me."

"Will definitely be interesting."

The shadows from the cottonwoods lengthened out into the brown water. A warm breeze stirred up a dust devil in the badland bluffs across the river. Jan stood up and took down a bottle of whiskey from the shelf of the boathouse. He unscrewed the cap and walked over to the edge of the dock. He poured the bottle slowly, regretfully, into the river. He doubted that it would work, but he was going to try it anyway. He threw the bottle far out into the water and walked over and sat down on the couch.

A breeze broke whitecaps on the river. The late afternoon heat warmed Jan to his bones. He closed his eyes and leaned back on the soft couch. He was thinking of Emma and Melissa and Monster and Bill Campbell and Ronald Hansen. The images floated together as though drifting by on the slow, dark water of the river— Emma was smiling peacefully at him.

Ginny watched him for awhile. When he began dozing she stood, looking down at him. She reached out and touched his hair. Then she turned and walked up the path to her car.